DEATH ON THE LAKE

A DCI SATTERTHWAITE MYSTERY

JO ALLEN

Also by Jo Allen

Death by Dark Waters
Death Eden's End
Death on Coffin Lane
Death at Rainbow Cottage

To Terry Lynn Thomas, as wonderfully supportive a writing friend as I could hope for. Thank you xx

AUTHOR'S NOTE

ll of the characters in this book are figments of my imagination and bear no resemblance to anyone alive or dead.

The same can't be said for the locations. Many are real but others are not. I've taken several liberties with geography, mainly because I have a superstitious dread of setting a murder in a real building without the express permission of the homeowner, but also because I didn't want to accidentally refer to a real character in a real place or property.

So, for example, you won't find Jude's home village of Wasby on the map; you will find the church at Martindale but not George's cottage nearby; you'll find Hallin Fell but you won't be able to place the Neilsons' property beside it; and so forth.

And although I've taken these liberties with the details I've tried to remain true to the overwhelming beauty of the

Cumbrian landscape. I hope the many fans of the Lake District will understand, and can find it in their hearts to forgive me for these deliberate mistakes.

CONTENTS

ONE

Ollie Neilson woke up groaning in the pool of sunlight that flowed through the cabin window and spilled over onto the bunk. Above the miasma of alcohol, the remnant buzz of a line of coke momentarily silenced him. He thought of Summer, rolled his naked body over and found the space beside him on the mattress empty.

She couldn't have gone far. For a second he lay with his mind racing in awed respect for Summer's body, the way she used it, the talent she deployed, the tricks she'd taught him. Freeing his tongue, which clung mustily to the roof of his mouth, he ran it round his lips again as his blood pulsed at the thought of what had passed. He was eighteen, rich and fancy free; he'd tasted heaven and was ready to taste it again.

The boat rocked as he rolled off the bunk and got to his feet. Or maybe it wasn't the boat. The sunlight had been the herald of a still, perfect May afternoon and the only thing to disturb them had been the gentle wash of the Ullswater steamer as it forged its way to Patterdale.

Hopefully none of the passengers had had a long lens on their camera — or rather, hopefully none of them knew who he was and thought it would be a prank to send pictures to his father. If they did that, he might have to re-evaluate the afternoon's activities. But even as he thought about it, even as he steadied himself with a hand against the bulkhead, his feet braced slightly apart, he knew that Robert Neilson's anger, though fierce, would be temporary; and the pleasure Ollie had had from Summer would live with him for a long, long time.

If there were pictures, though. He smirked. His mates would think a lot of him then. Him and Will. There was a bit of him wouldn't mind if there were pictures, as long as only the right people saw them.

Focussing, he managed a look around. The cabin looked as if it had hosted an all-night party. Half a dozen empty beer bottles and one still with a sad half-inch of vodka lay on the floor, rebuking him. Any unsteadiness was his and his alone, and the Seven of Swords rested too gently on the lake to disturb them.

Ollie looked further. Clothes — his, Summer's and Will's — lay strewn across the cabin floor. In a half-hearted attempt at restoring the damage before his stepmother got home, he picked up a pair of jeans and shook them into some sort of order. Summer's panties dropped from them and he made a half-hearted snatch, but the legacy of his overindulgence was too much, and they fell to the floor.

Bending down to pick them up wasn't such a good idea, and the scrap of pale gold nylon only reminded him that however fragile his head was feeling, everything below the waist was in enthusiastic fettle. He picked his way to the ladder that linked the cabin to the deck four feet above and heaved himself into the sunlight, where Will sprawled naked over the deck. Ollie grinned. At least he'd managed to fall comatose somewhere in the shade and wasn't going to suffer as his twin would, with a bad-tempered slash of sunburn flaming across the tender skin on the back of his neck. No doubt when Will came round he'd have the same thought that Ollie himself had had, and once Summer woke up no doubt they'd start all over again.

It was Will's turn first, though. They shared everything, and they did it fairly. Summer needn't be any different.

He hauled himself up over the last rung of the ladder, stretching in the sunlight, stirring his brother with his foot. 'Okay, Willie, boy. Are you up for more? What have you done with her?'

A yawn, a groan to match Ollie's own of a moment earlier, and Will resurfaced in the land of the living. 'Oh God. Oh my God.' He paused, shook floppy fair hair out of his eyes and grinned. 'Ollie. Jesus, that was some afternoon. That was fantastic.'

At least, Ollie thought, he could be reasonably certain that Will hadn't been shagging the girl without him. 'Where is she?' His gaze raked the deck and there was nothing there except a pile of discarded clothing and a pitifully small pool of vomit. That must be why Will had crashed out onto the deck, just falling short of the side of the boat. Ollie, who had managed not to be sick, filed that triumphant detail away for later. 'Where's Summer?'

'Isn't she down with you?' Will sat up, only to twitch forward again as his flaming back touched the rail of the boat. 'Shit. I'm burned.' He poked at the back of his neck with a tender fingertip.

'That's going to hurt later. Just as well you didn't crash out on your back, or your bits would be fried.' Briefly, Ollie considered the possibility that he'd somehow overlooked a naked woman in in his earlier survey of the cabin, only to dismiss it as bizarre. Nevertheless, as he reached for his shorts and briefs and pulled them on, he cast a quick look back down the hatch, only to crease his brows in a post-orgiastic puzzlement. The cabin wasn't large and there was nowhere she could have hidden.

Drink and drugs rot the brain, their mother had always warned them, but his must have rotted on the instant if he couldn't even see what must be in front of his eyes.

Must be. Because Summer's clothes were in the middle of the cabin, and his and Will's were on the deck, so if Summer had gone home she must have done it in the nude. And though she was a hell of a girl when the mood took her, he was reasonably certain the mood only ever took her in private and that walking five miles along the Ullswater Way with no clothes on was just not how she rolled.

Well. He shook his head. The fact he was even having that kind of interior monologue showed how smashed he must have been earlier on.

'Has she gone home?' In his turn, Will reached for his clothes, the follower not the leader in the major things as well as the minor. Ollie always capitalised on how the hour's difference in age weighed disproportionately in his favour, how Will endorsed whatever idea he came up with, no matter how mad, how he aped every action, sooner rather than later. Inviting Summer along for the afternoon had been Ollie's idea, and so had getting hold of some good-quality cocaine through a mate. No doubt in the reckoning — which, he now saw, was unavoidable — he'd be the one who took the lion's share of blame.

That was probably fair enough; but the reckoning was for the next day, or the day after, and the puzzle of Summer's whereabouts was immediate. 'She can't have done.'

'She must have done. She's not here.' Will picked up

Summer's bra, which had somehow got tangled in his discarded shorts, and twirled it round his finger, staring at it in adolescent fascination.

'She's left her clothes. And the boat.' They were moored fifty yards or so off shore, and the dinghy that ferried them to and from the landing bobbed at the back of the Seven of Swords. The line that tethered it hung limp in the silver water.

'She must have swum for it,' offered Will, by way of a solution.

Ollie's brain told him both that she must have done or she'd be on the boat, and that she couldn't have done because she'd left her clothes behind. The answer would be somewhere in between, but he was damned if he could see through his muddleheadedness to what it might be. Nevertheless, in a tentative search for a solution, he peered over the guard rail and down into the lake.

The answer was there all right. He opened his mouth to swear but all that came out was a child's whimper.

'Ollie?' Will hauled himself to his feet, joined his twin at the rail, froze for a second and repeated the exact same sound. On the far side of the lake, a queue of traffic snaked along the road from Glenridding to Pooley Bridge and the shadow of Gowbarrow Fell began its evening stretch, flexing dark muscles in the late afternoon. A yard below them Summer Raine floated face-down in the lake. Her blonde hair drifted around her head like the tentacles of a pallid jellyfish, stranded and helpless in the shallows, and the tattoo of a butterfly that graced the back of her left thigh shimmered under half an inch of water. She was naked. A dark strand of water weed curled like a wound across her shoulder blade.

It was the tattoo that did it. Some time not that long before — three hours maybe — Ollie had spent several enjoyable minutes familiarising himself with that tattoo. Now its sodden blurriness brought reality home to him. Summer had been in the water a long time, maybe all the time he and Will had been asleep, and now she was dead. He found his voice. 'Shit.'

'What do we do? What do we do?' Will could manage only an anxious bleat. 'Dad'll kill us.'

Robert Neilson, a man who was lighthearted and fun as long as he deemed the situation wholesome, was humourlessly upright when it came to morals. Maybe if he'd been more relaxed about things, thought Ollie in a moment of startling clarity as he stared down and watched a lap of water ripple the blonde hair he'd so recently laced his fingers through, there wouldn't have been so much to tempt them in what had seemed like a good idea. 'Yes.'

'She is dead, isn't she?'

'Yes.' Ollie's brain ticked. 'We need to get rid of her.'

'Get rid of her?' Will's jaw dropped. He looked about twelve years old.

If Ollie looked to his brother for leadership he'd do so in vain. One of them had to take a decision. 'Yes. Because Dad'll kill us. But he's not back until tomorrow night and Miranda isn't back for another hour or so and so we have time to get rid of the body.'

'But it was an accident. We'll make it worse if we hide it.'

'Just until the drugs get out of her system. And ours.' Ollie's palms were sweating and it wasn't the sun. 'We didn't hurt her. It's not our fault if she went for a swim somewhere on the way home. We'll take her in the dinghy and leave her. Someone will find her but the drugs will be out of her system by then. It'll look like an accident.'

'But Dad—'

Ollie folded his lips at the thought. 'Yeah. He might suspect. But he won't know for certain.'

Will gripped the rail with white knuckles, but Ollie knew he'd go along with it. He always did. After a second he saw sense, stood up. 'Her clothes. What about them?'

'We'll take them, too.' The decision made, Ollie dropped down into the cabin, scooped up Summer's jeans and pants and scrambled back up again to where Will, his face a mask of nausea and shock, stood at the back of the boat with the girl's sandals, bra and flimsy cotton top.

'Here's her bag.' Will poked it out from under one of the seats with his foot.

'Okay.' Ollie dropped it into the dinghy, jumped down and struggled to keep his balance as it rocked under his feet. 'Let's get her in here.'

As he looked towards the shore, the day got worse. Their stepmother's car was parked in front of the house. 'Miranda's back. We'll keep behind the boat and maybe she won't see us.'

He waited for Will to jump down into the dinghy and take his place at the stern before he unshipped the oars and manoeuvred them into the shelter of the Seven of Swords. The sun was beginning to dip, so it must be almost five o'clock. Surely they hardly had a prayer of getting away with it, on a summer evening in the Lake District, with a public footpath along the water's edge commanding one route of escape and their stepmother, who might be only slightly more forgiving than their father, having a full view over their path if she chanced to look out over the second? But Ollie was made of stern stuff, a teenager rapidly forming in the image of his father. There was no such thing as a hopeless case, no situation you couldn't bluff or bluster or bully your way out of if you applied yourself to it. He paused for a moment before he dipped the first oar in the water, rotating the dinghy and sending it alongside Summer's body. 'Grab her feet.'

'Her feet?' Will seemed mesmerised by the ripples from the oar, the way they rolled up to the girl and ran up against her bare arm and side, ran down her leg, unfurled around her head and them went on out into the lake in disarray, fading, fading, fading into oblivion.

'Yes. I'll get her head' Gritting his teeth, Ollie reached down and grasped Summer's shoulder. Hours earlier it had been living, pulsing, exciting; now it was queasily flaccid under his hand.

The dinghy rocked violently as they tried to roll her waterlogged body upwards and it took two attempts. At the second, they heaved her over the gunwales and she sprawled in the bottom of the boat, face upward, eyes wide and glassy.

Will, visibly gagging, sent Ollie a troubled look, but he said nothing. What was there to say? They were Robert Neilson's sons. Nothing defeated them. And, driven by the chilling sobriety of coping, Ollie began rowing and drove the dinghy, with its guilty cargo, into the shadow of the trees that overhung the shore.

TWO

'Breakfast in ten.' Jude Satterthwaite closed the door of his girlfriend's bedroom and his steps, firm and meaningful, descended the stairs to the kitchen. Left sitting at her dressing table, one towel wrapped around her body and another round her head, Ashleigh O'Halloran performed a quick calculation. Was ten minutes long enough to get dry, get ready for work and read the tarot cards?

It wasn't. In a sense it didn't matter; Jude would be quite happy chatting away in the kitchen to her housemate while he rustled up coffee and toast. He'd know what she was doing, because they'd been together for six months, and even if he didn't know he'd guess — or rather, deduce. He was a detective and knowing things was more than just a part of his job; it was rooted in his nature. Nevertheless, she'd rather not make it quite so obvious.

She towelled down her hair, tossed the towel on the bed and dried herself quickly, then got dressed. 'I'll just be a second,' she said to the cards that sat on her dressing table wrapped in a pile of purple silk, 'and I know I shouldn't rush it. But I value your advice.'

That was why she was discreet. It wasn't that he'd laugh, though he knew about the cards and teased her about them on a regular basis. It had taken her a while to persuade him tarot wasn't about fortune-telling but about concentration and meditation and making the best of all the available information, but nevertheless he couldn't quite bring himself to buy into them as the useful tool they were. For Jude detection was all about your brain and the evidence in front of it, whereas for Ashleigh the job benefited from intuition. You needed evidence but you needed intuition, too.

She never used cards for her work. It took a lot to keep your soul healed when every day carried with it the risk of coming across some kind of inhumanity, a crime perpetrated against the vulnerable or a violent death. The cards gave her a sense of perspective and kept her sane.

'I don't have very long.' She kept her voice low, because if Jude heard her, or if Lisa did, they'd mock her even more. 'So I'm afraid I'm going to have to hurry you.' No incense, no meditation, no time to stop and think. That wasn't the way to make the most of a reading but she might get something out of it, if it was only a whistle to call her unruly thoughts to heel. She slid the cards out of their box and dealt out just one. There was time only for the briefest reading.

She held her hand above the card for a moment before turning it over and flipping it down onto the dressing table. The Seven of Swords. At one level that was no surprise. The suit of swords came up far more often than it ought to, as if the cards were connected with the job she did. This, with its message of diplomacy and avoiding confrontation, told her nothing she didn't already know.

'My whole life is about avoiding confrontation,' she told the card, in mock-severity. And its alternative meaning was startlingly obvious as well, warning her of unknown opponents. 'I'm a detective. Of course I have unknown opponents.'

'Ash!' Jude's voice floated up the stairs from the kitchen. 'What the hell are you doing up there? Your coffee's going cold and your toast's about to burn, and you'll say it's my fault.'

'Just coming.' She cut the Seven of Swords back into the pack, stowed the cards away and went back to finishing off her hair. It didn't do to take yourself too seriously, and the cards didn't always deliver.

When Jude arrived at the office, separating from Ashleigh in the car park by mutual consent so as not to make their relationship any more obvious than it needed to be, he found Detective Inspector Chris Dodd, widely known as Doddsy, standing by the coffee machine in the corridor close to the office they shared. Doddsy's thoughtful look indicated that something had come up overnight — not so important that Jude, Doddsy's immediate boss, would need to know about it straight away, but something troubling nonetheless. 'Doddsy. Good weekend?'

'Aye, passed without incident.' Doddsy straightened up and examined the coffee in the cardboard cup as though he'd expected something better. 'Tyrone was on shift yesterday, so I got a load of work done.'

'Good.' Jude felt in his pocket for some change. He'd managed a whole weekend with Ashleigh with neither of them on call or having to go in to work for unfinished business so a trip down to the canteen rather than straight into work via the machine seemed an unnecessary luxury. His brow creased. It was only just eight o'clock. A former girlfriend's exasperation rang in the back of his mind. *For God's sake, Jude. You don't have to work every hour you're not sleeping just because you can.*

That remark was one of the reasons she was his ex, but she'd been right. If he'd listened, who knew how that relationship might have panned out? He'd cared about her. 'So what's on your mind?'

Doddsy ran a finger round his collar, a gesture that signalled slight awkwardness. 'I had a quick call from Tyrone just now.'

'Personal?' Jude kept his tone light. He'd known Doddsy for years and the two were close, but sometimes you had to tread carefully. Not everyone was as sanguine as Jude about the inspector's relationship with a policeman less than half his age. Sometimes Jude wondered if Doddsy himself was quite comfortable with it, but when the two of them found time to go out for a drink together, that particular subject was left untouched. Doddsy had never been one to talk about his private life, even to his friends, but these days he never opened up at all.

Fair enough. There were plenty of things Jude himself preferred not to talk about.

'No. Business. Something which came up first thing and he filled me in on it. Because he thought there might be more to it than meets the eye.'

'And you have a bad feeling about it?' Jude dropped two coins into the machine and was rewarded by a trickle of pale coffee that would do nothing to stimulate his brain. Thank God Ashleigh and Lisa had a decent coffee machine.

'We don't do feelings, though, do we?' Doddsy grinned at him. 'But yes.'

'You sound like my good friend DS O'Halloran.' Jude grinned. You had to give Ashleigh her due. It wasn't feelings that made her such a success, but an instinct for understanding the human mind and its follies, harnessed to an uncanny knack for persuading the most cynical witness to trust her, often to the point at which they succeeded only in incriminating themselves.

'I'll take that as a compliment.' Swilling the coffee round in his cup, Doddsy nodded towards the door of the office. 'Let's go in.'

Jude followed him in, assuming his seat, stretching out a hand to switch on his laptop and setting the coffee down on the desk. 'Go on then.'

'There was a missing person reported very early this morning from Pooley Bridge. A young woman. Her name is Summer Raine.'

Jude laughed.

'Yeah, I know.' Doddsy's own laugh was more sympathetic. 'Some people, eh? What they do to their kids. Anyway. She's up here for the summer, working down at the marina at Pooley Bridge. She's a sailing and surfboarding teacher, been here for the last couple of years. She was on a day off yesterday. She went out for a walk and hasn't come back.'

'And it was reported…when?'

'About half six. She lives in a bunkhouse just outside Pooley Bridge with a load of the other staff, but she has a boyfriend up in Howtown. It seem there was a bit of confusion. Her colleagues thought she was with him and he thought she was with them.'

'Who reported her missing?' Jude keyed in his password and sighed as a stream of notifications rolled across the screen like the closing credits of a long and complicated art house film, the price he always paid for staying offline for two days at a time.

'The boyfriend. He hadn't heard from her, so he called first thing when he got up. That was about six. She didn't answer, so he called one of her friends. Then he called 101. Tyrone and Charlie are heading down there later to see what's what.'

Later meant the matter wasn't deemed immediately significant, and whoever had assessed the initial report had judged that the unfortunately-named Summer Raine wasn't considered at risk. 'Tyrone and Charlie haven't even got there yet, and you're telling me there's something funny about it. What's the story?'

'It's the boyfriend. Luke Helmsley. You know him?'

Jude ran the name through his brain and found no obvious connections. 'I know of some Helmsleys over towards Appleby. I think I had some dealings with one of them years ago, when I was just starting out, but that was minor. Breaking and entering, if I remember. But it's not an uncommon name hereabouts.'

'No. But Tyrone knows of him. Not that they're of an age. Helmsley's a few years older.' He sighed. Doddsy had lived a long time as a quiet and celibate man and only found himself a partner as he approached middle age. Tyrone's youth seemed a permanent thorn in his flesh, inviting judgement and opposition on them where the same-sex relationship didn't. 'Twenty-seven. But you know how it is with Tyrone. He knows someone one who knows someone. He seems to know everyone.' A smile raced across his face and faded away. 'I ran Helmsley through the records to see what I could come up with. I thought I'd heard the name.'

'And?'

'Your man isn't exactly pure and spotless. He has a

couple of convictions for assault, both of them when drunk, both of them involving a woman. In one of them he took a swing at a guy he thought was staring at his then girlfriend — not Summer, but a previous partner. And in the other, he assaulted the same girl, who he thought was getting too friendly with one of his mates. Both of those were a few years back.'

'And yet the missing persons report—?' Jude prompted.

'I haven't seen anything that's come through on that. But I've suggested to Tyrone he might want to ask some searching questions.'

Jude sat back and thought about it. It irked him that he couldn't recall the Helmsley case, because he prided himself on the depth of his local knowledge and his recall of detail. 'What do we know about the girl? Is it unusual for her to disappear without letting anyone know where she is?'

'I imagine it must be, if he's bothered to report her missing.' Doddsy drummed his fingers on the desk. 'It may be nothing. She may turn up, and I'm going to guess there's nothing in her background to suggest she's at any kind of risk, or they'd have folk out looking for her already. And Helmsley may have been away the whole afternoon and not be a suspect at all, even if she doesn't reappear.'

Jude looked out of the window at a blue sky populated with animated white clouds blowing past in the stiff breeze. In the distance, to the east, the cobalt-blue line of the Pennine Hills rippled along the horizon. In the other direction, a dozen miles to the west, the hills around Ullswater would look equally inviting, hiding even greater dangers under their fifty shades of green. 'Yesterday was tempting, but it was cold up top. Ashleigh and I were out up High Street.' He paused to remember how they'd looked over the fluctuating fell tops, above the trough that held

Ullswater and towards the serrated edges that guarded the approach to Helvellyn. 'She may have gone for a walk up the fells and got caught out. Or a swim. The lake looks lovely but it's perishing when you're in.' And there were deep and treacherous currents. Things — and people — went into Ullswater and never came out again.

'She wasn't local.' Doddsy conceded that point. 'She may have misjudged. Maybe got lost.'

If that was the case she'd turn up safe and sound soon enough, perhaps dragged back by the mountain rescue team from a disingenuous-looking hillside, with a twisted ankle and an embarrassed smile and at worst a touch of exposure. 'But you think not.'

'Tyrone thinks not. And so I'm just warning you this one might be coming our way rather than be left with the guys in uniform.' Doddsy turned his attention to his coffee.

'Okay.' Tempted to follow it up, Jude nevertheless resisted the chance to run through for himself what Doddsy had already done. He turned to other things, wondering how he was going to manage to fit in this kind of missing persons enquiry if it ever reached his level, but his period of concentration lasted only until he'd opened the first of the weekend's accumulated emails. That was the point at which the door opened without ceremony and Detective Superintendent Faye Scanlon walked in to the room.

Despite a bad beginning, Jude had recently realised he liked Faye. She was brisk and demanding; she could be both antagonistic and defensive; she was spiky and ambitious; and he had a natural dislike of authority which she seemed to sense. To make matters worse, she brought with her a shedload of baggage in the shape of a past relationship with Ashleigh O'Halloran — something which wasn't exactly a secret but to which very few people were privy, and something he personally would rather not have known. But he knew and she knew he knew, and the resulting tension was always there between them.

And yet he liked her. Faye was a competent and effective police officer, a terrier at management and one who got the best out of her staff. If it wasn't for the scandal that had trailed around after her affair with Ashleigh, with both of them married at the time, then she'd have been in a bigger job or in the same job in a bigger force, but life wasn't like that. A twist in the sequence of events that had sent Ashleigh to start a new life in Cumbria had landed Faye upon them a few months later, and after the first moment of intense irritation she'd rolled her sleeves up and got on with the job. Jude's dislike had turned to respect and the respect was mellowing further. He couldn't see himself ever enjoying a social situation in her company, but he could work with her. 'Faye. Anything I can do for you?' He waited.

Faye looked pointedly at Doddsy, who'd just picked up his phone. It was, Jude suspected, more of a tacit observation on the faint smell of cigarette smoke that the chain-smoking inspector took with him wherever he went rather than a request for privacy, but he was wrong. Seeing Doddsy wasn't for moving, she stepped back out again. 'If you could spare me five minutes in my office.'

He logged out of his emails and followed her the three doors along the corridor. Faye had an office to herself but like him she was rarely in it, straying around the building making sure she knew what was going on, always preferring a face-to-face briefing to an email one and catching up on the paperwork late in the evening when there was no-one around from whom she could learn something directly.

'Sit down.' She closed the door behind him, an indication of something either serious or secret. 'Something got passed up to me this morning and I'd like to keep an eye on it. Or rather, since it's way below my pay grade, I'd like you to keep an eye on it.'

When she first arrived, that remark would have put his back up. He internalised his smile. 'What is it?'

'A missing person.'

Something told Jude a mighty coincidence was about to unfold in front of him. He downplayed it. 'I think you'll find that's way below my pay grade, too.'

She waved that aside. 'Yes, probably, but it's something I'd like some discreet input into from the non-uniformed side, and I'd like you to oversee it even if you aren't directly involved. Does that satisfy your professional pride?'

'Yes.' He took a speculative punt. 'Is it Summer Raine?'

She looked surprised. 'How did you know?'

He allowed the smile to break out. It was always particularly satisfying to be a step ahead of Faye. 'Just a guess. Doddsy was telling me about it.'

'Doddsy was? How did he know? Information runs amok in this place, and nobody seems able to control it.' Her irritation was obvious.

'You want to keep this missing person inquiry quiet rather than ask around to see if anyone's seen her? Am I understanding this right?'

'Of course that isn't what I said. I suppose it's no surprise Doddsy knew about it. It's his boyfriend who was dispatched initially, I think.'

'Yes.'

'Good. If that's all, I don't need to worry. I hear nothing but good things about young PC Garner, but I'm sure Doddsy has enough sense not to tell his young man anything confidential.' She hit a couple of buttons on her laptop and the printer in the corner whirred and spat out a sheet of paper. 'So. Summer Raine was reported missing this morning at about half past six. PC Garner and PC Fry went down to talk to the girl's boyfriend first thing this morning and have just filed this report.'

He was intrigued. Someone — possibly Faye herself — must have prioritised Summer's disappearance since Doddsy had heard about it from Tyrone. He scanned the two sheets of paper she handed him. A blonde woman, young, dyed hair with dark roots trapped in braids from which it had begun to escape, was laughing in a photograph, bathed in sunshine. Behind her, the brown hills of the Lakes loomed large. 'Is this picture recent?'

'It's a couple of weeks old. She's twenty-two, and left Exeter University three weeks ago. She comes from London. She'll graduate in July and in the autumn she's enrolling on a masters degree in feminist politics, but she's a watersports enthusiast and was planning to spend the summer teaching sailing and surfboarding at the watersports centre up at Pooley Bridge. It's her third summer there. Last year she entered into a casual relationship with a local man, Luke Helmsley. He says this was the reason she came back again this summer. By all accounts she's an independent young woman, more than capable of looking after herself in this kind of terrain in summer conditions. Yesterday was her day off. She spent the morning at the watersports centre and in and around Pooley Bridge, and then went out. She told her colleagues she was going for a walk and a group of them saw her heading up the Ullswater Way on the Sunday. There was a subsequent sighting, further along the route. That was by Luke Helmsley.'

Jude raised an eyebrow. 'Last person to see her alive, eh?'

'So far, yes, but he claims to have been with someone at the time. We've yet to confirm that.'

Jude flicked through the rest of the sheet. Summer had been wearing jeans and a light top, carrying a small leather backpack and wearing sandals — definitely not the right clothing for anything more challenging than the road, or possibly the marked route along the lake. 'There's no previous history of going missing? No vulnerabilities?'

'Nothing.'

'And nothing special about Summer herself? No reason why anyone might want to abduct her?'

'Not that I'm aware of.'

'Then what's so special about the case?'

She sat back in her chair and looked at him with a steel-grey gaze. 'It's a little awkward, Jude, and I rely on your total discretion. Even internally.'

'Of course.'

'Very well. I know very little about the case I'm about to talk about. I'm involved in it only at the margins, largely as a matter of courtesy because it comes onto my turf. Assuming Luke Helmsley is telling the truth, when Summer was last seen she was beyond Howtown and heading towards a lakeside property owned by a man named Robert Neilson.' She looked at him with a raised eyebrow, as if questioning him.

'Local lad,' he obliged. 'Filthy rich. New money. Brought up in Pooley Bridge. Parents scraped everything together to send him away to boarding school and he went off to the City to make his money. Came back not that long afterwards able to buy a huge property and a few tens of acres with one of the best views in the Lakes. Married, divorced, remarried. Twins from the first marriage, I think.'

'You're astonishingly well-informed.'

There was nothing astonishing about it. Jude had been accumulating information about the countryside and the people who lived in it since long before he'd ended up in the police. Thirty-six years of insatiable curiosity had matured into a store of rock-solid local knowledge. Luke Helmsley had slipped below his radar but the more intriguing Robert Neilson had not. 'The kids are eighteen, I think. Spoiled brats, according to Mikey. My kid brother,' he added, for clarification.

'I see. Well, I'm interested to hear what the local gossip is on Mr Neilson. He's one of several subjects of a wide-ranging, very hush-hush, investigation into fraud and money-laundering on an international scale. Our colleagues delving into organised crime are very interested indeed in what he's been up to, how he's managed to make so much money so quickly and what he's spending it on. I'm not entrusted with the details of it, and I'd probably find it too difficult to understand if I was.'

'But you've been asked to keep a watching brief?'

'I've been asked to keep them informed of anything unusual I hear about the Neilsons and anything unusual that goes on at their property. I don't want to attract too much attention to it and of course, you're right. You're far too senior to be directly involved at this sort of investigation at this sort of stage.' Her nod did duty for an apology for her earlier slight. 'I did think, however, that it might be smart to send a detective down to join your two constables. Send someone junior. That way we can pretend it's normal procedure. He won't know any different.'

There was an obvious candidate. 'I'll send Ashleigh.'

'Hmm.' Faye stared over his shoulder into the distance, as if they hadn't both slept with Ashleigh O'Halloran and weren't both fully aware of her charms as well as her skills. 'She does have the talent for getting people to talk, doesn't she? I imagine she'd do the job very well.' Mention of Ashleigh seemed to have unnerved her. She nodded towards the door, a subtle signal that the interview was over. 'She doesn't need to know why, of course. I'm sure you can think of some reason why we might want a detective on the case.'

'There's already a very good one.' Jude pushed back his chair and folded the missing persons report in half, as if that would make his interest in it look casual to any passer by. 'Her current boyfriend, Luke Helmsley, has a record of violence and as far as I'm aware it's associated with sexual jealousy.'

'Is that right? Well, goodness. How interesting. And yes, a very good reason to send someone down to run an eye over the dale,' she said, and turned back to her desk.

THREE

The old dry stone walls that marked the edge of the road up to Howtown and beyond towards Sandwick gave way, very suddenly, to a set of imposing and incongruous wrought iron gates. A slab of carved slate announced this magnificence as Waterside Lodge. After a moment's pause to consider her surroundings, Ashleigh negotiated the cattle grid with care and drove slowly along the driveway that unwound ahead of her to offer her views of trees, of the steep rising slope of Hallin Fell, and at last of the silver sheet of Ullswater.

A marked police car was parked in the paved courtyard in front of the house. She pulled up beside it, noting the two-faced nature of the property in front of her. Old slate on the lower storey paid homage to its humble origins, with brighter, newer slate, carefully-chosen to match but not quite aged, showing just how much the original building had been extended. As she paused before getting out of her car, she snatched a glimpse through one of the downstairs windows and saw plate glass beyond. So the house was one of those, all traditional at the front and daringly modern at the back to make the most of its lakeside setting.

She sighed. Life had been kind to her and her parents had enough money to give her and her brother everything they could possibly have needed, even if not everything their young souls had yearned for, but the family's three-bedroomed holiday cottage in North Wales was a hovel compared to this. It was rare she coveted anything, but the Neilsons' summer mansion brought out the worst in her. How well did such ostentation go down in the rest of the dale where, her drive had shown her, there was money but not a lot of it and some people still seemed to scrape an existence that depended from year to year on how many other people visiting were rich?

She snatched a final glance at her notes. A girl had gone missing. The boyfriend (the violent boyfriend, Jude had observed) had reported her; but that meant nothing. Summer Raine was young, she was fit and she was adventurous, possibly too much so. In normal circumstances she'd expect the girl to turn up, sheepish after some unplanned adventure.

Jude clearly didn't think these were normal circumstances. His briefing had been casual at most, but she sensed he hadn't told her everything. *Go along and help Charlie and Tyrone out*, he'd said to her, as if either the vastly experienced Charlie Fry or the talented rookie Tyrone Garner needed any help from anyone in a routine enquiry. She smiled. Tyrone had been in the force for less than a year and already she'd heard people muttering, not completely in jest, about how long it would take him to rise to the rank of Chief Constable.

Still, whatever was going on behind the scenes, she was there to be a presence. She was there to look official and — she guessed — show a rich local family there was nothing to worry about. Fine. She could spend the morning sitting drinking coffee and looking at the view while Charlie and Tyrone took statements. It was a rare opportunity to do something more interesting than paperwork.

She got out of the car and crossed to the door, which opened before she had a chance to ring the bell. A woman whose shoulder-length brown hair rang with copper highlights, chic in a creaseless sky-blue linen frock that skimmed her knees, stood in front of her. A diamond the size of a pea hung, round and fat, on a gold chain around her neck and her perfectly made-up face bore an expression somewhere between sorrow and irritation. 'Good morning. I'm Miranda Neilson. You must be the detective they said they were sending along. I do hope something terrible hasn't happened to that poor girl. But do come in. I'm afraid my poor stepsons may have been the last to see her.'

Ashleigh introduced herself, then followed Miranda Neilson through the house into the huge kitchen. 'One of your men is talking to Will in the lounge. The other is with Ollie in here.'

There were voices from the living room — Charlie's deep, local one, and the high-pitched, slightly nervous tones of a youth. In the kitchen, sitting opposite a young man with floppy hair, a pale face and dark rings under the eyes that the beginnings of a summer tan couldn't erase, Tyrone paused in his note-taking and gave her a reassuring smile.

'This is my stepson, Ollie.' Miranda waved a hand in his direction. 'Ollie, I'm sure there's nothing to worry about, but Sergeant O'Halloran is here to supervise the search for Summer. Though of course I've every confidence she'll be found safe and well. Coffee, Sergeant?' She turned away to the coffee machine at Ashleigh's nod.

Ollie Neilson, with the manners drilled into him by a

good education, bounced to his feet and offered Ashleigh a hand, but he didn't meet her eye. Guilt, she recognised, was all over his face. The previous night must have been a sleepless one for him. 'Ollie, nice to meet you. There's nothing to worry about, just routine. Carry on talking to PC Garner, and I'll listen in.'

Tyrone waited a polite moment while Miranda brought coffee and Ashleigh took her seat, then coughed politely. 'No need to wait, Mrs Neilson.'

'Of course.' She backed away. 'PC Garner has already spoken to me,' she said. 'I was away yesterday afternoon, with friends in Kendal.'

The door closed behind her and the heels of her sandals clicked down a stone-floored corridor. A moment later she appeared in the garden that sloped down towards the lake.

Turning back to Ollie, who was folding his fingers endlessly together like a nervous bride, Ashleigh was struck by the woman's self-confidence. What kind of a relationship did Miranda have with her stepsons? A good one, judging by the way Ollie had looked after her when she left, as if he was desperate for her not to go. Or maybe she was the only person there he thought would support him.

'So, Mr Neilson.' Tyrone was barely three years older than Ollie, but the difference in maturity was palpable. 'Let's just go over it again for Sergeant O'Halloran. You said you spent yesterday afternoon with Summer.'

Ollie Neilson, catching his breath, gave Ashleigh a sidelong look that rather too obviously took in her assets, and allowed himself the kind of snigger that young men with one thing on their mind never quite realise anyone else can hear and interpret. 'Yes. Will and I are up here for the summer. We've both taken a year out before we go to uni and we got back last week.'

'You're eighteen?' Tyrone asked, surely for Ashleigh's benefit because he must already have gone over that.

'Nearly nineteen. We went to school young. Ahead of most of our year.' Ollie sounded like a man not short of self-belief. 'Last year we bummed around in Australia for a bit, went to South America, the Far East. That sort of thing.'

'And you knew Summer,' insisted Tyrone, politely.

'Yeah. We met her last year. She taught — teaches — watersports at the marina and Will and I like a bit of that. We went down there last week when the weather was good. Sunday was her day off, and her boyfriend was working, so we said she could come up and we'd have the afternoon on the boat. Miranda was away, and Dad's in Frankfurt.'

'Do you know her boyfriend?' Ashleigh asked, watching Miranda as she stood and stared across the water.

'No, only that he lives along in Howtown and works on one of the farms down there. But if he'd been free we'd have asked him to come along, too.' The way he shifted in his seat clearly indicated that Luke Helmsley was never intended to have any part in what the twins might have planned for Sunday afternoon.

'And so Summer came along at…what time?' Tyrone made rapid notes at the side of his pad, reminding himself of things to ask.

'About noon. We went out on the *Seven of Swords* and had some lunch and…stuff.'

'The *Seven of Swords*?' Despite her intention to leave the questions to Tyrone, Ashleigh intervened. The constable had missed that little detail, but then again, he would. As far as she knew he was a man for intense practicalities, and he couldn't possibly know the card she'd drawn that morning.

'Yeah, that's our boat.' He jerked a head towards the lake where a sleek, white vessel sat fifty yards or so off the lake in front of the house. 'We keep her up here.'

'Oh, I see. Thank you.' She nodded to Tyrone and let him take over, smiling a little at what must be coincidence.

'Yeah. So we had something to eat.'

'Which was?'

'Err…sandwiches and stuff.' Ollie went pink. 'And a beer. Maybe a couple of beers. I fell asleep and Will must have done, too. When we woke up, she wasn't on the boat.'

'Okay. And what time was that?'

'About five o'clock.'

'And weren't you worried?'

'Nah. We thought she'd need to get back and she must have decided not to wake us.'

'And the boat,' pursued Tyrone, in patient explanation, 'was out on the lake, where it is now?'

'Yeah.'

'And you get there by a dinghy.'

'Yes, but it was tied to the boat.'

'And so how did Summer get to the shore?'

There was a long pause. 'Don't know.' Ollie pushed his chest out in what was obvious defiance, snatched a sideways look at Ashleigh, who returned it with interest just to let him know she was already onto the probability he was lying, and turned back to Tyrone. 'I never thought of that. I just woke up and she'd gone.'

'Perhaps your brother rowed her over to the shore.'

Ollie snorted. 'Will was way more drunk that I was. I had to wake him up.' He brightened. 'She must have swum.'

'In her clothes?'

'Yeah, why not?' The youth brightened, as if a solution had occurred to him. 'She was really sporty. I think she went wild swimming and stuff. Or maybe she rowed over with her bag and stuff and then returned the boat so we could get off, and then swam back and got dressed and walked home. That would make sense.'

'Perfect sense. You didn't think to check she'd got home safely?'

'No, because…well, I didn't think. It didn't occur to me. To tell you the truth, I didn't think anything, much. I'd had quite a lot to drink. Beer. And it was hot. Goes right to your head.'

'Anything other than beer?'

Ollie squirmed in his seat. 'Summer brought a bottle of vodka.'

'And anything else?'

'No.' Ollie's ears flamed scarlet.

'Okay. But it's fair to say you were drunk. And Summer?'

'Very drunk. I hope she's okay. Maybe she fell asleep somewhere on the way home.'

Tyrone looked at Ashleigh, received a nod, and put his pen down. 'I'm going to ask you to read over this statement as I've written it, and initial it as a true representation of everything you've told me today. If Summer doesn't turn up somewhere in the very near future, I expect we'll be back for more questions.'

'Because we were the last people to see her, yeah?'

'The last that we know of.' Tyrone handed the sheet of paper and the pen to Ollie, who barely scanned it before signing his name at the bottom of it. He must be keen to get rid of them. And then he'd be checking with his twin to make sure they'd said the same thing although, she realised with a sigh, they were probably both smart enough to do that before they started.

Summer might turn up, but she had the distinct

impression Ollie knew more than he was letting on. She pushed her chair back. 'Thanks a lot, Ollie. You were a great help.' She smiled at him, a full-on smile he tried and failed to return. The blush deepened. Ollie Neilson was a confident young man, and she didn't think a smile from a woman usually sent him that beetroot colour. Yes; surely he had something to hide.

'Thanks, Sergeant. Constable.' He nodded them out of the kitchen, grandly. 'I'll go and get Miranda. She'll want to see you off.'

In the living room, Charlie was wrapping up his interview with Will. 'Thanks, lad,' he was saying. 'That's all I need just now.

Will bounced up with obvious relief and the slightest nod passed between him and Ollie, as if each had concluded their side of a bargain, as he flung open the french window and yelled for his stepmother.

Miranda had been waiting for the summons, and was in the room in half a dozen strides. 'Thank you, Ollie. Will.' She dismissed her stepsons with grace, and they withdrew without any sign of the tension common between teenage children and a second wife only three years into their lives. Maybe they were glad to get off so lightly. Instead, she addressed herself to the three police officers. 'Thank you for being so helpful. And so understanding. I'm afraid the boys don't seem to have covered themselves with glory yesterday.'

'Boys will be boys.' Tyrone nodded his head as if he were twenty years older.

'We don't encourage them to drink a lot, and they've yet to learn to handle what they do drink, it seems. And I believe the young woman brought spirits. Of course, if I'd been here this wouldn't have happened. Or not in the same way. I worry I cut them too much slack, but I try to turn bit of a blind eye. They're so young.'

And she was their stepmother and didn't have the authority their father would have. 'When is Mr Neilson expected back?' Ashleigh asked, as Charlie and Tyrone got into the patrol car and headed off to make further inquiries in the village.

'He was due home on Friday, but I spoke to him earlier and he's coming back straight away.' The faintest scowl crossed her face. 'He won't be pleased. I'm afraid he can be a little puritanical. They like to have fun. I think the party on the *Seven of Swords* was Ollie's idea.'

'That's a wonderful name for a boat.'

'It's a tarot card. A fortune teller drew the card for me at a fair, years ago, and I liked the name.'

A short silence hovered between them. 'Thanks for your help.' Ashleigh moved towards the car.

'No, thank you, Sergeant O'Halloran.' A pause. 'I do hope you find the poor girl safe and well.'

'We'll do our best.'

Ashleigh slid into the car and started the engine, noting how Miranda watched her all the way along the curve of the drive until she was out of sight. It wasn't until she was off the premises and could park up in a field gateway that she called Jude. The phone rang three times before he answered it, seconds she spent looking out through the window and down over the lake to the *Seven of Swords*, now the last place that Summer Raine had been seen alive. 'Jude. I've just been at Waterside Lodge with Tyrone and Charlie. The Neilson place. I smell a rat.'

'Do you indeed? What sort?'

Many things attracted Ashleigh to Jude Satterthwaite and his voice, whose sharpness was underpinned with humour that most people failed to pick up, was one of them. Today, rather to her surprise, she didn't hear his usual enthusiasm and readiness to listen but instead identified a thread of weariness, as if the rat was a problem too many for a Monday morning. 'We've spoken to the two Neilson boys. They had Summer round for drinks yesterday.'

'I see.'

She'd expected him to be more forthcoming. 'I'll be damned if it was just drink. I'll lay a little wager they were smoking something at the very least. I'd like us to have a wee look around.'

Jude was a stickler for the rules and the law, a man who never flinched from difficult territory even when there might be personal cost. Today even the hint of illegal substances didn't tempt him into action. 'I don't think so.'

'No, listen. I know what you're thinking. I know there's nothing to suggest Summer's vulnerable and I know she's capable of looking after herself. But if she went home off her head on drink and drugs then something terrible could have happened to her. We need to find out what she took, if she took anything, and where she got it.'

In a silence at the other end of the phone she imagined him weighing up the pros and cons, balancing out arguments, some of which would be unknown to her. 'Fair point, and from what you say it does seem as if she may have come to some harm. I'll escalate it. I'll get the mountain rescue people on it. Divers, too, if you think we need them. But no search of the Neilson property.'

'Jude. What if they—?'

'Do you have any evidence they were using drugs?'

'No, none.'

'Right. Then no search. Not until you come up with something better, or unless you can give me any real suggestion that we might find her there. Sorry.'

He could have done it. In Ashleigh's view they had clear grounds for suspicion. 'Is there something I don't know?'

'Clearly,' he snapped back at her, uncharacteristically sharp. 'Otherwise we'd know exactly where to find her, wouldn't we?' And he ended the call.

FOUR

The police came back in the early afternoon, with boats and divers under the supervision of Ashleigh O'Halloran, who stood on the shore with a radio and a clipboard. When Miranda went up to the first floor and looked out from her bedroom she spotted another boat, just off the shore further down the lake path, and figures in hi-vis vests tramping through the fresh green curls of early summer ferns. At the edge of the lawn Ollie, looking exactly like his father, stood with his hands in his pockets and, she suspected, a frown of deep thought on his face, watching them with Will hovering just behind him like a downtrodden handmaid. The boys must know something and the police might know they knew.

This is all getting too difficult, Miranda said to herself, taking another look over the silver sheet of water, rippling in the stiff breeze. The boats from the sailing school weren't out today, maybe as a mark of respect or maybe because Summer's former colleagues were too busy answering the police's questions. She could tell by the severe look on Ashleigh O'Halloran's face that they weren't expecting to find Summer alive.

Where could the girl have gone? People didn't just disappear. And somehow, her instinctive response was one she couldn't share with the police, no matter how much she might want to. The fear that lay like a rock in the pit of her stomach wasn't one that anyone else could understand. *It'll be me next.*

Miranda wasn't a woman for leaving things alone. She strode down the stairs with purpose and out into the garden to where the twins were standing. Will, she could tell, would rather be anywhere else and only Ollie's bullish determination kept him there, tethered to his brother by an invisible tie. Of the two of them she liked Will the better, but he was the weak link. Even at the age of eighteen Ollie, a formidable businessman in the making, was the one she could deal with. 'Will, would you pop in and put the kettle on? Maybe offer the police a coffee or something.'

'Keep them sweet, eh?' muttered Ollie as Will took advantage of the loophole and scuttled back towards the house. 'Great idea.'

'It never does any harm to be hospitable.'

'Right.'

When Will had gone, he turned to her and stared, cool brown eyes weighing her up. She often thought she was glad Robert loved her and today a similar thought occurred to her about her stepson. *I'm glad he isn't my enemy.* 'Are you okay, Ollie? Yesterday must have been shocking for you.'

'Sure was.' He showed the faintest sign of weakness, biting his lip, but he didn't take his eyes off her. 'Just as well you were out all afternoon, eh, Miranda?'

'And just as well it was only alcohol and not drugs you had on the boat, eh, Ollie?' she rejoined, deadpan.

His face cracked into a wary smile. 'Do you think you can keep Dad sweet for us?'

'I doubt it. He'll assume the worst and act on it. You know what he's like. But I promise you I'll try.'

He sighed. 'Okay.' One day in the not-too-distant future he'd be brave enough to challenge his father, the young stag taking on the old, but they all knew he wasn't ready yet. There would be drama aplenty in the Neilson household when that day came. 'And in return I promise I'll forget I saw your car outside the house when you said you were still in Kendal.'

She nodded him a gracious acceptance, but the conversation terminated as the sergeant strode up the lawn towards them. Beside her, Ollie allowed himself the lowest of wolf-whistles, unwilling to let a sexy woman escape his notice yet not quite daring to antagonise the law. Scrutinising her with care, Miranda judged his appreciation to be well-earned. The woman had curves many other women would have envied but which must send a low rumbling through a red-blooded male. She wasn't what Miranda herself would have called beautiful, but she had an earthy attractiveness. There was a sensuousness about her that reminded Miranda of Elizabeth, her long-ago best friend.

But Elizabeth was dead and Summer was probably dead too. *Am I next*? wondered Miranda, as a chill threaded itself around her spine and up to her neck. *Could there possibly be a connection*? She shivered.

'Are you all right, Mrs Neilson?' The detective reached them and must have read Ollie's body language and found his thoughts unwelcome, but she could look after herself, brushing his smile of welcome aside and turning her back on him. This show of spirit, this putting the bumptious young man firmly in his place, was admirable and Miranda warmed to her. 'You look pale. I'm so sorry we have to do this. Please don't feel you have to stay here.'

'It's all right.' Miranda kept half an eye on Ollie, who'd taken a step back and was eyeing the woman up from the rear, now, with obvious appreciation. She wished she dared scowl at him. 'I quite understand. But it's so distressing. The poor girl. An accident, you suppose?'

'I don't suppose anything,' the woman said, words that surely came from the dictionary of stock phrases for reassuring the public.

'But you're looking for a body.' Miranda didn't know why she was harping on about it. It was better to let it go, not to show anything other than a stranger's shock at an overly-close death.

Ashleigh O'Halloran was looking at her carefully and to her shock Miranda suddenly found herself wanting to tell the woman all about Elizabeth and what she'd done, about how she'd died, and about the guilt Miranda herself would carry with her until the day the past caught up with her. One day, perhaps one day soon, the police might be probing the cold depths of Ullswater looking for Miranda herself. 'Sergeant O'Halloran.'

'Yes?'

Thank God Ollie was within earshot. Otherwise she might have done it, might actually have committed the cardinal sin of telling the police the truth they hadn't asked her for. 'This poor girl. You will find her, won't you?'

The detective looked at her again, long and hard, but decided to let it go. 'I hope so.'

'And you think she may have had an accident.' Any question, even an old one, would do to to deflect this woman's attention.

'The signs certainly point to that. After all,' (a hard stare towards Ollie, who remembered in time that it would become him to be humble and composed his face into a suitable expression of sorrow) 'it does appear everyone on the *Seven of Swords* had rather more to drink than is good for them.'

'Bit judgemental there, Ashleigh,' Ollie muttered under his breath, but if she heard him she ignored it.

'Perhaps she fell in the water, if she was very drunk.' Miranda flicked her eyes closed for a second.

'Perhaps.'

A call from down by the water sent Ashleigh down there at speed, but she'd barely reached the water's edge before the drama seemed to be over. Her heart in her mouth, Miranda turned to Ollie. 'For a moment I thought they might have found her.' But he was shaking his head, as though that thought had never crossed his mind.

FIVE

Monday morning's sunshine had turned to afternoon rain, and low cloud had clamped down over the Lowther Valley as Becca Reid drew up outside her cottage on Wasby. Ryan was already there, sitting on the wall with his scarlet rain jacket on and his hood up, and although he was early rather than she late, the abject misery of a man stranded in the Lake District wilderness made her feel bad about herself. She'd thought she'd have time for a shower and a cup of tea, at least, but the long day at work was about to stretch into a long evening doing her cousin yet another favour. A tinge of resentment coloured her good nature, regret at a promise she wished she'd never made. She pulled up the car, opened the door and got out. 'Sorry Ryan. Have you been waiting long?'

'Nah.' He beamed at her. 'Walked down from Askham. Just got here.' His Australian accent had a cheerful twang to it. Perhaps, after all, he found the drizzle different and invigorating.

'Good.' She walked up the path and Holmes, her cat, streaked out from his shelter into the porch, pressing his nose to the crack in the door while she fiddled with her key. She felt no sympathy for him. It served him right for refusing to come in the morning, falling for the false promise of sunshine. Like Becca herself, Holmes was old enough to know better. 'You can stand in the kitchen and drip for five minutes while I get changed. Have a coffee if you think you've got time to drink it. I'd rather get down to Howtown sooner and back sooner, and George is early to bed these days. But I warn you, if he's in the mood, he can talk for Westmorland.'

George Barrett, their mutual great-uncle, could lie for Westmorland, too, but at ninety-five his tall tales had become a source of amusement and entertainment for family and friends, as well as for George himself, so she didn't grudge him the exaggeration. She ran upstairs, changed and ran down again to the kitchen where Holmes was standing beside an empty bowl scowling and Ryan leaned against the kitchen unit checking his phone. With a sigh, Becca forked food into the bowl, mopped up the drips from the floor and picked up her own raincoat. 'Okay. Let's go.'

Outside, as she turned the key to lock the front door, her bad mood intensified. A dark blue Mercedes drew up outside the cottage opposite and Jude Satterthwaite and his girlfriend got out. Becca had ditched Jude after an eight-year relationship four years before and so she had no right to feel resentful, either of Ashleigh O'Halloran for falling into the lap of so charismatic and intriguing a man or of Jude for having, after a respectable interval, replaced Becca herself with an altogether higher-spec model. That didn't stop her feeling irritated every time she saw him, and she saw him more often than was comfortable because she lived opposite his mother.

'Hi Becca.' It was Jude's standard greeting, neutral, polite and yet somehow unforgiving.

'Hi,' Ashleigh said, more brightly, and took three steps up the path towards Linda Satterthwaite's front door.

'Hi.' Becca felt in her pocket for her car key and it wasn't there. Beside her, Ryan loitered next to the wall. His silence, and Jude's presence, forced her into social interaction. 'This is my cousin, Ryan.' But Jude would know that, because he had an irritating habit of knowing everything and an even more irritating habit of largely keeping it to himself. 'Ryan, this is Jude. He's an old friend.' Because that was all he was.

'I've heard all about you.' Ryan heaved himself off the wall with reluctance that verged on rudeness and went straight to the car door.

'All good I hope.' There was a smile lurking on the edge of Jude's lips, as if he found this whole awkward situation amusing. As well he might.

'Nah, mate. Not much of it.'

Becca closed her fingers on the key card, flipped the doors unlocked and saw Ryan disappearing into the car with no further ado. 'Ryan's Australian,' she said to Jude, as she walked past him to the driver's door. The smile was full on now. He could afford to laugh at her. 'They speak their minds.'

'Obviously.' He turned away before she had the chance to add to her apology. 'Okay, Ash. I'm coming. No point in standing out in the rain.'

With relief, Becca slid into the car and started the engine. 'Did you have to say that? Jude's okay.'

'I thought you'd fallen out with him.'

That was what the story was but the story was never quite the whole truth. 'Yes, but it was years ago, and we're both grown up enough to be civil.'

'Yeah, Becca. But I've never been a great fan of the pigs.' He paused. 'Though that girl he's picked up is a bit of all right.'

Becca drove out of Wasby and up towards Askham, still disproportionately annoyed. Dislike of Jude Satterthwaite was something she regarded as her prerogative, because he hadn't valued their relationship as highly as he rated his job. A more general dislike of the police didn't carry quite the same credibility, especially not from Ryan, who was ex-army. Or maybe that was it. Maybe the one branch of authority instinctively despised the other. Either way, his tactless but accurate appraisal of Jude's new woman hadn't helped.

In good weather and light traffic it was twenty minutes to Howtown, but today the cloud had clamped down on the road that climbed around Askham Fell and flooded the Eden Valley to the east. The road was slippery with mud and flooded where the water had surged down the hillside.

Their progress was further slowed by obvious police activity as they wound their way down the narrow road to George's cottage in Martindale. There were two cars parked near the marina and another two pulled up on the verge by the Sharrow Bay Hotel.

'Something up?' Ryan inquired, raising a hand to wipe away the condensation from the inside of the passenger window and serving only to blur what little Becca could see in the wing mirror.

'It looks like it.' It couldn't be important, or Jude wouldn't have been spending his evening taking Ashleigh round to visit his mother, but even as that thought occurred to her, Becca suppressed it. Jude's devotion to his job was excessive, but he wasn't involved in every case and maybe he was learning, albeit too late for the two of them, that there was value in getting away from the job.

Or maybe that was all he and Ashleigh ever talked about. Maybe, after all, he hadn't learned the value of downtime and his only chance of a successful relationship was to build one with someone who shared his priorities.

Three more police cars were parked at the pier in Howtown and the signs of activity here were more intense. Becca had to slow down to squeeze her way around them. There was a cluster of police officers, and a small motorboat sitting fifty yards off the shore. As she glanced across, a diver tipped backwards over the edge and disappeared below the surface with barely a splash. A policeman she vaguely recognised as one of Jude's uniformed colleagues was leaning against a dry stone wall holding a reusable cup in one hand and clamping his radio to his ear with the other.

'Looks like someone's fallen in the lake.' Ryan turned to crane his neck backwards as she turned the car up the hairpin bends that took them from Howtown and down into Martindale. 'Someone misjudged the countryside I bet. Rookies.'

It had taken a week for her cousin's continual chirpiness, which he seemed to think did something to offset his constant requests for favours, to begin to grate on Becca's nerves, and she was the most tolerant of her family. That was why most of the favours seemed to devolve to her. Normally she wasn't remotely bothered about popping along to see George, but she preferred to do it at a time of her own choosing and one she knew would be suitable to him. Ryan had a tin ear to other people's convenience. She dropped down the steep hill past the new church of St Peter's, a mere hundred and fifty years or so old, and turned along the lane to Martindale and the much older St Martin's, its churchyard walls standing reassuringly solid a bare twenty yards from George's cottage. 'I'll warn you. He can be a bit grumpy.'

'Ruth told me about that. He'll be fine with me.'

'You can turn your legendary charm on him.' She pulled the car up and turned to him with a smile that was meant to take the sting out of her words. Ruth, her mother, was already losing patience with their distant cousin.

'I told you. He'll be fine.' He smiled back, the full stare, the cheeky wink. Cousin or not, Becca knew when she inevitably had to introduce Ryan to her current boyfriend, there wouldn't be a lot of love lost. Adam resented everyone who challenged him for her attention — even Holmes. 'She said he can get grumpy in the evenings. That's all. We'll be ready for it.'

Becca got out of the car and locked it. When her mother had issued Ryan with a coded warning to watch his step with George, the suggestion that the evening wasn't a good time had been meant as a firm instruction not to visit, but Ryan, who was bright enough to pick it up, had chosen to disregard it. Fair enough. He'd already shown he had the sensitivity of a rhinoceros to everyone else around him, so why would he care about George?

'Come on then.' Resigned to a short, blunt visit, she led the way up the path and round the two-storey house to the side door he used to avoid the front step. The window frames needed attention, especially upstairs, but George hadn't been upstairs for a good two years, so it didn't matter. He'd be far better out of the place but no-one dared suggest it. She opened the door, always left unlocked and stepped into the dark rear porch. 'Uncle George! It's me, Becca. I've brought someone to see you.'

He was in the kitchen and she waited until he replied before she left the narrow hallway. 'Who is it? Not that new boyfriend of yours?'

'No.' Becca had brought Adam Fleetwood along to meet George on one previous occasion, and she wasn't about to do it again, not because they hadn't got on but because the last thing she wanted to do was allow anybody to jump to the conclusion there was any permanence in a relationship she now realised she'd primarily entered into to put Jude Satterthwaite's back up. It hadn't worked, and now she was looking for a way to disengage herself from it with grace. 'Much better than that.'

'Better? You haven't brought Jude to see me, have you?'

He was provoking her. She held firm. 'Even better. I've brought Ryan. Sharon's Ryan. You know. From Australia.'

'I've just finished my tea and I was thinking about my bed.'

It was half past six but Becca, a district nurse, knew all too well how people like George could spin a routine to cover three hours. 'Why don't you and Ryan sit and have a blether? I can clear your tea things up, if you like.'

George was sitting at the table, an empty plate in front of him. He wore every one of his ninety-five years like a badge of honour, tissue-thin skin stretched over a fragile frame of bone, scant white hair that had grown too long, eyes that had once been blue but had faded to the pale colour of melting spring snow, but he nevertheless showed why he was good for many years more. His facial expressions were quick and sharp, his movements slow but precise, and he wore a pair of scarlet braces over his faded checked shirt in some sort of challenge to Father Time.

'Ryan, eh?' He didn't get up, though he reached out a

frail hand to shake that which Ryan offered him. 'Your mam didn't tell me you were coming. Not that she writes to me more than Christmas.' He sniffed in disapproval.

'Evening George. No, Mum's not a great correspondent,' Ryan said, shaking his head. 'I'm not so good myself, either. I think I maybe forgot to tell her.'

'You forgot to tell your mam you were coming halfway round the world?' George's expression cracked into a sneer.

'The world's a lot smaller than it was in your day, mate. I was due some leave so I thought I'd drop everything and roll. It's how life is, now. It moves on.'

Becca moved to the kettle and George's hand snapped up in a gesture of obstruction. 'Don't bother with that. I don't take anything at this time of night.'

Unsurprised, yet without any great sense of vindication, Becca registered that she was right and Ryan had struck entirely the wrong note. All to the good. Once they'd got through the minimal painful formalities, they could go home and she might be able to salvage something from her evening. She turned to make herself useful while she could, picked up George's plate and cutlery and placed them in the sink. 'There's a lot of police activity along the lake shore today. Any idea what's going on?' And he would know, because even though he barely left the dying house he'd chosen for himself, he would come out of his garden like a spider snapping up a fly when one of his neighbours wandered by, and the couple who kept the next-door farm were in and out every day, keeping an eye on him. In his retirement, George's whole life was absorbed in other people's business.

'Aye.' He perked up at that, turning his attention away from Ryan. 'Some lass from down at the marina went out for a walk and never came back. The police came up this morning to ask me if I'd seen anything, but she was never by the end of this road. I was looking out this morning and I'd have seen. Tom Fenton reckons she fell in on the way back by the lake path and drowned.'

'Fell in?' Ryan, clearly determined to make amends by sounding interested, leaned forward. 'It's not steep along that way.'

'And how would you know?'

'I walked along that way the other day, when I got here. First thing I did. She might have tried to swim and drowned, but there's nowhere to fall.'

Ryan was wrong and there were plenty of places where you could fall, but you didn't get anywhere with either him or George by arguing. 'Awful,' Becca said, to try and make peace. 'The poor girl. Are they sure she fell in the water?'

'No, but she spent Sunday afternoon drinking with those useless young bucks up at Waterside Lodge so she'll not have known right from wrong by the end of it.'

'She might have fallen, somewhere. Or wandered off the path.' Ryan wouldn't give up. Couldn't he see he'd already irritated George close to a point way beyond the possibility of forgiveness? 'She might still be alive. I do know a bit about that, you know, George. Being in the army. I'm a survivalist.'

'I was in the army myself.'

'Yes, but times have changed. You must have done National Service. I signed up as a regular.' Ryan stretched his hands, flexing his fingers together so that the muscles rippled up to his elbows and onwards underneath the short sleeves of his tee shirt.

'Leave the plates, Becca. Sally can do them in the morning. I'm wanting my bed, and I daresay you'll be wanting to get home and put your feet up, too.' He got up from his chair, his movements careful but stable, and turned his attention to the pill box on the table. 'I'll take my tablets and be off to bed.'

Becca poured him a glass of water. 'At least you got to see Ryan.' And it been relatively painless.

'Aye. And maybe next time you come skulking up the dale and hanging around near my cottage like you did last week, lad, you'll call in when it suits me, not when it doesn't.'

'I wasn't skulking. I just came for a walk to ease off the jet lag. Got a bus to Pooley Bridge and walked to Howtown and back.' Ryan stayed seated, even when Becca nodded pointedly towards the door. 'George, mate. I can see you're tired. Sorry if we disturbed you. But I wondered about you doing me a favour.'

That came as no surprise. Becca reclaimed the glass, placed it in the sink and turned to the door. 'We really do need to go. I'll call in some time soon, Uncle George. And let me know if you need anything.'

'What I was thinking,' Ryan pursued, leaning forward, 'is that I might be able to do you a favour. I like this part of the area. It's where my roots are. Where my granddad was born.'

'I don't need you to tell me my family history.'

'No, course not, mate. Sorry. But this is what I was thinking. I could maybe move in with you for a few days. We could get to know one another. I could help you out around the house a bit. Because I need somewhere to stay. I can't impose on Ruth for any more than a week.'

'Aye.' George glared. 'So you think you're going to come and impose on me instead?'

'I don't see it like that.' Ryan had adopted a wheedling tone. 'I thought we could help each other out. Thought you might be able to tell me a bit about the family and all that sort of thing. I love this place. I want to spend a bit more time here. Get back to my roots. You know?'

'You're supposed to be a…what did you call it? A survivor?'

'Survivalist.' Ryan's face was contorted, a struggle between keeping a charming front to try and improve his chances of getting George onside, and sheer irritation at the way the old man had received his suggestion. 'I was just trying to help.'

'Help yourself, maybe. If you're a survivalist and you want to get back to your roots, get yourself a bloody tent and camp out. But make sure it's somewhere I don't see you.'

'Come on, Ryan.' Becca raised her voice, as she might have done with a child who was pushing her patience. 'I think it's time to go.'

He pushed his chair back. 'Yeah, okay. Sorry for caring.' A trace of petulance flickered in his voice.

'The only one you care about is yourself. I know why you're here. You've turned up when you've never seen me before, out of nowhere, and you're trying to see what you can get from me.' George's voice rose to a shout. 'Well, you're wasting your time. I don't have anything but this house, and if I did I'd be leaving it to people who care about me!'

'Uncle George.' Alarmed, Becca crossed the room and stood between the two of them. She could see Ryan was twitching with fury but she trusted him not to turn violent with an old man. George was a different matter. He might be too frail to do Ryan any harm but he had a notoriously bad temper and she could see him working himself up into a sufficient state to harm his health. 'We're just leaving. Ryan didn't mean any harm.'

'That young lad is just like his grandfather. I never want to see him again.'

'I'll call in next week.'

'Aye. You know I'm always glad to see you.'

Thank God the visit was over. Becca ushered Ryan outside and down the path and the two of them lingered for a moment at the roadside while she waited for some sign of contrition from her cousin.

'I ballsed that one up, didn't I?' He flipped his hood up against a further surge of rain that rocked and rolled its way across the bleak dale towards them. 'I thought the old guy would want to get to know me.'

'It's not your fault.' Now they were out of the house Becca's good nature triumphed, as it always did, usually to her detriment. 'He's very old, and he hates having his routine disturbed.' Sometimes she thought their great uncle's bursts of irrational fury were all he had left, rage his only weapon against impending death. That was why she still kept coming along to see him, despite his undoubted malice.'Besides, I think you struck a raw nerve with him. Mum says he never got on with your grandfather.'

'You reckon that's it? That it wasn't me?'

'I think you probably rushed him a little. And maybe you remind him a little of his brother.'

'You think I do?'

'I don't know.' She considered. The Barrett brothers existed as youths only in one or two sepia photographs, taken before Ryan's grandfather had died in the 1950s and his widow had emigrated to Australia with their children. Ryan had a long thin face that sat strangely above his muscular torso and bore no resemblance to their matching square jaws, but he had sandy hair and she remembered her mother saying they'd been a trio of redheads. That might go some way to explaining George's short fuse. 'I wouldn't take it to heart.'

'Well, I'm here whether he likes it or not. I won't bother him again if you think I shouldn't, but I thought it would be a good thing for both of us. He's not getting any younger and I won't be here for ever.'

'I can't see George agreeing to it, I'm afraid.' Becca took another look down towards the shore, her thoughts briefly with the girl missing on the lake. The police should come along and ask George about her, because if she'd gone past the cottage and he was awake he'd almost certainly have seen her. The cottage dominated the route down through Howtown to Sandwick and he liked to know what his neighbours were up to.

'Maybe you're right. And maybe he was right, too. Maybe I should get a tent and camp out for a bit. It's so different to Down Under. I could learn to love it, but yeah. I don't need a roof over my head. Not right now.'

Tactless he might be, but at least he could see sense. On balance, Becca thought she was entitled to heave a sigh of relief this ordeal was over. 'Since you're here, would you like to have a quick look at the church.'

'Is it open?'

'No, not at the moment. But we can look at the graveyard. Your grandfather's buried here. So is mine.' In time George would be buried next to them in a long-reserved plot, possibly the last of the residents of the dale to find eternal rest within it. Becca's lips twitched at the thought of the three brothers bickering into eternity. She led Ryan around to the church, through the ancient gate with a heavy stone on a spring to close it. 'Look how they do this. It's a self-closing gate? Isn't it clever? They have to be careful about keeping it closed, or the sheep get in.'

'Doesn't seemed to have worked,' he said, looking round.

The nettles and brambles that burgeoned around the low slate building had been trampled and someone had forced back the branches of an ancient yew tree so that one of them had snapped and hung forlornly, glistening its rain. 'I expect that's the police, looking for that poor girl.'

'They've made a right mess.'

They had, but Becca was glad of that. It spared her the thought of stumbling over a body, lying in the long wet grass that whipped around her legs. She led him to the two gravestones set close to the rear wall. 'Here you go.'

Frank Barrett had died relatively young and lichen had had the better part of seventy years to climb over the unyielding surface, but his name and his date of birth were clear. There was nothing else, other than the terse note that he was of the parish — no words of love or comfort or regret from his widow and children. There must have been a reason why everyone disliked him, but for all that he was her family. Next time she came, she'd try and remember to bring some flowers.

Ryan spent ten minutes standing by the grave looking contemplative. Leaving him to enjoy whatever thoughts he could muster of his late grandfather — because something told her he wasn't usually the thoughtful, sensitive type — Becca strayed out of the churchyard, past a couple of curious Herdwick sheep and up to the top of the rise where George's house sat. The frantic activity still seemed to be ongoing at the lake, and as she watched a Range Rover eased over the bridge at Sandwick and through the electric gates at Waterside Lodge.

'Okay,' Ryan said, appearing beside her. 'That's me done my duty by the old bugger. I said hello and goodbye to him, and that's all you can do, isn't it? It's not like I ever met him.'

As they headed back to the car the drizzle turned once more to rain and the wind flayed the drops into slingshots that came at them with force. With relief, Becca made the comfort of the car and as they headed up the dale she saw George, in his eyrie on the front room window, gesturing vigorously. He might have been waving, or he might have been shaking his fist. With George, you never knew.

SIX

There was no shortage of opinions in and around Pooley Bridge and plenty of folk were keen to share them with the police. Though Summer Raine had passed only briefly through the lives of the villagers, many of them remembered her as an ever-cheerful, ever-bubbly, skimpily-clad visitor from the previous year and had been happy enough to see her back again, some of them for the full force of her personality but others, Ashleigh suspected, for the opportunity it gave them to be scandalised. But most of the flak that was incoming towards the unfortunate Summer wasn't personal. Most of it was directed towards her boyfriend, Luke Helmsley.

'No-one likes the guy,' Tyrone said to Ashleigh, handing her a sheaf of scrawled witness statements as she stood beside her parked car in the centre of the village. 'Have a look through. They say he's rude. They say he's aggressive. They say he drinks a lot and drink doesn't suit his nature. Most of them think he's done her in, though none of them can say why, or when, or how.'

'Most of them don't know where she was on Sunday afternoon, then,' Ashleigh observed, accepting the papers and looking down at the top one, which bore out exactly what Tyrone had just been saying. 'If they did they'd be putting two and two together and getting five.'

'Doing our job for us, eh?' Having completed his mission, Tyrone turned back again towards the main street. 'We've spoken to anyone who was up Howtown way and might have seen her, but there's no sign of her.'

Ashleigh reviewed the route in her head. She'd never been there but she'd scanned the map. 'She might have come back along the lakeside path, then.'

'I spoke to a few people who were out on it between about three and five. Nobody saw her.'

'Those boys were lying about how much they drank,' she said, thinking aloud. And drugs. She was sure there must have been drugs involved. Jude's refusal to accept it still irritated her.

'She might have been so drunk she went the other way, but if she did that she'd have had to go across the bridge at Sandwick and then she'd have realised.'

'You think? Those boys looked pretty rough when we spoke to them and that was the day after.' She frowned and recalled the map again. It would have been all too easy for Summer to have disappeared off into the hills.

'We'll all just have to keep looking.' Tyrone squinted along to the hills. It was May but the nights were still cold and Summer hadn't been dressed for the outdoors. She'd been gone for almost forty eight hours.

'Yes. No point in giving up hope.' Ashleigh checked her watch, her mind already flitting ahead to what would need to be done next. There was a huge area to cover and her gut instinct was that it was fruitless and that drink and drugs and folly had sent Summer stumbling to death by misadventure. If she'd survived, surely someone would have found her.

Her phone rang. 'Thanks Tyrone. Keep going. I'll need to answer this.' She turned away, raising the phone to her ear. 'Hello.'

'Bad news.' It was one of the uniformed policewomen engaged in the search up at Howtown. 'We've found a body.'

'In the lake?' Ashleigh's heart dived into a sick, horrible place. The first knowledge of death, accidental or otherwise, never got any easier, though when she'd joined the force she'd thought it would. 'Is it Summer?'

'Yes. Young female, long blonde hair. Tattoo of a butterfly on the back of the left thigh, another butterfly on the left collarbone. Naked.'

Oh God. 'Whereabouts?'

'In the water just off the lake path. Near a spot called Kailpot Crag.'

Dead, naked. How much were the Neilson twins lying? How far out of hand had their mini orgy got? 'Any signs of injury?'

'Nothing obvious. But her clothes and her bag were there, all in a neat pile on the shore. Purse and phone on there, so it doesn't look like anything's been taken. The bank card is in the name of Summer Raine.'

'Okay. I'll get down there as soon as I can.' Ashleigh ended the call with a further bout of instructions, even though the constable on the other end of the line would know exactly what to do and would have a uniformed sergeant on hand to ask if she didn't. 'Tyrone, you keep on here. They think they've found her.'

She walked round to the driver's side and slid into the seat, clicking the seat belt fastened before putting in a call to Jude. 'I don't know if you've heard yet. It looks as if we've found Summer's body.'

'No. I hadn't heard.' There was pause, as though he was mentally rearranging his day, which would mean that Summer's death was potentially far more significant than just an accidental death. 'Where are you?'

'Pooley Bridge. They found her in the lake just under Hallin Fell. I'm just heading down there.'

'Okay. I'll come down and join you. Just to see what's going on.'

So she was right. Jude wouldn't normally ditch whatever he was doing to come and take an interest in the discovery of a body. There were plenty of people on site, apart from herself, capable of doing whatever needed to be done and plenty more to whom he could have delegated the job if necessary. 'It was at Kailpot Crag, apparently. You know it?'

'Yes. It's midway between Sandwick and Howtown if you go by the lake route. About a mile, either way. Did anything come from the witness statements?'

'Only that they all seem to think it was the boyfriend whodunnit, even though there's absolutely no evidence of any foul play.'

'Interesting. Okay, I'll let you get on. You carry on. I'll be about fifteen minutes behind you.'

Ashleigh started the car and drove, without any particular urgency, along the narrow lakeshore road. On another day she'd have spent more time appreciating the beauty of one of Ullswater's moodier days. The previous day there had been sun and the fresh green shoots of spring, a shimmering ripple of turquoise where bluebells were about to burst out, but today a clag of thick wet cloud smothered the tops of even the lower fells and shower after shower blew in on the westerly breeze. It took her ten minutes to reach Howtown, where she parked at the side of the road.

Carly Bright, the uniformed policewoman who'd called her, was waiting for her. 'We've closed the path to the public at both ends. I'll take you along and show you the lie of the land. If you ask me it's pretty clear what happened. She decided to go for a swim and couldn't get out. Cramp, maybe. The water's cold if you're not used to it.'

Ashleigh let the woman's assumptions go unchallenged. It might be all there was to it. It might not be. Only a rigorous examination of the evidence would give them an idea and even then the circumstances of Summer's death might never be established.

Turning up the hood of her raincoat against the drips from the trees where the path entered the wood, she followed her uniformed colleague along the narrow path. About a mile, Jude had said, and the quick glance she'd snatched at the map showed her that it was, indeed, as far from the road as possible. That sparked a warning at the back of her mind.

As they squelched through the last few yards, she saw Carly and her colleagues had been busy. The path had been closed off and blue and white tape fluttered in the breeze. A boat was just beginning to motor off down the lake and, from their elevated position, Ashleigh saw the black body bag inside it. She shivered. 'Where did you find it?'

'The divers found it. About fifteen yards off the shore.'

They went no closer to the scene, but there was a clear enough view from the path. Not that there was much to see — just wind-driven wavelets running up to the shore and the drip-drip of overhanging trees. 'They're taking the body off now?'

'The ambulance will meet the boat at Pooley Bridge

and they'll get it up to Carlisle. We've photos, of course.' Carly took out her phone and flicked through them, her face a mask of forced indifference, but Ashleigh gave them barely a glance. There would be plenty of time for that later. 'What about her belongings?' There was no sign of them. 'You haven't moved them?'

Carly allowed herself a look of sheer outrage at the suggestion. 'They're down below us. You can't see them from here. They were stowed under an overhang. To keep them dry, maybe. I haven't been down there but some of the lads came at it from the lake.'

But it had been a beautiful afternoon and if the Neilson twins were to be believed Summer had been very drunk. Carly had photographs of Summer's clothing, and Ashleigh was more ready to look at them — a pile of clothing, denim shorts, bra and pants, white cotton top.

'Everything's looking shipshape down here. You've done an efficient job.' Jude's voice, brisk and devoid of any emotion, drifted along the path behind them. 'I can see it's all under control. I won't come any closer. I'm sure I'll see everything there is to see later.' He stood on the edge of the path and frowned down at the shore. His expression was one Ashleigh was too familiar with — concentration and faint discontent. Something was troubling him. 'I overheard that last bit. It looks as if you've got everything organised. Site secured and everything. Excellent. I've asked for a CSI team to come down here as soon as possible.'

'A bit of a waste of time, if you ask me,' said the PC. 'It's pretty obvious what happened.'

'Well, maybe.' Jude seemed unperturbed. 'But until we know any better we'll just treat it as something a bit more sinister. Call it overcautious if you want. Most people do. But it's procedure.'

Carly must know that, and a light went on in her eyes, as if she'd suddenly realised what was odd. It would be that a chief inspector was down on site and taking an interest in a situation that was unarguably tragic but also routine. 'Sir.'

'You just carry on. I've asked DI Dodd to come down and help out here as well. Not,' he added to Ashleigh in a undertone, as he turned away, 'that I think you aren't capable. Far from it. But as there seems to be very little doubt about the identity of the body, and as the buzz on the street seems to be that her boyfriend is a bad 'un, I'd like to go down and talk to him before he knows that she's been found and where. And it goes without saying I'd like you to come with me.'

Leaving the scene in the hands of others, they walked back along the path. Jude had no hood, but he turned the collar of his coat up against the drips. 'It's the trouble with drowning, isn't it? You never get to see the body in situ.' He paused for a moment. 'If it was drowning, but the PM will tell us that.'

'Yes. I'll say one thing for PC Bright. She made sure she had photographs of it from every possible angle. She was flicking through them like they were her holiday snaps.'

'Excellent,' he said with a cheerfulness that had to be false. 'Tammy and the CSI team will get the shoreline covered and checked. Interesting, though. I didn't see any sign of anyone having gone down there from the path. Not even our lot. Although I expect we've lost a lot of evidence already, with the rain, and God knows who was along the path on Sunday afternoon.'

'Evidence? Do you think it was murder?'

'Did I say that? I think it's a suspicious death. And until

we've done everything possible to to establish what happened I'm keeping an open mind.'

'I wondered if the body could have been hidden.'

'It's such a convenient spot, isn't it? As far as possible from either end of the road.' He frowned. 'Yes. That was the first thing that struck me. The trees overhang. You can't see it from the path unless you're actively looking to see what's down there, although there's a clear enough view if you step off a bit. And it's an extraordinarily odd place to choose for wild swimming when there are so many other, easier places to get into the water.'

'And out of it.'

'Yes. Though of course, if you're right about drugs there's definitely something suspicious about it.'

'Jude.' Ashleigh ran a few steps to catch up with him, just as the path emerged from the trees and onto the shore. 'Level with me.'

He stopped. 'Yes, if I can.'

'I've got two questions. Firstly, why are you getting involved in what looks for all the world like an accidental death and secondly, given that you are involved, why wouldn't you authorise a search of the Neilsons property when I asked you?'

'We didn't need a search of the property to find her.'

'It must have occurred to you that there's a possibility she didn't die accidentally. That she was killed elsewhere and the body was brought here. And even that she might not have died until recently.'

'You saw the pictures of the body. I accept you aren't a pathologist, but would you say she'd been in the water for longer than, say, twenty four hours?'

Ashleigh allowed herself a shiver that she hadn't dared give way to under PC Bright's deadpan stare. 'Yes.'

'Okay. So we wouldn't have found her if we'd searched Waterside Lodge. But as it happens, I can answer both of your questions, and the answer is the same, although you won't find it any more satisfying than I do. Faye has a bit of a bee in her bonnet about the Neilsons. I think I can tell you that. So she's asked me to both keep an eye and keep my distance. Satisfied?'

'Obviously not, but I imagine that's all you're going to tell me. There are a lot of lies being told up at Waterside Lodge.' Most of them by two teenage boys who'd done some foolish things and were terrified their father would find out what they were.

SEVEN

To save time, they drove the few hundred yards from the pier car park to the farm where Luke Helmsley worked. Jude listened to Ashleigh's succinct briefing with only half his attention. In a sense, she was right and he didn't need to be there. She was right, too, about the Neilsons' property. When he'd looked over the twins' statements they'd had a pattern of phrasing that suggested they'd been agreed beforehand and that in its turn implied they had something to hide. Not the drink; they'd admitted to that. Drugs, then. Ashleigh was right about that, too.

He pulled the car up rather too sharply at the farm gate. A few years before he'd found himself in a similar situation, when he'd discovered Mikey with a stash of soft drugs. His response then had been the one that Ashleigh was so insistent on now, and he'd done exactly what she wanted him to do now and pressed forward with it.

When he'd marched Mikey up to the police station those few years before, it hadn't turned out the way he'd expected. Mikey had got away with nothing more than a slap on the wrist from the police and an almighty dressing down from his mother, but there had been ramifications. The supplier of the drugs had turned out to be one of Jude's own friends, and the police acted less charitably to those who dealt drugs for profit than those who experimented by way of rebellion.

Adam Fleetwood was out of prison now, his feet firmly under Becca's table. That was something else Jude hadn't anticipated when he'd delivered his brother to the desk sergeant at Hunter Lane. He'd never thought Becca wouldn't support him, that she'd see his actions as over-zealous and align herself firmly on the side of those who believed that you should live and let live.

Mikey hadn't got into any serious trouble, and all the signs were he hadn't been tempted back into the wrong sort of company, though he still hung around with Adam and his mates, as if to make a point to Jude that he didn't need his older brother looking after him. That was the only positive he could see that had come from it.

'Okay, Jude?' Ashleigh had got out of the car while he was still turning over the past, and was looking at him as if she understood.

She probably did. He realised he'd been gazing down at the lake and the *Seven of Swords* as it floated so serenely just off the Neilsons' manicured garden. Those kids, spoiled and entitled, believing themselves invincible, weren't too different to Mikey at a slightly younger age and if Ashleigh was right they were already on a slippery slope.

'Fine.' He got out of the car and came round to join her

'If the toxicology reports show there were drugs involved, will you have the place searched?'

'That's for Faye to decide.' But there was a curl of yellow cowardice to the edge of his soul. He didn't want to go through all that again, with someone else judging him if the drugs turned out to be locally supplied, and Faye's insistence that he should stand back from the Neilsons looked as if it was all that was protecting him from it.

'Hmm.' She looked unimpressed.

He managed a smile, though it was an ironic one, at the thought of the one girlfriend castigating him for not being tough enough on drugs where the former one had cut him off for precisely the opposite reason. 'Let's get on with the matter in hand, shall we?'

The farmer directed them to a field a further half mile up the dale where Luke Helmsley, clad in wellies that were thick with mud, stained overalls that might once have been blue and a hat sodden with the last of the rain, was standing back and surveying a bulge in a dry stone wall with a pensive expression on his face. The cloud had thinned and the strong May sun was beginning to muscle its way through for the next phase of the day's weather.

'Mr Helmsley?' Ashleigh called as they got out of the car.

He looked at them, and waited as they approached, scanning them with the dispassionate eye of a stockman at a market. 'Aye. You must be the police.'

'Yes. DS O'Halloran and DCI Satterthwaite. We've come to talk to you about Summer, ask you a few questions.'

Jude stuck his hands in his pockets. This kind of thing was best left to Ashleigh, with her knack of gaining people's confidence. All the indications he'd seen from his quick glance over the witness statements had suggested Luke hadn't been the sharpest tool in the box academically, but the way the man was looking at them implied an innate cunning. Even without that, he must surely know that, as a potentially jealous boyfriend, he was first in line for questions if Summer was dead and the automatic prime suspect if she turned out to have been murdered.

'Okay.' Luke took his cap off and turned it over in his hands. He was a tall man, and broad shouldered. His hands were those of a workman, blunt-fingered, calloused and with broken nails. A dirty fabric plaster was wrapped around a finger. 'You've been looking for her. Have you found her?' He spoke matter-of-factly.

'Yes. I'm afraid we have.'

'Dead?'

'Yes. I'm very sorry.'

Luke who, Jude thought, had a limited range of emotion, paused for a second to process the information. 'I reckoned that would be the case, if she didn't come back. Out drinking with the Neilson kids, they say.'

'Yes.' There was no point in denying anything when the local gossips were onto it.

'Did you know she was there?'

'Nah.' Luke shook his head. 'Didn't know where she was, only I seen her going along the road. I was with Tom. He seen her too.'

Jude nodded. Luke seemed to think this cleared him, but it didn't account for his later movements.

'She'd said something about going up to talk to Mrs Neilson about her masters degree,' went on Luke, 'but I reckon that was a line to get into the place and have a look round. Turns out she didn't need it anyway, if she got in with the twins. Didn't surprise me when I heard, though. She was more their sort than mine. Rich. Posh. What happened to her? Off her head and had a fall?'

'It looks as if she went for a swim and drowned.'

'That's a real shame.' Luke's face creased into the briefest expression of sadness. 'She was fun.'

'You knew her quite well, didn't you?' Ashleigh was

turning on the sympathy now.

'She called me her boyfriend. But I never thought I was the only one.' Luke laughed. 'She wasn't the only one for me, either. If there was anyone else around I'd have been interested. And she was only here last summer for the sailing season. She never said she was coming back, but she turned up looking for a shag. No strings. Why would I say no?'

Luke's convictions for violence, Jude recalled, had both related to the same woman, implying his jealousy might be specific, rather than inherent. He certainly didn't seem bothered one way or the other about the death of the woman he'd been sleeping with, and Summer hadn't been worried enough about his reputation to let it stop her having an afternoon of unleashed fun with the Neilson twins. 'I'd like to ask you a couple of questions, Mr Helmsley. About Sunday afternoon.'

Something — fear? — flared briefly in the man's face. 'I thought it was an accident.'

'It looks that way.' Ashleigh jumped in to soothe him. 'It's procedure, Mr Helmsley. that's all. Trying to pin down when and how it happened. Just boxes we have to tick.' She made a face, as though she was confiding in him. 'We'll be asking the same of her colleagues. It's in case anyone saw her.'

'I didn't see her after when I told you. Tom sent me further up the dale and I was there 'til about six o'clock. Then I went home.'

Jude had fished a notebook out of his pocket and was jotting down a brief summary of the conversation. 'When did you see her last?'

'Saturday. We went to the pub for a couple of drinks. I went back to her place after that. Then I went home. I was working Sunday. Had to be up early.' Luke rubbed a thoughtful hand around his chin. The stubble, Jude noticed, almost hid a swelling bruise.

Ashleigh noticed it, too. 'There was a bit of excitement in the pub, wasn't there?'

'One of them in the village tell you that, did they? Some folk can't help but badmouth their neighbours.' Luke touched the bruise again, as if there was no point in trying to hide it now he'd given himself away. 'You might call it excitement. Just normal for me.'

The definition of exciting varied from person to person and it was pretty clear Luke regarded a Saturday night punch-up as the rule rather than the exception. 'What was it about?'

'Some Londoner getting loud. I hate the bastards. They get mouthy when they've had a drink.'

'Aye, some folk do,' Ashleigh said. She'd changed her voice, Jude noticed with amusement, picking up a trace of a local accent in place of her usual private-school one, and Luke responded to it. 'It all got sorted, your man at the pub was telling me.'

'I bet he hates these folk as much as I do. But he can't say anything because of the money. I better get on.' He bent down to pick up a slab of stone and forced it into into a gap in the wall. 'You want to ask George down at Martindale. Mardy old beggar, he is. But he sees everything from that cottage.'

'We've already talked to him.' George had seen Summer heading up the dale but not back again.

'Is that right?' Luke had lost interest in the conversation.

'Thanks, Mr Helmsley.' Ashleigh backed away. 'I'm so sorry about Summer, again.'

'I'll miss her I suppose. But there are plenty of other lasses.' His brow did darken at that.

They left him staring at the wall, picking up bits of rock and weighing them in his hand, evaluating them and the spaces he wanted to fill. 'It's a dying art,' Jude said, as she started the engine and drove along the narrow lane towards Howtown, 'dry stone walling. Young Mr Helmsley is a bit of a craftsman. If I knew more about it I could have had a chat with him about it.'

'He wasn't very forthcoming, was he?'

'Did you think not? I think he pretty much told us everything he had to say. I don't know if he's capable of hiding anything, although he's one of those people that are naturally suspicious of the police.'

'Probably with reason. I bet he drove back from the pub on Saturday night, and I bet he didn't restrict himself to a tidy half pint.'

"I'm sure you're right. Fortunately the only person he's likely to do any damage to on this road is himself.'

'For what it's worth, I believe him.'

'Yes. And let's face it, there's no suggestion at this stage that what happened to Summer wasn't an accident.'

'True. But I do wonder why she chose to go swimming of that particular piece of shoreline when it would have been so easy to go from somewhere else.'

'I know. That niggles at me, too. I'd like to check up on her phone records. That's one thing we can do. I'll get young Chris onto that when I get back to the office. And you'd better head on up and break the news to the Neilsons. It'll be interesting to see how those two lads react.' But as he stopped at the pier at Howtown to let her out before he headed back to Penrith, Jude knew that unless the post-mortem or the crime scene assessment showed any signs of foul play, Summer's death would be deemed an accident and go unresolved. And he, like Ashleigh, would find that profoundly unsatisfactory.

EIGHT

The hubbub on the lake path had died down, but there was a brooding sense of doom hanging over Waterside Lodge. It wasn't over.

'What do you think's going on, Miranda?' Will asked. His face had a pallor about it, and his usual chirpy attitude was subdued. The twins were only eighteen, Miranda reminded herself as she watched Ashleigh O'Halloran's car drawing up at the front of the house, and death was very shocking at that age. At any age.

'Come to arrest us, I bet.' Ollie was the type who became morose when things got him down. 'Hey, look on the bright side. It's that sexy blonde detective. I'd quite like to be handcuffed to her.'

'Ollie. That's totally inappropriate.' Miranda moved to reach the door before Ollie could say anything else to antagonise the woman. She herself had no fear of the police and it was always her policy to be polite to everyone, to keep on their right side. You never knew when you'd need a helping of good will, or who might unexpectedly turn out to be your guardian angel. 'Good morning,

Sergeant O'Halloran,' she called, and checked her watch. Yes, it was still just morning, a couple of minutes to noon. 'Is there any news?'

The detective closed and locked her car and approached the door before she answered. Miranda read that as a precursor of bad news. 'I'm afraid so. We found Summer in the lake, just below Kailpot Crag.'

There was no need to ask if she was dead. 'Oh, God. I'm so very sorry.' For no particular reason, Miranda remembered Elizabeth. 'Do we know what happened?'

'It looks like an accident,' Ashleigh O'Halloran said. She took a look over Miranda's shoulder to where Ollie and Will lurked in the hallway, neither of them daring to come forward but yet not having the grace to step back. They were like that, always egging one another on until there was trouble. 'Of course we have to investigate it thoroughly to be sure, and there will be a post-mortem and so on, but that's certainly what it seems like at present.'

'It's such a tragic start to the summer. The boys will be devastated.' But she thought they'd get over it pretty quickly, because neither of them had really cared about Summer and the world was too rich and exciting a place for them, with too many distractions.

'I'm sure they will. We'd like to talk to them both again, at some stage.'

From behind there was a whisper and a snigger. The detective shot a reproachful glance over Miranda's shoulder and her fingers tapped on the notebook that stuck out of her jacket pocket, as if to indicate that everything they said or did was noted. The snigger stopped.

'I'm sure that'll be fine. Although,' said Miranda with a weary sigh, 'I don't know that any of us can tell you anything new.'

'It's really just to go over the statements and make sure

that there's nothing else you can tell us. There may be some further questions now we know where she was found. I'll send someone down to do that later on this afternoon, if that's all right.'

'Oh...you won't be doing that yourself?'

'No. I'll be up in Howtown.'

Miranda's positivity sagged a little. The spectre of death weighed on her, but she'd thought talking to Ashleigh O'Halloran in private might have eased her. If she couldn't tell her about Elizabeth she might at least have been able to glean some kind of reassurance that Summer's death really was accidental, and that the shadow she felt upon her heart was a pale one from the present, not the dark one from the past. 'Thank you for your help. And for coming to tell us. I do appreciate that you're very busy.'

Fear. Fear was the worst thing. As she watched Ashleigh O'Halloran get back into her car and drive away, Miranda shivered. In her pocket, her phone pinged with a text. *Flight just landed. Back by four o'clock.*

That was something. At least with Robert home she had nothing to be afraid of, and there would be plenty of drama to distract her. 'Ollie. Will. That's your father. He'll be home in a few hours.' A conspiratorial smile shifted their expressions from apprehension to optimism. 'I'm not promising anything. But leave it with me and I'll see what I can do to keep him sweet.'

Robert, in the end, could not be kept sweet, though she did her best and she could tell by the look on the twins' faces that they appreciated her efforts. In the end, when the storm that had broken within minutes of his arrival and endured throughout the evening meal had failed to blow through by dusk, Miranda had withdrawn from the battle, vanquished. While Robert was taking a business call, scowling with irritation at having been forced to come home because of his sons' immaturity, she took her glass of wine and strayed out to the garden.

After the rain, as so often, it had turned into a beautiful day, though not as hot as the Sunday which had seen the death of Summer. The wine — it was her second glass — had failed to slow her heartbeat and all it did was stir those old memories. Her pulse quickened. Fear. Again.

If Summer's death — if Summer's presence at Waterside Lodge — was in any way sinister, what did that mean for her? They would be coming for her, but where from? From the lake? From the narrow road that wound up the dale, a single track into a dead end that left her waiting on the lakeside like a rat in a trap? Or over the trackless hillsides from Boredale or Martindale?

But she'd been wondering that for years, a fear so far without foundation. No-one would come for her now. All that had changed was that Summer's death had raised the ghosts she'd thought were long laid.

'All right?'

Behind her, Robert's soft footsteps made her twitch with nerves before she realised who it was and remembered that with him at home she was safe. 'Of course.' A pause. 'I'm so sorry about what happened. I really don't think the boys meant any harm. I should have looked after them better.'

'Why?' Robert was a man with a keen sense of justice, one who never placed blame where it didn't belong. 'You're their stepmother. You have a far better relationship with those boys that I ever imagined you could, but I don't expect them to recognise your authority. For God's sake, they don't recognise their mother's. And they're eighteen.'

Ollie had made that point in the early part of his defence, before he'd allowed Will's rapid submission to drag him down with it. 'I know. And I'm fond of them. But they—'

'They're pushing the boundaries. Fine. Now they know where they are.'

She paused and swirled the wine around in her glass. The lights from the picture windows stretched out to compete with the last of the sunset over behind Helvellyn. The artificial light would inevitably win the battle as the world turned and the darkness consumed them for another night. 'When will you be away again?'

'Not to Frankfurt for a while. London, for a couple of days next week. They'll be long days, but I'll be back to keep cracking the whip until I'm sure those boys have learned their lesson.' His smile showed how proud he was of them, deep down. 'No, scratch that. I don't want to leave you here alone after what's happened. I'll ask Aida to come up from London and we can work from here. I won't ask her to stay, and she won't be in your way. I'll put her up somewhere decent. Penrith.'

Not too close. That was good news for her peace of mind. Aida Collins, Robert's PA, was fifty years old and looked older, grey-haired and forbidding and not remotely a threat, but she was someone whose presence was so severe, whose attitude very much that of a gatekeeper for her employer's secrets, that she left Miranda feeling intimidated. *All I want is peace*, Miranda pleaded, to no-one in particular. 'Perhaps the police will leave us alone now.'

'I hope so.' His lips narrowed.

Robert staying was a security blanket, as well as easing the pressure of dealing with her challenging stepsons, but maybe he had other reasons for keeping an eye on goings-on. Miranda looked away, in case there was something in his expression she wouldn't like. She never asked questions about his business. If there was anything dubious about where her husband's money came from, she'd be better not knowing.

In a strange way there would be comfort if she did. Shared secrets allowed you to love someone for what they were, just as confession cleared your conscience. If only she had the courage to trade secrets with Robert, so their marriage could be strengthened by the knowledge they kept, the ability it gave them to save and to betray one another. Then perhaps she might not be so afraid.

Because fear, like loyalty and friendship, made you do terrible, terrible things.

NINE

At the police headquarters in Penrith, the missing person inquiry had become a matter of suspicious death and Faye Scanlon, on hearing of it, had made her usual point of going straight to the horse's mouth.

'Okay, Jude.' She stalked into the office he shared with Doddsy, who was elsewhere, and positioned herself squarely in front of his desk. 'Let's hear it. Did the girl die by accident?'

'It looks like it to me. I haven't seen the PM results yet, but they'll go to Doddsy.' He looked down at his watch. 'He and Ashleigh and Chris are coming along in a few minutes for a quick briefing. And Tammy's going to pop round and tell us what they've uncovered at the scene. Hopefully we'll have a clearer idea of what's going on after that.'

She put her head to one side as if deciding whether to say more, then perched on the corner of Doddsy's desk. 'I do hope your people didn't cause too much alert and alarm.'

'You really don't want them putting Robert Neilson's back up, do you?'

'It isn't so much that. I don't want him misinterpreting our interest in what happened at his property as being interest in his financial activities. That's all. Hence the reason why I really don't want to know what kind of thing his sons get up to at this particular stage. There may be questions to answer later. But the National Crime people don't want him getting wise to the fact that they're looking at him.'

'Can you tell me any more about why?'

'Only what I know myself, which is that he has a lot of links to a lot of very dodgy businesses, and also that his accountants are the very best in the business and act for some very interesting people. And I always think if someone's prepared to spend as much money as he must do on a firm of accountants, it can only be because it's worth their while. So for my money, if Robert Neilson isn't a big-league crook himself, he's knowingly playing the part of the acceptable face of a dodgy organisation and benefitting financially from it. Does that make sense?'

Jude nodded. Thank God he wasn't in that line of work. His own job was filled with long stretches of fruitless paperwork but there could be little more dull than spending years unpicking the enmeshed digital trail of someone determined to hide the source of their money. 'Strange, though. By all accounts he's obsessively moral about the behaviour of those two kids.'

'I don't think it's strange at all. It's just a different sort of wrongdoing. He'll have persuaded himself that what he's doing is somehow okay, just as those kids will have persuaded themselves there's nothing really wrong with taking drugs. People are very quick to persuade themselves that something illegal really ought not to be and therefore it's okay to do it. You must see it often. The illusion of victimless crime.' She jumped down from the desk.

In Jude's view, motive was usually more complicated than that. He knew a little of Robert Neilson, who had a reputation locally as strong-minded, charming and ready to put his hand in his pocket for a good cause while managing to keep himself at a distance from the locals. This was telling, given the close-knit nature of the community where he'd grown up. 'Are you sure you don't want me to find some pretext to go down and chat to him?'

'I really think not. I know you're curious, with reason, but we have to treat this case exactly as what it is — a death that looks like an accident. If it turns out to be suspicious we'll rethink. But I'm sure Neilson is streetwise enough to know a chief inspector wouldn't normally be overlooking something so straightforward. Keep on eye on it by all means, but now we have the body and it seems relatively innocent, keep your distance.'

'And if there are drugs involved?'

'Get Doddsy to follow it up, of course. As normal'

When you lifted a stone you uncovered all sorts of things that you'd rather not know about. Once more Jude recalled that exactly this sort of operation had led, in the past, to landing Adam Fleetwood in prison for supplying Class A drugs. 'And if it leads back to Robert Neilson?'

'That's a very interesting point, but I don't think it will. If he has anything to do with drugs, which he may well do, it'll be at a high level and he'll be careful not to dirty his own back yard. Which might, of course, explain why he takes such a moral high standard on the subject with his children. I'll lay my house he's a criminal, but I'll also lay the rest of my financial assets that his sons are capable of sourcing their own narcotics.' She turned to the door.

'Here's Ashleigh. This must be your team meeting convening. I'll leave you to get on with it.'

Jude stifled a smile, as much at the sight of Ashleigh as at the obvious fact that Faye didn't want to hang around too long while her ex-girlfriend was there. Ashleigh had no inhibitions about her sexuality, but Faye thought it mattered, or at least thought it might be damaging to her career. 'I'll keep you informed.'

'You know where to find me.' Faye whisked out of the door, holding it open for Ashleigh and her fellow detective sergeant, Chris Marshall, and failing to make eye contact.

Even people as tough as Faye Scanlon had their insecurities. The only surprise was that she'd let it show. Jude turned his attention to the matter in hand, to an inquiry that was surely a foregone conclusion. 'Okay, then. Let's have it. I'm hoping this one's going to be fairly straightforward. Where's Doddsy?'

'He was just behind us.' Chris, who had already come in, popped his head out again and then lingered, holding the door open until Doddsy's long strides had brought him to the office and he'd taken his place at his desk.

'Okay,' Jude said. 'First up, I'm only part of this meeting because Faye asked me to keep an eye on this case, for reasons I can't be explicit about. So carry on. Doddsy, you're in charge of events on the ground.' Even giving an apparently routine case to an inspector without strong evidence of foul play might raise the odd eyebrow. 'Run us through it, would you? Beginning with some pastoral care. Do her family know?'

'Yes. Her parents have been told. They've seen the body and given us a positive ID, they've been allocated a liaison officer and they're away back to London now, to try and come to terms with it. Obviously they want the body for burial as soon as possible, so we've had to break it to them there's a chance it's suspicious.'

Jude sat back. 'And is it suspicious?'

'The PM results are just in.' Doddsy looked to his computer and ran a quick eye down them, absorbing all the available information. He could deal with this kind of case in his sleep if he had to. 'Cause of death, drowning. Time of death, not certain but probably some time on Saturday afternoon. No evidence of any external injury other than occasional bruising, consistent with what you might call rough sexual intercourse. Not enough to suggest that anything was forced. Technically, of course, one might suppose the girl was raped while unconscious, but there's nothing in either the twins' stories or in Summer's reputation to suggest that might be the case.'

'Ollie had what looked like love bites on his neck,' Ashleigh supplied, 'which seems to me to confirm a good time was had by all.'

'Okay.' Jude tapped his pen in the desk. 'And the toxicology tests won't be through yet, I imagine.' Though they'd almost certainly show alcohol. 'There may be traces of drugs, in which case I think discreet inquiries from the boys about where they came from are in order.' He felt Ashleigh's eyes upon him, judging him. It was a balancing act, a small injustice against a larger one. 'There's no need to get heavy handed with the kids. I suspect they didn't get whatever it was locally. If they tell you, you can pass it on to the narcotics team.'

Ashleigh looked outraged. 'But—'

'We don't have the resources to spend too much time on an accidental death.'

'If it is accidental.'

'Unless there's evidence to the contrary, yes.' Usually her instinct for a crime was an asset but today it was a thorn in his conscience. He offered an olive branch. 'Though there are one or two things that trouble me about it. One is the location she was found. She went to Waterside Lodge by the road and her shoes weren't suitable for that path. Even if she was off her head with something, she'd got a long way along it.'

Doddsy looked again at the post-mortem report. 'Blisters on her feet, in fairness, but she could have got those walking there rather than walking back.'

'It's a hell of a spot.' Chris spent most of his work life inside and most of the rest of it outside, and Ullswater was one of his favourite playgrounds. 'I go wild swimming in the lake quite a lot and there are plenty of easier places to get to than that.'

'And she'd climbed down the bank, while drunk, taken off her clothes, folded them, placed them neatly underneath a tree root and gone into the water.' Ashleigh chewed the end of her pen. 'Folded them. That's the thing. Not dropped them on the floor or stuffed them into her bag or gone into the water fully clothed. But that apart, no. It's easy to see what happened.'

'Deepish waters,' Chris supplied. He'd brought along some prints of the photographs Carly Bright had taken of the body, and he spread them out on Doddsy's desk. 'Colder than she thought. Slipped, went under, panicked, got caught up in a branch. Couldn't get out. Especially if she was very drunk.'

Another set of heels tapped along the corridor, another knock came on the door. 'Jude. I can give you five minutes.' Tammy Garner, leader of the CSI team, breezed into the room, smiled at everyone except Doddsy for whom she reserved the chilliest of nods, and declined the offer of a seat. 'I can let you know what happened down at Kailpot Crag, and I can take three questions. Then I'm off.' She smiled at him as if she needed to indicate it was a joke. Since Doddsy had begun dating Tyrone, her son, she'd been very frosty with her former colleagues, as if they were taking sides against her.

Jude, who was very much of the opinion that Tammy's objections had no place in the workplace, refused to give ground. 'This is Doddsy's case. I'm only here to make the coffee.'

Professionalism asserted itself. In a simpler life, Tammy had got on with Doddsy well enough, but the fact that he was only a couple of years younger than she was and a clear quarter of a century older than Tyrone strained her temper whenever she saw him. This time, as always, she took refuge in briskness. 'Fine. But no need to make one for me. I won't be here long enough.' She turned towards Doddsy. 'So. We've completed the investigation on the path. As you know there's been quite a lot of rain since Sunday afternoon and if she left any footprints they've been washed away. There's thick bracken along that way and some of it was broken down.'

'So she did go down from the path?' Chris sat forward, alert.

'I wouldn't swear to it. There wasn't a clear area where she might have got down to the water, but the vegetation springs back pretty quickly, especially at this time of year. There are other explanations. We might not think it's the easiest way to get to the water, but a lot of people walk their dogs along there, and some of them are pretty big. They don't think twice about galloping up or down the slope.'

'The branches,' Ashleigh said, looking at the picture of the body as it floated face down in the water. 'That big one there. Could she have got trapped under that?'

'I didn't see the girl in situ, but yes, she could have done.'

'And the clothes?'

'Maybe she was neat and tidy. All I can say is, we didn't find anything to suggest anyone else had been down there at the waterside with her. But we didn't find a lot of evidence that she'd been tramping around much, either. Sorry if this doesn't help, but bluntly, I'm wondering why you felt the need for a full crime scene investigation on a case like this.'

'I thought you might be bored.' Jude grinned at her. None of them was ever at a loose end.

'Aye, that'll be right. I sit twiddling my thumbs all day.' But she grinned back at him. 'It looks straightforward to me. I'll write up the full report, but as far as I'm concerned, everything you need to know will fit on one sheet of paper. And if that's all, I'm off to twiddle my thumbs somewhere else.'

'I never trust something that looks straightforward,' Doddsy said, with a sigh.

'The clothes bother me.' Ashleigh was still frowning. 'They really bother me. And there's something else. Jude, do you remember when we spoke to Luke Helmsley? He said Summer had talked of going to see Miranda Neilson about her dissertation.'

'Yes. He said that.'

'She left university in the summer.' Doddsy checked the missing person report. 'And was due to embark on a masters degree.'

'I got the call log back from her phone,' Chris said. 'She called Miranda's number on Saturday and left a message but there's no reply. I don't know where she got the number from. One of the twins, I expect.'

If Summer had found out something about Robert

there might have been a case to have her removed, but what could she have found out that Faye's connections in the organised crime agency didn't know? And it wasn't Robert that she'd tried to contact, but Miranda.

'Miranda Neilson wasn't there on the Sunday,' said Doddsy. 'According to her story and the twins, she didn't get back until after they'd found Summer gone and started sobering up. But it might be worth asking if she had any idea what that call was about.'

'What did you make of the Neilsons?' Jude asked Ashleigh. 'Co-operative?'

'Extremely. I thought Mrs Neilson was particularly concerned, although she never mentioned having met Summer. I got the impression most of her worry was about how to handle things internally — tough father, kids showing signs of rebelling, that sort of thing. But actually I thought she was pretty much together. She struck me as someone who intended to use her position as stepmother, which might be a weakness for some, as a position from which to broker some sort of compromise. I think she's a strong and capable woman.'

'Interesting stuff. But if Summer didn't die by accident there has to be a motive, doesn't there?' Chris pointed out.

'There does indeed.' Doddsy turned once more to Ashleigh. 'What do we know about Miranda Neilson? She's couldn't be the jealous type, could she? Summer seems to have been fairly easy come, easy go when it came to sex by all accounts, and her boyfriend was, too.'

'Yes, he certainly wasn't jealous, which is interesting given he does have a history of jealous rage. But that all seems to be directed towards the same woman, not Summer. I think Luke's a simple soul, but I think he's probably still trying to fight his way out of falling in love with someone who isn't interested.'

Jude allowed himself a moment for reflection. Someone needed to take Luke Helmsley to one side and tell him the only way out of that kind of situation was patience and, eventually, acceptance, but he knew from his own experience that it was harder to do it than think about it. Most of the time he managed to keep his mind free of Becca Reid and when she did trouble his thoughts it was almost always out of the office, but she'd crept under his defences. It was because her old uncle lived up in Martindale, and he'd been up there plenty of times to visit the old man when he and Becca had been together. He allowed himself a smile. George was a one-off. His views on the goings-on, and in particular the meteoric rise of local boy Robert Neilson, would be worth hearing.

He looked up and caught Ashleigh's eye and knew, by the sudden irritated pink that flooded her cheeks that he'd caught her thinking along the same lines. She'd never got over the breakup of her relationship, either, and the fling she'd had with Faye was her own way of lashing out at life. Maybe, after all, it was simpler to do it Luke's way, to hit out with your fists and have done with it.

'Luke might not be jealous,' Doddsy pointed out, 'but what about Miranda? I don't hear anything about Robert Neilson being a womaniser, but suppose there's something going on there.'

'The Neilsons were away most of last summer.' Jude frowned. 'I remember hearing that. They were getting that vast extension built to the house and they decamped to the South of France. They do say the rich are different.'

Summer could have met Robert Neilson somewhere else, of course, or there could be a whole lot more to learn. But there was a practical line that he had to navigate, one that took heed of time and resources. If Summer had been murdered, or even if there was any realistic suspicion that she'd been murdered, he might have been able to justify expanding the inquiry into her character, and Miranda, and the twins, setting Chris to follow a line of investigation that might show motive, or some connection between a drowned woman and a very wealthy family whose lives had barely touched. But there was no evidence at all that the death was the result of foul play. 'Then it looks to me as if we hand this one over to the coroner, pending the toxicology tests and leave it at that.' Because, as Tammy had reminded them, it wasn't as if they didn't all have more constructive things to do with their time.

TEN

'The least I can do is take you out for a drink.'

After over a week in which she'd felt as if she'd spent every spare moment running around after her cousin while the rest of her family pleaded alternative arrangements, Becca couldn't help thinking that a drink was, indeed, the very least that Ryan could offer her. 'Better make it an Appletiser.' Living out in the country, she was inevitably the designated driver and ended up ferrying everyone else back home. 'Thanks.' And she gave him a warm smile, because life, on the whole, was good. She was a social being, and here she was in the pub with a group of friends. What more could she want?

'Thanks mate. Mine's a pint. One of us needs to keep the breweries in business.' Interpreting the offer as a general one, Becca's boyfriend, Adam, slid an arm around her and accepted with a beaming smile. As she'd expected, there was a frisson between the two of them. Ryan was overly in-your-face and Adam tended to the possessive, but the posturing was soon over and done with and the pint sealed the deal. Adam was officially in a good mood. 'Move along, Becca. Let Ryan sit down.'

Moving along meant snuggling up close to Adam, something Becca was increasingly reluctant to do. When she summoned up enough courage and found the right moment, she'd need to sit him down and talk things through. A break from the relationship would be good for both of them. She needed a bit more time to get her head round her infernal jealousy of Jude and his new, blonde, curvy woman.

Not so new, either. It had been going on for a few months. When she'd first heard about it she'd imagined it would blow over in no time, because she thought she knew her ex pretty well and she'd have bet Ashleigh O'Halloran was the type of woman who'd catch his eye but not be able to keep it. It wasn't the first time she'd been badly wrong about Jude, so maybe she didn't know him so well after all.

'Enjoying your visit?' Adam resumed, once Ryan had delivered the drinks. The pub was busy, and the group had split between two tables, half of them to the left with Becca, Ryan and Adam at the second table to the right. In between, Mikey Satterthwaite, Jude's much younger brother, sat on a wobbly stool, part of neither one conversation nor the other.

'Yeah, it's great. Reckon I've stayed in town long enough though. I might go down and stay in Howtown for a few days, where the folks come from. Get to know it a little bit better. When I get back to Oz I don't know how long it'll be before I get enough leave to come here again.' Ryan laughed, uproariously.

'For God's sake, don't try and talk to George again.' Becca begged him. 'I'd forgotten he and Frank didn't get on. I did know, but I must just have assumed blood's thicker than water.'

'Brothers are always best friends, aren't they? Eh, Mikey?' Adam laughed.

Mikey lifted an eyebrow in a way that added fifteen years to his age and made him look, for a second, Jude's image, but when the eyebrow dropped again and the smile returned, he was back to being himself. 'Yeah, sure.'

Mikey was all right, and the continued socialising that Becca allowed herself with him was the sop to her conscience. He hadn't long turned twenty-one, very much younger than the group he was with tonight, and she was fully aware that Adam nurtured their friendship just as he did his relationship with her, and she hers with him — to be a constant irritation to someone who no longer cared. When Jude and Adam had fallen out the one had moved on and the other, refusing to forgive, had not. Since coming out of prison Adam had turned over the newest of leaves, working in a charity for rehabilitating drug users, and Jude lifted a cynical eyebrow exactly as Mikey had just done whenever Becca reminded him of it.

'Old George will come round,' her cousin said with confidence. 'I'm not my granddad. I'll pop back some time before he's had his tea and his tablets.'

'I really don't think you should.'

'Christ, Becca, you don't believe what he said about me wanting something from him?' Ryan made a convincing job of looking hurt.

'No, of course not. But it isn't about what I believe. It's about what he believes. And people sometimes get more entrenched in their views as they get older. George never could abide being argued with.' She took a long sip of her Appletiser. 'Bluntly, you're much better off agreeing with whatever he says and leaving him be.'

'I think it's a great idea, staying with him.'

Becca thought not. If nothing else, George was entitled to his privacy, and Ryan had already shown himself to be a man who had no idea of how to behave on other people's territory. Or rather, she thought he knew exactly how to behave in order to get what he wanted, manipulating people with a smile and a constant, subtle pressure. He'd done it to her, with great effect, targeting the person least likely to resist, but she was thirty-two and resilient and George was ninety-five, argumentative, and set in his ways. 'I know it seems like it. But he won't have it.'

'There's got to be someone down in Howtown who'd take me in. Cumbrians are supposed to be a welcoming bunch.'

Becca took that as an implied criticism but Adam, his hand on her sleeve as if he sensed it, laughed. 'We are. But most of them down there aren't locals.'

'Is that right?' Ryan drew the back of his hand across his top lip, and the foam from his pint collected on his fingers, which he wiped fastidiously on his jeans. 'There are all those kids that come for the watersports, aren't there? Where that girl died.'

'Yeah, they come every year. You might find a space in the bunkhouse.' Adam laughed again, good mood but bad taste. 'If you don't mind sleeping in a dead woman's bed.'

'What about up in Howtown itself? Any B&Bs?'

Becca shook her head. There was something troubling about Ryan's fascination with Howtown, even though there shouldn't be. It was his ancestral home, just as it was hers. 'Maybe George was right. You should get a tent.'

'Either that or kip down with the Neilsons.' Adam shook his head. 'They're locals, though you'd never know it by listening to them. Or the way they interact. Because they don't.'

'Do you know the Neilson boys, Mikey?' Becca asked,

to draw him into the conversation. 'They're a bit younger than you, aren't they?'

Mikey shook his head, almost in contempt. 'Nope. Not my sort of guys. Spoiled pair of crackheads.' He shot a nervous look across at Adam as he did so, the look of a young man who knew he nearly made the mistakes that led him into the same sort of trouble, or would have done if he'd had the money.

'But local crackheads.' Ryan threw his head back and laughed very loudly.

'Yeah.'

'All of them the same? Mum, dad, kids?'

'The woman's the second wife.' Mikey was like Jude in his extraordinary capacity for acquiring information even when it didn't particularly interest him, and for once Becca could see that without any kind of irritation. 'The first wife came from Patterdale, and she was great. She was a teacher. They were childhood sweethearts. But then they got rich and he dumped her for someone else.'

'That's the woman who's down there now? Miranda, is it?'

'Nope. It was some woman he met when he was working abroad, and he ditched her pretty sharply as well. He met Miranda down in London. She's quite a bit younger than him.'

'Hell, you're a mine of information, aren't you?' Ryan turned to Mikey in what passed for awe. 'You should be on some quiz show. *The Lives of my Neighbours*, we could call it. That would sell to all the networks, and you'd be rich.'

'Nah. I just remember things I hear. Folk round here talk because they've nothing else to do. And I listen for the same reason.'

'Collecting incriminating knowledge runs in the family, doesn't it?' A little jibe from Adam probably wouldn't get back where it was intended to, to Jude, because Mikey's relationship with his brother wasn't an easy one, but Adam must deem it worth the try, leaving it there to fuel Mikey's resentment. He was a more subtle operator than Becca had thought.

'I just remember things,' Mikey repeated, defending his position.

'Mikey's brother's a detective.' Adam ripped open a packet of peanuts and helped himself. 'Anything we say may be taken down in evidence and used against us.' He laughed.

'Oh, right.' Ryan gave Becca sidelong look. 'That detective?'

'Yes,' she said, annoyed, 'that one.'

'Better not tell you what I think of the police then, eh?'

'Say it if you want. You're among friends.' Adam had had a pint too many to have a care for Mikey's sensibilities and Becca's restraining scowl passed him by. 'It's a fair bet I'll share your opinion.'

'Aw, nothing much. Just that I don't have time for jobsworths who spend their lives getting in the way of five minutes of harmless fun. Fifteen miles an hour over the speed limit? A couple of pints when you're okay to drive home? These guys need to give us a break and catch the real criminals.'

'It's because they want the easy targets,' agreed Adam. 'Not the ones who cause them any hassle.'

Becca's eyes met Mikey's and each silently reproached the other for not standing up for the man they'd both fallen out with over his attitude to exactly such things. She looked away first.

'I'd better go.' Mikey stood up, hooked a finger through his leather jacket and flung it over his shoulder. 'I forgot. I'm supposed to be meeting someone. Ryan, mate. I know it's my round next. But I'll buy you a pint before you go back.'

'Don't do anything you shouldn't,' Ryan called after him. 'The boys in blue will get you if you do.'

Mikey was staying at home in Wasby over the summer and Becca had arranged to give him a lift. For a moment she was tempted to go after him, either to persuade him to stay or to go with him and make some kind of stand against the low-level niggling, but she stayed. Because, after all, she agreed with everything Ryan and Adam were saying even if she didn't like the way they were saying it, and Mikey was old enough to make his own way back home without her.

'I'll get his brother eventually,' Adam said, confidentially. 'Don't worry about that.' He cracked his knuckles, an unpleasant sound. 'I learned a few things when I was inside. Made a few friends.'

'Patience,' Ryan said to him, with a laugh. 'Patience.'

'Oh, don't worry. I've got all the time in the world.'

ELEVEN

'See you in the morning.' Jude hovered on the doorstep for one last kiss and Ashleigh, obliging him, wondered about asking him to stay. He'd have agreed. She knew it. He was as reluctant as she was to spend the night alone. But she didn't want to risk getting too close, and a dose of independence was healthy.

'Okay.' She added a bonus kiss, just to make sure he knew she still wanted him, though there was no reason she could imagine he'd think otherwise. Or maybe it was just to leave herself with that last taste of him to see her through the evening. 'Don't be late in tomorrow. After all, we've got loads to do. Lots of routine cases to over-investigate.'

He groaned. 'Don't remind me. Though it looks like we can lay poor Summer to rest, now. Pending the toxicology reports.'

They'd show some kind of drugs, Ashleigh was sure, with every case creating more work. And there was still something troubling her about the neatness of Summer

Raine's clothes, piled at the very edge of the steep drop to the water. 'Let's hope so.'

'When are we next off at the same time? It reminded me that I haven't been walking up that way for years. We should go down to Martindale and do Pikeawassa and Beda Fell. Just Pikeawassa, if you don't want to do the whole thing.'

'You know me. A good walk doesn't have to be a long walk. If we just do the morning I'll treat you to lunch in Pooley Bridge.'

'It's a deal.' He lingered for a satisfying second longer before he turned and headed down the street towards his car.

'I'll be in early,' she called after him, watching as he strode down through the evening and the last pale light of the fleeing sun, and got a brief wave in reply.

It was barely nine o'clock. She turned back into the house and went through to the kitchen where Lisa was pottering about with the dishwasher. 'I'll help clear up.'

'No, on you go. You know the rule. You cook, I clear up.' Though it had been Jude who'd done the cooking, turning his hand to a speedy and tasty macaroni cheese. 'Anyway, I'm listening to the football.' To emphasise the point, Lisa turned the radio up.

Like Ashleigh's ex-husband, Scott, Lisa was a Manchester United fan. Ashleigh frowned. This was the third time that day she'd thought of him. The first had been when her phone had pinged her through a notification she didn't need, didn't want and thought she'd turned off, alerting her that it was his birthday. Then there had been Jude's remarks about Luke and his jealousy, the thought she knew they'd shared about how hard it was to leave real love behind. Now it was the triviality of a meaningless football commentary on the radio when all the winners and losers of the season were already decided and there was nothing left at stake.

Foolish things always reminded her of Scott. It must be because she'd loved him. But unlike Jude's romance with Becca, Ashleigh's relationship with Scott had ended at a time of her choosing, a conscious moment when she realised the effort of committing to him wasn't worth the pain of his perpetual philandering, and that the charm and tenderness which she so adored in him would never only be for her. Over two years later she had her regrets, but they were never about ending it — only that she'd had no choice.

When she'd first arrived in Cumbria he'd tried to follow her but he'd been silent since then, other than a bunch of flowers by way of an apology. She'd bumped into him in a pub in Alderley Edge on a visit to her family, and they'd managed a civilised conversation. He'd been with a woman, of course, because he always was, and for the first time in years she'd parted from him without awkwardness. Maybe it was time to forgive and forget. She picked up the phone and hesitated before downgrading her magnanimity from a phone call to a text. *Happy birthday. Have a good one. A.* No kisses, though. It was never a good idea to offer him unnecessary encouragement.

Still carrying the phone, she ran upstairs. 'I'm going to have a bath,' she called down to Lisa, 'and put my pyjamas on. I'll be down in a minute.' And she'd take a moment to read the cards, because the melancholy that came over her when she thought of what she'd walked away from always meant her common sense needed shoring up, and her decision required validation. She was in the mood for positive advice and knew exactly where she'd find it.

The phone rang in her hand and she looked down at it. There had been a time when she'd thought about blocking his number, but she'd never quite been able to bring herself to do it. 'Scotty. Happy birthday. Are you having a good one?'

'I thought you wouldn't call.' Sometimes there could be a trace of self-pity in his voice but though she listened carefully, today she could detect nothing but cheerfulness. 'I wouldn't blame you if you didn't. But it's great to hear from you.'

'You, too.' A slow tide of warmth crept over her. She hated unfinished business and if she couldn't afford to have Scott as her lifetime partner, she still wanted him as a friend. Jude might have something to say about that, but he was in no position to preach. 'How are you doing? Out for the evening?'

'Just down in the Crown with some of the guys.'

They'd had a few evenings out together in the Crown. 'I bet they've forgotten all about me.'

'Never. We were talking about you earlier.'

'All good, I hope.' She laughed and sat down at the dressing table taking the tarot cards out of their slot in her top drawer and unwrapping the purple silk that bound them with her right hand.

'Yeah, all of it. I saw you in the paper, talking about that girl who went missing. Found drowned, is that it?'

'Yes.' Scott's curiosity was always superficial, and there was nothing about the case that was secret. It was safe to answer his questions. 'Poor girl. Horrid.'

'I don't know how you cope with it. I couldn't do your job, even if I could do hers. Watersports instructor, wasn't she?'

She laughed again. It was a long time since she'd found two separate things to smile about in a conversation with Scott. He'd been a watersports instructor when they'd met, but the cold, grey waters of a Cheshire reservoir hadn't sat easily with his sun-seeking nature, and he'd upgraded his qualifications and taken off to the Mediterranean to crew yachts instead. It was no wonder the marriage hadn't worked. They'd been apart so much they'd surely have failed, even if he'd been able to keep his trousers on with so much beautiful female flesh around him. 'I can just see you. You'd be shivering, even in August, and that handsome tan would fade.'

'The tan's gone. I'm not going back to the Med this year. Just looking at a bit of this and that, wherever I can get it.' For the first time he sounded forlorn. 'You know what, Ash? It isn't the same without you.'

Alarm bells rang. 'You'd freeze your favourite bits off in Ullswater.'

Lisa flung the bedroom door open without knocking, and her questioning expression rapidly turned to a scowl. '*Get off the phone*!' she mouthed.

Ashleigh raised a questioning eyebrow. 'Sorry, Scott. What was that?'

'*Off the phone*,' Lisa hissed, maybe loud enough for Scott to hear. '*Now*!'

'Okay. I have to go. Enjoy the rest of your birthday.' She flicked the call off and turned to her housemate. 'Is something the matter?'

'Something the matter? I'll bloody say so.' Lisa, tall and stick-thin, stood with legs braced apart, hands off hips, looking like a strange runic symbol from an ancient grave. 'That was Scott, wasn't it?'

'Yes, but it's his birthday. That's all it was.'

'He called you, and you answered. Ashleigh O'Halloran, what in the name of all that's holy do you think you were doing?'

Ashleigh put the phone down and spun round in her chair. Lisa was only articulating what her own better judgement was struggling with. 'I was wishing my ex-husband a happy birthday. Because we're adults and we're civilised.'

'I thought you'd let him go.'

'I have.'

'Really? Well, I've got news for you. When you let someone go you don't call them to wish them a happy birthday.'

'He knows there's no chance of me taking him back. Do you want me never to speak to him again?' Ashleigh spun back, picked up the cards and began to shuffle them, cutting and intercutting. The Queen of Cups dropped out of the pack and she scooped it up and put it back.

'Yes.' Lisa was never afraid of expressing her opinions. 'That's exactly what I want. Because you've forgotten how awful he was to you. You've forgotten how miserable he made you. And I haven't.'

Ashleigh pursed her lips. If she had any courage she should ask the cards about Scott, but she wasn't sure she wanted to know the answer. 'It's nice of you to be concerned.' She struggled to keep the irritation out of her voice. 'But you don't know what went on in my marriage.' Only she and Scott knew that.

'No, but I know what you were like when it all went wrong. I know what he did to you.'

'He didn't do anything. You're talking as if he's a domestic abuser and I'm some defenceless child. He was just never there.'

'Ash.' Lisa must have realised that shouting would get her nowhere, so she dropped her arms and composed herself into an altogether more appeasing shape, leaning against the door frame, head tilted archly to one side. The landing light shone behind her head so her short dark hair glowed like a halo. 'Come on. You know how upset you were. You don't know how worried we all were about you.'

It was sometimes hard to be so rational, trained to analyse the evidence. There was no denying Ashleigh had come closer than she dared to think to a breakdown when she'd realised nothing she could ever do would change Scott's character, that fidelity was an impossibility for him. 'You had no need to be. It turned out okay.'

'Yes, but you had to give up your job.'

'That wasn't Scott.' That had been because of Faye Scanlon, a woman with emotional problems of her own who'd tumbled into an affair with her junior officer and then ended it the moment she sensed any risk to her career. *God*, Ashleigh thought, looking at her reflection in the mirror, *I may have nearly lost it over Scott but it wasn't him who made me go*. And if she could handle Faye, who'd kicked her when she was down, she could surely handle Scott, who was only ever true to his nature.

'I just don't want you to get hurt again.'

Ashleigh softened again. Lisa was thirty-two and had never, as far as she knew, fallen in love, so how could she understand what madness came on you when you lost your heart to someone? But friendship came with just as many commitments and compromises as marriage, though a different sort. 'Yeah, I know. I appreciate it.'

'I just don't want him to treat you the same way again.'

'He won't get the chance. I've learned my lesson. I don't love him any more, but I still like him and I want to be his friend.'

'Hmm.' Maybe Ashleigh hadn't been as convincing as she'd hoped, because Lisa radiated scepticism, but she didn't press the matter. 'Okay. But if I think you're back with him—'

'If I get back with him —which I won't — it'll be nobody's business but mine and his. But if it makes you feel better you can give me a piece of your mind.' Ashleigh cut the cards one final time and then dealt them out. 'I'll be down when I've had my bath.'

'I'll put the kettle on. We both need cocoa.' Lisa turned and whisked out.

Without thinking, Ashleigh had laid the cards out in two rows of two. To get anything out of a reading you needed to think beforehand about what you wanted to from it. Still, she'd started, so she'd carry on, and she certainly wasn't going to risk interrogating the cards, or anyone else, on the subject of Scott Kirby.

She turned the first card up. 'What's worrying me that shouldn't?' she asked, the first question that entered her head.

The Four of Pentacles, a beast of an image if ever there was one. An old man, clutching treasures to himself, was the representation of avarice and possessiveness, of materialism and manipulation. No-one could ever accuse Scott of being materialistic, she thought outraged, then remembered it wasn't about him. 'Good. I don't need to worry. So if there was anything, it's behind me, right?' So what did it mean? Faye perhaps? Or just life. But it was heartening advice, and if she was going to draw the Four of Pentacles anywhere, it was in a position where it stood for the past.

'Next. What's over and done?' She hovered her hand over that one for a moment, not sure which part of her life she was so keen to find closure in, and then she turned it over. A calm feeling came over her as she did so. The Two of Cups, one of the better cards. Two lovers, smiling at each other. Normally she'd have been delighted to find it. 'I'd have liked to see this one in the future,' she remarked, aware that she was only talking to herself, that she lacked even the gratitude to be grateful for the good things she'd had. 'And where do I go from here, then? I wouldn't have minded that card next up. I'm not going to lie.'

She turned up The Sun with a beaming smile. It was the most positive card in the deck, one that highlighted communication and positivity, everything good, everything focussed on herself. 'No mention of a relationship, thank God.' It would be churlish to reproach the fates for not offering her that.

And to move from the past to the future, from bitterness and corruption alongside the completed happiness, towards the promise of a sunny future, there was a final card. She turned over the Hanged Man.

It wasn't a bad card, certainly not in the way that the uninitiated always seemed to think it was, though when she'd turned it up on previous occasions it had never proved particularly auspicious. But if you were to read it in the context of emotions, as she was inclined to do, it fitted very nicely with everything else she'd read and — irritatingly — with everything Lisa had just been shouting at her. *Let go of your emotional baggage.*

But she'd done that already. She had Jude as a lover and surely she could afford to keep Scott as a friend?

TWELVE

'I appreciate the favour.' Ryan gave Becca his best, broadest outback smile, white teeth shining in his tanned face. 'I don't deserve you. But it's the last one I'll be asking.'

'That sounds very dramatic.' If she was a betting woman Becca would have put a couple of pounds on the fact it wasn't the last, because Ryan had a unique assumption that it was normal to turn up without notice on the doorstep of family members he'd never met and then expect them not just to put him up but to cater for his every possible need. He might well justify it to himself on the grounds that he'd pay them all back if the situation was ever reversed, but he must know it never would be.

'Nah. But I was thinking about what George said.'

'I hope you didn't take it too much to heart.' Becca tucked her Fiat 500 in behind a caravan as they passed the turn for Howtown and Martindale, and dropped down the hill in to Pooley Bridge. She couldn't see any signs of police activity, so the drama at Howtown must all be over. A sensitive soul, she spared a thought and a prayer for a young woman she'd never met.

'What, that he shouted at me? No. I do get it. I forgot he's old, and he doesn't have that attitude we Aussies have. Just take it as it comes, roll up and someone will look after you.'

'I know he can be difficult. I suppose I've known him so long I've just learned to deal with his idiosyncrasies.'

'Must be it. But I'll not bother him again. Shame, because he's family, but that's the way. But I do want to get to know the country, and it was a smart suggestion of his. I'll get a tent.'

'And camp down at Howtown? You might get a bit bored in the dale.'

'There's a lot more to see of the old country than Martindale. I thought I'd take a couple of weeks and bum around the fells a bit. Walk the Coast to Coast route, maybe. So I can say I've walked across a country.'

Becca tried not to show her relief. If Ryan disappeared for a week or so she'd have her evenings back, without being obliged to operate as his personal chauffeur or keep him occupied when all she wanted to do was sit down with a glass of wine, something on the telly and Holmes curled up her lap. There was a downside, and that was that Adam would be looking to occupy her free time and so she'd have to make her mind up about what to do about him, but she'd have had to do that sooner or later. 'How long will that take?'

'I reckon I could do it in a few days if I set my mind to it, but I'm in no hurry. I've given myself a couple of weeks to wander around. Communicate with nature. Look at the scenery. Smoke a bit of weed.'

Becca flinched. Somehow the conversation seemed to

keep coming round to illegal substances. 'Just don't get caught.'

'No-one'll find me. England's small compared to Oz, but it's big enough.'

'And busy enough, too. It'll be heaving. Even if you're wild camping you'll hardly be alone.'

The caravan pulled in to a lay-by and she put her foot down, anxious about the time, keen to get to Glenridding while the outdoor shop they were heading for was still open so that she could get her cousin off her hands that evening rather than have to come back and try again the next day.

'Trust me. I know how to disappear.'

The outdoor shop was still open when they arrived, and so was the local grocer. Armed with a list, Becca went in and stocked up on suitable foodstuffs to see Ryan through to the east coast while he went in to buy the camping kit. She was out before he was, and strayed over to the other side of the road to look over the lake. The lower slopes of Hallin Fell were bright with new ferns, the upper ones a more subtle shade of green, and the speeding clouds rolled over it, sending shadows rippling on the grass like waves. Nestled in a twist of the shoreline, the Neilsons' home commanded the lake.

'Okay?' Ryan appeared beside her, his old, well-worn rucksack bulging with his purchases. A tent was strapped to the bottom, a carry-mat to the top, a water bottle each side. 'I've got the lot. Maps, compass, water purifying tablets, everything.'

'I remembered matches, though you'd better find something waterproof to put them in.' Becca handed over the carrier bag of supplies and Ryan began to stow the contents meticulously in the rucksack. She really shouldn't patronise him. He could probably light a fire from two sticks. 'The folk in the shop must have thought it was Christmas, the amount you've bought.'

'The guy thought I was a rookie. Told me I shouldn't be going out there without help and support or I'd end up dead.' Ryan laughed, and the laugh held contempt. 'I know what I'm doing.'

'Do you disappear for long in the outback on your army training?'

'Weeks on end. Okay, it's not the same as this, but I'll take my chance on a fog here rather than the desert over there. At least you've got landmarks to steer by.' He thrust the last item into the bag, pulled the flap down and clipped it shut.

'You don't want a lift anywhere else?' Becca really couldn't help herself. No wonder everyone thought she was a soft touch. She was relieved when he shook his head.

'Nope. I'll just start from here. I'll head up Glenridding and camp for the night. Helvellyn tomorrow.' He hoisted the pack up onto his shoulders. 'At this time of year I'll be up and back before breakfast.'

'You'll let me know where you are, though?'

He gave her an amused look, as though he was the one who'd lived in the Lakes all his life and she the newcomer. 'I doubt it. Even if there's anywhere I can get a signal I'm not planning to be anywhere where I'll charge my phone. Or not often.'

'We still have public phone boxes in this country. It would be nice to know you're still alive. And anyway, someone might need to get in touch.'

'I'll be in touch when I'm back. Tell your mum I'll bring all my washing.' His laugh was, at least, self-effacing. 'I'll see you.'

He crossed the road and strode across the car park, pausing only to check the signpost, and swung out through the village with a wave. Her last sight of him was from the car, a solitary figure following the path across a field, heading into the hills.

She sighed, and set off back to what she hoped would be normality.

At ninety-five and a half George was feeling every moment of his near-century, and it manifested itself in discontent. Becca hadn't been to see him since he'd hounded her and that brash Australian great-nephew off the premises, and while he didn't give a damn about the boy, he missed Becca's eternal patience and what seemed to be the genuine pleasure she took in his company. It was his fault and he knew it, but nevertheless he allowed himself to take offence. He was old, and people ought to make allowances for him.

It was a pleasant enough evening, and he was tired of being alone, so he shuffled out of the kitchen and into the garden. The sun was warm but declining. He rested a hand on the stone wall and looked down the lane to where a figure was striding towards him. George beamed with satisfaction. Luke Helmsley, on his way home from work, was always a figure to poke at, always one who would give you a rise if he was tired, as surly and ill-tempered as George himself, but without the excuse of age. 'Evening Luke.'

'George.' Luke stopped and met him with a scowl, even before George had the chance to rub his natural irritability.

'What's up with you then, lad? You're looking right sour tonight.'

'You'd be looking sour if your neighbours were dishing the dirt on you to the police.' Luke approached the wall and laid both hands on it, facing up to George in a way that challenged him.

To his chagrin, he found himself forced to step back. 'No more than you deserve, I daresay.'

'Oh, you do, do you? And were you one of them, granddad? Were you one of the bastards who've been telling the police I'm a violent sod who can't keep his temper?'

There was a figure strolling along the lane towards them. Seeing it made George brave. 'It's no more than you are.'

'Is it, aye? Well, now they're asking me questions about Summer, and folk who call themselves my neighbours are saying I killed her. I bet you were one of them.'

George hadn't specifically suggested to the police officer who'd interviewed him that Luke might be a killer, but nor had he held back his views on the boy's bad temper. 'And did you kill her?'

'Did I hell! She does what she wants and I do what I want. If she wanted to hang around with the posh kids at Waterside Lodge, that's up to her.'

'What else is up with you, Luke?' George goaded him. He could see, now, that the approaching figure was Miranda Neilson, which made the conversation potentially even more delicious. 'Jealous, are you? Do you wish you'd been invited down there yourself?'

'Nah, why would I? Can't stand any of them. He calls himself a local boy and comes back with a pair of spoilt rich boys and a posh tart in tow. He's not one of us.'

Rather to George's disappointment, Miranda showed no signs of having heard herself described as a posh tart. 'But that girl of yours. She got on all right with them. Not surprising, though. She was worth a dozen of you.'

'Doesn't matter, does it? She's dead.'

George paused, waited until he was sure Miranda was within earshot, and carried on. 'I bet I know why you were so keen on your girl hanging around down there. It was to see what you could get out of it. I've seen you hanging round the place. Casing the joint were you?'

Luke lost his temper, as George had known he would. He leaned over the wall, made a snatch at the old man's jacket and missed by a whisker. 'You shut your mouth, granddad, or I'll shut it for you! You think I care anything about how much they've got down there? What I care about is them filling some innocent girl up with drink and drugs and leaving her to drown. And about my so-called neighbours grassing me up to the police for something I never done!'

'And if anything goes missing from the Lodge, I bet we'll know where to find it. The police won't need me to tell them where to look for it, will they?'

'The place is like a fortress. You can't get through them gates without being seen.'

'Sussed it out, have you?' jeered George, then stepped back, dipped his head, and smiled. 'Evening Mrs Neilson.'

'You bastard!' White with fury, Luke made another, futile swipe in George's direction and gave the old man the satisfaction of seeing Miranda Neilson step in to break it up. 'Luke. It is Luke, isn't it? Goodness, don't be so angry.' As he stepped back, she moved forwards, placing herself neatly between Luke and the wall. 'Of course, I understand why you're angry. Let me tell you. I'm just so sorry about what happened to Summer.'

There was silence.

'I know it must have been very hard for you,' Miranda continued, her brisk tone infused with just the right amount of sympathy. 'Of course you're upset.'

'I'm upset because this old goat has been telling the

police I done it.' Luke flung another contemptuous gesture in George's direction.

'The police are so persistent. I'm sure nobody really thinks that. Everybody knows it was an accident.' She held up a warning hand to prevent Luke getting any closer to the wall that separated him from the cottage garden. 'It was just unfortunate. If the boys hadn't fallen asleep they'd have made sure she got home safely. Or if I'd been there—'

'If you'd been there?'

Fascinated, George picked up the very slight emphasis on the word *if*, the obvious sneer that accompanied it.

'Yes.' Miranda's tone was light. 'I didn't get back until after she'd left.'

'Is that right? Then it must have been someone else I saw driving your car along this road that afternoon.'

'There are plenty of people in the dale on a Sunday afternoon.' Miranda turned away from him. Her face was expressionless. 'I expect it was someone driving a similar car.'

'You can get on your way, now.' George flapped a hand at Luke. Having a witness made him brave, and he was relieved to see Miranda could stand up to Luke's bluster. 'No doubt you'll want to get down to the pub and fill yourself with drink, and be bold and brave like you always are when you've had a skinful.'

'George.' Miranda lifted an eyebrow at him. 'This isn't helping anyone. Is it?'

He liked Miranda. Yes she was rich, yes she was posh, yes when she came to the dale she'd approached everything with the wide-eyed nervousness of Johnny Town Mouse abandoned in the country, but she'd done her best to adapt. She'd been friendly to her neighbours — far more than Robert had ever bothered to be, even though he'd known some of them all his life — and done her best to settle in, and it wasn't her fault people like Luke refused to accept her, deliberately and sneeringly reinforcing her perceived different status by steadfastly rejecting her invitation for them to call her by her Christian name. And there was something about her that appealed, that made him feel young again. Perhaps it was that she treated him with respect but not awe, and never patronised him. 'Maybe not. But he can't speak to me like that.'

Luke had resumed his place leaning on the wall, and he pushed himself off from it like a swimmer from the edge of the pool and gave himself a good five yards down the road before he turned. 'If I hear anyone's been spreading lies about me, George Barrett, I'll know who it is and I'll be back. One way or another you won't do it again.'

He strode out, his shadow lingering behind him, reached the turn of the road and headed towards home, leaving George face to face with Miranda.

He missed company, and sometimes he thought she must be lonely too, with her husband so often away. 'Come by and have a cup of tea.'

She paused for a moment, her expression pensive. 'Oh, why not?' she said, after a moment, and followed him up the path and into the cottage.

'I do hope Luke didn't upset you.'

They'd got through the formalities quickly and easily enough and now Miranda, cradling a china cup that was as frail and translucent as George's own skin and was probably at least as old as he was, finally managed to bring the conversation round to where she wanted it without raising George's suspicions. At least, she hoped so.

'No.' His cup trembled in his fingers, she noticed, and she suspected he wasn't as robust as he wanted people to think. She'd stop by and visit more often in future, make sure he was okay.

'It's none of my business, of course, but it must be difficult for you living alone. If there's ever anything I can do—'

'I'm all right. Ruth — my niece — comes sometimes. My great niece comes more often. They make sure I'm looked after.' George pushed the biscuit tin across the kitchen table. 'Sometimes Ruth brings me her home baking. Becca brought these. Malted milk.'

It was evening and Miranda associated biscuits with the morning, but it would have been impolite to refuse, so she took one and turned it over in her fingers, looking at the raised image of contented cows. 'Do you argue with Luke often?'

'It's not just me. He falls out with everyone. All the time. Trust me, you don't want to get on the wrong side of him.'

Miranda bit into the biscuit and found it had the taste of her childhood, a flashback to a time when nothing could touch her and no-one could harm her. The comparison with now, with ten years of haunting, sent her heart hammering. 'Surely you don't really think he killed Summer?'

George put his head to one side, considering. 'Could have done, I suppose. No question of that. But if he'd done it he'd have hit her straight out and not cared who seen him do it. He doesn't have the wit to pretend.'

'The police are saying it's an accident.'

'You don't think that?'

'Oh, I don't know. You see.' She paused. 'Do you know George, sometimes I'm scared.' It was out, and she hadn't intended to say it, but there was something about the cosy warmth of the cottage kitchen, the dimness of its enclosed walls, the dreamy strand of a climbing rose across the window, that made her feel secure. No wonder he loved it there. 'Now you'll think I'm ridiculous.'

'The countryside can be a scary place,' he agreed, setting the cup down and helping himself to a biscuit. 'Owls. Sheep bleating. That kind of thing.'

'When we first moved here I heard a fox crying at night and I thought it was a human being.' That had upset her, so that even when she realised what it was she'd hardly slept for a week afterwards. At that point she'd almost told Robert the whole story but it had been too soon. Was now the right time? Or had she even left it too late, kept her secret so long the truth would damage her? 'But that wasn't what I meant.' She couldn't tell George the secret, either, but that was all right. There were plenty of other things that scared her. 'Those boys of mine. Robert's, of course. But I think of them as mine.'

'They've fallen into bad company,' he agreed, elongating the *a* in bad, until his voice mimicked the bleating of a sheep.

'Yes. Not here, of course. But they have some friends I don't approve of.' And the friends would no doubt have found them whatever drugs they were taking, unless they'd done a deal with some disreputable Mancunian in a pub in Keswick or Penrith.

'Their friends don't come to the house, then.'

'No. And obviously I can't control what the boys do when they're not here. At friends' houses for example. Or when they were away.' Their gap year would have been full of various sorts of exotica unfit for the ears of an older generation. 'But for Robert's sake I so want to make Waterside Lodge a refuge for them. Because the world can be a terrible place, a really tough one, and one day they'll need it.'

'Is it a refuge for you?'

She hesitated. 'Yes.'

'From terrible things?'

'Not what you'd call terrible.' George, she vaguely remembered, had fought in the War as a very young man. D-Day, the desert or the Western Front; it didn't really matter. It was a safe bet he'd have seen worse things, and probably even done worse things, than she had. 'I'm afraid I belong to a very spoiled generation. I increasingly find modern life very difficult and very challenging.'

'You don't work,' he said, after a while.

'I used to. I worked for a merchant bank. It was all about long hours, high expectations, and intense pressure. I suffered from burnout. A very modern problem, but it's a problem nonetheless.'

'And then a man came to rescue you.' He was old enough not to regard that as in any way demeaning.

'I wouldn't say he rescued me. But marrying Robert meant I was able to do something different, more worthwhile, and take on the job of bringing up his boys. Which is why I'm so worried about them. That they might go off the rails.' And so they'd got back to the point of the conversation. 'I wanted to ask you. Your house is so wonderfully set, and you're so acutely observant.'

'I've an eagle's eye.' In Miranda's experience all men responded well to flattery, and George proved himself no different.

'Yes. So I wondered if you'd seen anyone strange in the dale recently.'

'Strange!' George laughed out loud so that the cup

trembled in the saucer he was holding, and he slid it from his shaking hand onto the table. 'Bloody place has been full of strangers, and you want me to tell you if I've seen any odd folk!'

She laughed at herself. 'Oh, of course I don't mean the police. Or even that poor girl's family.' She'd seen them, or the people she'd assumed to be them, getting out of a car at Howtown pier and heading with slow steps and bowed heads along the lake shore towards Kailpot Crag. 'I meant anyone else. Anyone you wouldn't expect to see.'

'Apart from them carloads of tourists.' George got up and shuffled over to the windowsill, retrieving a pipe, a tin of tobacco and matches. 'Too old to give up,' he said, as if a justification for not asking her if she minded.

'Nor should you. It's your life.'

He laughed, plucked shreds of tobacco out of the tin and began to stuff the bowl of the pipe as he thought about it. 'There's just one person you might be interested in.'

'Oh?' Miranda's nerves tautened, as if they were the strings on a violin and a violinist was pulling them ever tighter, the pitch increasing. Any minute now and they'd start screeching, like the background music in *Psycho*. Plenty of tourists came to Martindale in a day but if George could pick one out as suspicious, she trusted his observation. 'Who was that? And what were they doing?'

He tamped the tobacco down with his thumb once, twice, a third time. 'Taking pictures of your house.'

'What?'

'Aye.' He struck a match and the flame flared up in the gloom. 'A woman. Parked up at the turning and then walked up to get a good view. She had a camera. Took a lot of pictures. I didn't think she looked like a drug dealer, though. And I've seen her more than once.'

'What did she look like? What was the car like? When did you see her?'

He considered, puffing slowly on the pipe. 'A red car. I don't know the make. I don't drive now, so why would I? But it was a small one, not a local's car. Wouldn't have stood up to the weather.'

'And the woman?' Miranda found that her heart hurt her, the fear was so great.

'Tall, for a lass, unless she was wearing heels. I couldn't see. Short grey hair. Quite a bit older than you, I'd say. And in a business suit. That's why I noticed her.'

The tension snapped. Miranda's laugh was far higher-pitched than it should have been, but hopefully George wouldn't read too much into her sudden hilarity. 'Oh! That'll be Aida. Robert's PA. Sometimes if he wants to spend time here rather than in London she comes up for a few days. She's at the house just now.' Something had cropped up, Robert had said, that needed his attention, and Aida had arrived after their evening meal and the two of them had disappeared into his study. 'It's why I came out for a walk. Maybe she wants the pictures to show her family where she's working. And it is very beautiful.'

'Had you worried, there did I?' He was sitting with his back to the window but she could just about pick out the smile on his face, although the slight red glow from his pipe played tricks with the shadows. If he hadn't been so old as to be harmless she'd have seen evil in it.

'You did. I was scared someone might be coming to the dale to…' she paused. 'To sell the boys drugs.'

George puffed away. 'You're a young woman, Miranda. You've a lot to learn.'

She was forty and already knew more than she could handle, but she let it pass. 'Oh?'

'Aye. When you've lived as long as I have you'll know it

isn't strangers you need to look out for. It's the people under your nose.'

'Is that right?'

'Aye. Because there's trouble brewing in this dale, too. So if I was you it might be others I was looking at. That young buck, Luke. He's been sniffing around your house. Looking for something to steal, no doubt, though he's so thick you'll soon catch him if he tries.'

'Well, thank you for the warning.' George hadn't mentioned what Luke had said about seeing her car on the day Summer had died. Was that deliberate? Had he just failed to hear it?

'And not just him.' George puffed out a long, long cloud of smoke. 'I saw my great-nephew kicking around that week, too. He'll be up to no good, just like his granddad. But that'll be me he wants to do away with, not you.'

'George.' Her own fears relieved, at least as far as her neighbours went, Miranda felt able to be robust. 'Why would anyone do that?'

'Wants me in an early grave for my money, I expect. But he won't get any. He might think I'll split it with his side of the family because I never had bairns of my own, but why would I? I've never met any of them. They've been over to England and not troubled to visit. They never even send me a card on my birthday. It's my niece and my great nieces who look after me. They'll get the little I've got.'

'No flies on you, George. Good for you. You leave it to the people who care about you.' She stood up, carried her cup over to the sink. 'I'd better go, before it gets dark.'

'Shall I walk you home?'

It was a joke, but she would have welcomed the company. 'That's very gallant, but I'll manage. It's not far.'

'Pop by and see me again some time, if you want.'

'I will. And you let me know if you have any more trouble from Luke.'

She let herself out and wandered down the path towards the sunset, wreathed in the scent of his pipe smoke and the freshness of cut grass, and headed down towards Waterside Lodge. George's observations had temporarily lifted the greater weight of nerves that were troubling her, but they didn't help. Just because you didn't see someone didn't mean they weren't there, but might only mean that they were smarter than you thought. It was a relief when she reached the electric gates, flicked them open with her key fob and stepped inside to safety.

THIRTEEN

Miranda, thought George, was a deeper woman than she wanted people to think.

It had been a couple of days since his confrontation with Luke and although he'd seen him passing by on the way to and from his work up at the farm, he'd taken care to avoid any sniff of trouble. Luke's temper was well-known and he seemed on edge, more so than he ought to be now the police appeared to have laid the case to rest. The sad death of Summer Raine had, the local newspaper informed him in a bare inch of type tucked at the foot of one of its inner pages, been referred to the coroner; the inquest had been opened and adjourned. The police cars had gone and the windsurfers, dinghy sailors and kayakers had started out again from the marina, the passing of the poor young woman barely observed. In his old-fashioned way George thought it shocking, but the more pragmatic part of him understood how things moved on, and put younger people under new pressures.

That was what Miranda had hinted at when she'd talked to him about the strain she was under, but he wasn't sure he was convinced. There was obviously something troubling her, and he wasn't so sure it was the boys. If they were hers it would be different, but other people's children were, at the end of the day, other people's problems. He regretted having no children himself, and he was lucky he had Becca and, less often, her mother and her sister to come and cheer him up, but he didn't miss the sleepless nights children would have given him when they were young. And older, too.

He stared out of the window. The heavy overnight rain had eased and the day had turned rapidly from dark to light. Family entitlement was something you earned, in his book. That was why Sharon's boy, Ryan, had put his back up so much, swanning up and expecting to be taken into the bosom of the family without making any effort to learn about them or listen to how they did things. And as for that idea of moving in…he'd read about that sort of thing in the paper. Drug dealers moving in with vulnerable people and using their homes to push their wares. Cuckooing, they called it. But if that was what Ryan had been trying to do, he'd been thwarted. *I'm many things*, George chastised himself, *but I'm not vulnerable.*

A sound startled him from upstairs. Upstairs? No-one went upstairs in his cottage. The dust would be as thick as March snow up there, and after he'd gone whoever came to clean up would be able to roll it up like a mat and throw it away.

At ninety-five he should expect his hearing to play tricks on him. He shuffled his way into the kitchen to fetch his pipe and have a cup of tea. It was nearly ten and Becca, he knew, had every second Saturday off. When that happened, she'd call in and see him in the morning and spend a bit longer with him. He always looked forward to that.

The noise came again. He shook his head, irritably. It might be a bird, but if it was it must be a hell of a big one. A pigeon, maybe. More likely something had gone wrong with the roof. When he'd moved in all those years before repairs hadn't seemed too important because he'd expected to be carried out in a box long before he had to deal with that problem. But that was how it went. Life played silly buggers with the smartest plans, and if he'd spent all that money and gone through all the hassle he probably wouldn't have lived long enough to be grateful there were no raindrops falling on his head; but if the roof had gone he had a problem. The previous night's downpour would have done a wild winter storm proud, and the rain had hammered so hard on the cottage it had sounded like someone was in the room above his head. The accompanying wind could easily have lifted a tile or two. When it rained again, as it would before another day had passed, he'd have problems. If there was a serious leak, Becca and her mum wouldn't let him stay there, and if there was one thing he was set on, it was spending his last days in the dale where he was born and the house he'd been born in.

It would save on the funeral costs, he thought to himself, if they only had to carry the coffin the short distance down the lane to the church.

Putting the pipe down, he shuffled towards the stairs.

The last hurrah of the overnight gale was whipping white horses to life on Ullswater as Becca came around the south side of Hallin Fell and down into Martindale. She frowned as she got out of the Fiat, because she'd been right and the car that had been following her for the last mile or so was Jude's Mercedes, and the woman in there with him was

Ashleigh O'Halloran. Her heart flickered in a moment of anxiety, as if she expected him to bring bad luck. Surely there couldn't have been another mysterious death?

He stopped his car in the same lay-by. That meant she'd have to talk to him and she wasn't in the mood — not when she'd failed to find the courage to have that crucial conversation with Adam the night before and so, in consequence, found herself ever more deeply embedded in the wrong relationship. She hated to hurt people's feelings, and if she'd known how difficult it would be to terminate her relationship with Jude she probably wouldn't have tried. And it would all have gone toxic. The right thing to do was almost always not the easy one.

This complicated train of thought, backwards and forwards, didn't help her out of her present predicament. She was still going out with Adam Fleetwood and, in the immediate future, she would still have to be polite to Jude Satterthwaite.

'Morning.' She stayed by her car as he and Ashleigh got out of the Mercedes. They were dressed for walking. At least that meant there was no trouble to be had. 'Off for a walk?'

'Yep.' Jude opened the boot of the Mercedes and lifted out a small backpack, which he swung over his shoulder, and a pair of walking poles which he handed to Ashleigh. The two of them looked as if they trusted the weather. She was wearing walking trousers and a thin tee-shirt that showed the dark shape of a bra that might have been red, and he'd opted for shorts and a tee shirt. 'I've never taken Ashleigh up onto Beda Fell and Pikeawassa, and as we've both managed to get the weekend off together, I thought I'd show her the view.'

Ashleigh O'Halloran didn't have the legs of a hill-walker, thought Becca spitefully, though Jude undoubtedly did. 'It's going to be a lovely day now all that rain has cleared. It looks as if you might need your sunscreen.'

'Yes, nurse.' Ashleigh felt sufficiently familiar to risk the joke, and she and Jude exchanged glances and smiles over it. Becca smiled back. She was grown-up enough to understand there was no way back from the way that she'd treated Jude and generous enough to hope he found some kind of happiness with someone else. It was just that she was surprised by the woman he'd chosen.

'Enjoy your walk,' she said, nodding at them.

'Say hello to George for me,' Jude said. He divided the people around him but George, who prided himself on his cussedness, liked him, probably because so many other people didn't. 'I'd pop in and say hello, but…'

That would be a recipe for discord. The last thing Becca needed was George telling her she'd let a good man slip through her fingers. 'I've brought him some of Mum's millionaire shortbread. I didn't stay long last time, so I owe it to him.'

'I expect we'll see you around.'

'I expect so.' She turned and marched up the path, the plastic tub of shortbread under her arm, and rapped hard on the door before she opened it and went in. 'Uncle George, it's Becca.'

There was no answer. Instantly concerned, she lifted her head and listened for the sound of him snoring, but there was nothing.

He might still be in bed, unable to get up. A slow dread filled her, because she was almost certain she knew what she'd find. She was a district nurse and she stumbled on the dead too often for comfort, but she was used to it. It was different when it was one of your own. She'd feared this moment for a long time. 'Uncle George?'

In passing she laid her hand on the kettle and found it

just warm, with George's pipe abandoned beside it. Crossing the kitchen, she opened the door that led out into the hallway and found him, sprawled at the foot of the stairs.

He was still alive. She saw that immediately as she dropped to her knees beside him but she checked the pulse anyway, and found it weak. His face had collapsed into a travesty even of what it had been before and his skin was grey where it had once been white. Breath rasped in his throat.

'Uncle George, it's Becca. I'm going to look after you until an ambulance gets here.' Tweaking his top button free, she rolled him gently into the recovery position, then ran through to fetch a blanket from his bed. On the way back she diverted out into the front garden and looked along to where Jude and Ashleigh were still standing, she tying her walking boot, he watching. 'Jude!'

He must have recognised the sound of an emergency, because he turned on the instant. 'Is something wrong?'

'Yes. George has had a stroke.' She'd thought she was calm but her own breathlessness surprised her. 'Can you call an ambulance? I can never get phone signal up here and he doesn't have a landline.' He was a stubborn old man who believed his neighbours owed him their help and support and who was determined to die in his house instead of in a hospital. And now he was reaping the whirlwind.

'Sure.' Jude was already reaching into his pocket for his phone. 'What else shall I tell them?'

'It looks like a bad one. I don't think he's been there too long, and I don't think he's hit his head or anything. I've put him in the recovery position and I'll keep him warm.'

'Right.'

She ran back in, returned to her knees beside him and spread the blanket over him. 'Uncle George. Can you hear me? It's Becca.'

He shifted a little. She leaned in towards him. If she'd been a little earlier she might have got there in time. She might have been able to do more for him. Time was crucial and she didn't know how long had passed. 'You've had a stroke, but it's all right. We'll get you to hospital and you'll be fine. I expect you'll be able to come back here before very long.' A lie, because there was no way anyone would allow him to come back to the house unless he made a full recovery, and she couldn't see that happening. *Over my dead body*, she imagined her mother saying, outraged. 'Can you move your arm?'

A convulsive twitch of the face was the only reply.

'Okay.' Watching the second hand on her watch ticking on, Becca understood. The worst was happening and she was watching his life ticking away with it. 'The ambulance must be on its way by now. Jude called it. You remember Jude? A friend of mine.' She searched his face for some flicker of recognition and saw nothing.

'Becca.' From her place on the floor she saw Ashleigh O'Halloran's walking boots — expensive ones, relatively new — stopping at a discreet distance. 'Jude's on the phone to the ambulance now. Is there anything else I can do to help?'

'I don't think so.' *It's too late.* Becca fought back a tear. There was nothing she could do to help him, probably nothing anyone else could do to help him, and all she could offer was calm professionalism and affection to see him out. She didn't even know if she could deliver that. She reached for his hand and held it, the frail fingers listless in hers. 'Uncle George. I brought you some of Mum's millionaire's shortbread. I'll make sure we take it in the ambulance so you can have it in the hospital, all right?'

There was some kind of response, half-cough, half choke. 'Don't try to talk. It's okay.' Surely it was forgivable to lie to the dying? 'There will be plenty of time later.'

'I'm going to make you a cup of tea,' Ashleigh said. 'The ambulance might be a few minutes yet.'

'I have to stay with him.'

'Of course. But you can have a cup of tea at the same time.'

'When you're in the ambulance,' Becca said, aware of her voice beginning to tremble, falling prey to a cold feeling in her gut and a gathering sense of loss that was premature but not by much, 'I'll call Mum and get her to come up and meet us at the hospital. And when you're well enough to have visitors Kirsty will come, too. They don't really allow babies in the hospital but maybe I can have a wee word with whoever is on duty and they'll let her bring Rosie in to see you. They might do that, for me. And you'd like that, wouldn't you? Because she's such a sparkler, and you always make her laugh.'

The stone floor of the cottage was cold and hard under her knees. In the kitchen Ashleigh clattered about. Becca's heart beat heavy and hard and painfully in her chest and George wheezed again, each breath more of a struggle than the last. 'Uncle George, it's okay. There'll be plenty of time to talk later.'

'Okay, Becca.' Ashleigh was back, and the chink of china on china suggested she'd tried and failed to find a mug. 'Here's a cup of tea.' She set cup and saucer down on the floor.

It was too quickly made, no doubt, and would taste disgusting, but Becca had done that herself in an emergency. She hated being treated like a layperson when she was the health professional. 'Thank you.' Gently, she stroked George's hand. 'It'll be okay. We'll get you to hospital.'

'I think he's trying to tell you something.'

'What?' Becca sat back on her knees, still holding his hand. 'He shouldn't talk. Uncle George, it's okay.'

'He's trying to tell you something,' Ashleigh repeated, a frown of perplexity on her face. 'Look. Poor man. Can you see? He's distressed.'

'He can hear us,' Becca hissed at her. Hearing was the last sense to go. For God's sake, please let neither Ashleigh nor Jude say anything stupid and let George know how little time he had left. But then it dawned on her. If, as she was so sure was the case, George was dying this was the last chance he'd have to tell anyone anything at all. 'I love you so much,' she said to him, and that was the cat out of the bag. If he had any comprehension left, he'd know, because he never encouraged any kind of emotional input, but this was all about last chances. Yes, he should stay calm. But he was dying and there shouldn't be things you never said. She wouldn't let him go without love. 'Is there anything you want to tell me?'

His hand twitched, his mouth convulsed and a pulse quivered in the edge of his mouth. Spittle trickled down his cheek and Becca, unable to reach into her pocket for a tissue, dabbed it away with the corner of the blanket. A strangled groan was all he could manage.

'Uncle George,' she pleaded. 'What is it? Did something happen?'

Jude's feet joined the scene. His boots, unlike Ashleigh's, were worn and well-fitted. 'That's the ambulance on the way. They say to keep him warm, but you'll know that.'

George twitched. Tears rose in Becca's eyes. 'Uncle

George. Speak to me. Tell me what you want to say.' Even if it was only goodbye.

A last, convulsive gasp. George was gone. She knew it. She touched a finger to his still-warm skin and the pulse was absent. 'It's too late.' She lifted a hand to dab at her eyes as the walls of the cottage seemed to close in around her.

'Jude, Becca's not okay.'

'I know.'

'I'll wait here for the ambulance. I think you should take her home.'

They were talking over her, as if she wasn't there. 'I'll wait with him,' she snarled up at them, but her voice let her down, breaking as she spoke. The edge of the blanket did duty as a hanky for her, too, wiping away the tears she couldn't stop and shouldn't shed. Falling apart wouldn't help George. But nothing could help George now.

'No.' Jude bent down and placed a cool and impersonal hand under her elbow. 'Ashleigh's right. This is about you, now. You're upset. I'll call your mum and tell her I'm bringing you home and she can get back to look after you. You've done what you can for George and you should be proud of it.'

'Don't you dare patronise me. I'm only doing my job.'

'Yes, I know that. But it's harder this time, because I know how much you care about him. So let's make this about you, and make sure you're all right.'

To her shame, she gave in, allowing Ashleigh O'Halloran to take her place at George's side and letting Jude tow her out of the cottage and guide her into her car, sitting in the driving seat until he'd phoned her mum.

'I'll drive,' he said, in that neutral policeman's voice. 'I'll take you home and wait until someone gets there to sit with you, and then I'll leave. Ashleigh's going to bring my car and pick me up from my mum's. Okay?'

That was so typical of Jude, doing everything by the book as if she was a victim of crime. They were friends, or they were supposed to be. But she didn't have the energy to resist, sitting in the car with her hands folded in her lap and staring out of the window, seeing but not paying attention. Even the ambulance they gave way to on the narrow road to Pooley Bridge didn't merit more than a glance.

'Okay.' They'd reached Wasby as if through some strange time-slip, the journey taking forever and yet no time at all. She sat in her seat until he came to open the door for her, reached for her handbag, rifled through it for her keys, opened the cottage door and then came to help her up the path. 'I've left the door on the latch for when your mum comes. You go and sit down and I'll make you a cup of tea.'

'I don't need you to make me tea. I'm perfectly capable of doing it myself.'

'Of course you are. But I want to help. Just to make it a bit easier for you.'

His phone pinged and he looked down at it. Jude had the knack that she envied, of keeping his expression inscrutable, but she'd always been able to sense what kind of emotion he was trying to hide. 'Is that Ashleigh? Is there news?'

'Yes.' He replaced the phone in his pocket and stared at her, thoughtfully, before bending down to offer Holmes the briefest of acknowledgements as the cat rubbed round his legs. 'I'm sorry.'

'He's dead, isn't he?' As if she hadn't known. The paramedics' verdict was just a confirmation of her failure to save him.

'I'm afraid so.'

Still her heart refused to accept the evidence of her eyes and the response of the paramedics. 'Why did you let me leave him? I should have waited.'

His expression answered her, but he was too kind to repeat the brutal truth.'You were upset. And if he'd been aware of that it would have upset him more. Sometimes it's better that way.'

'I was not upset. I should have stayed with him.'

'Becca. You're in shock.' He snatched a glance through the window, as if anxious for someone to appear and relieve him of his duty of care. 'Don't beat yourself up about it. You didn't do anything wrong.'

'I'm a healthcare professional. How dare you tell me whether I've done anything wrong or not!' Grief and self-loathing overwhelmed her and she launched herself at him, fists clenched. 'How dare you? Who do you think you are? Who? Who?'

Tears blinded her. Jude's hands closed around her wrists as he held her off. 'Becca. Calm down. This isn't helping anyone.'

'Nothing will help now!' she shouted back at him. 'Don't you see? Nothing. Nothing! I couldn't save him! He's dead, and we'll never get him back, and I'll never see him again. And it's all because of everything that's been happening!' It was Ryan giving him hassle and the police asking questions. It had been the shock of Summer's death and the disruption that had come upon peaceful Martindale. 'It's your fault, too!' But he didn't answer, just continued to hold her at a distance. Fury changed to tears and her misery erupted into a huge sob. 'Jude. Oh, Jude. What am I going to do?'

He released her and she collapsed against him, clinging to him and sobbing. It took a second before he responded, a hug that was so cold and impersonal as to hurt more than anything else, the kind of hug you give people at a distance when they embarrass you. 'Oh God, Jude. I'm sorry.'

'No need to apologise,' he said, still with that cool lack of engagement.

She'd loved him for so long and now he was distant. When she relaxed her hold, he stepped back with obvious relief, and she almost hated him for it. 'I'm sorry if I inconvenienced you.'

'Not at all. But I'm going to leave, now. It looks like there's someone here to help you.'

Becca turned towards the door and found the presence of her current boyfriend chillingly less comforting than that of her ex. 'Adam. What are you doing here?'

'Your mum called me and asked me to pop by and make sure you're all right.' He walked past Jude, who'd stepped back still with that same infuriatingly neutral expression on his face. Her tears had left a dark mark on his tee shirt. 'That's what I'm here to do. What a hell of a shock for you, my darling. Poor old George. No wonder you're struggling to cope. But at his age it was probably the best thing, with him living in that house all on his own.' He flicked a knife-like look at Jude. 'Okay, pal. You're not needed.'

'I'll see myself out.' Jude was already in the hallway. 'Becca. If you need me you know where I am.'

There was a click as he dropped her car key on the hall table and then he was gone, with the grey shadow that was Holmes ghosting down the path at his heels.

Jude crossed the street to his mother's house in a state of deep thought, and leaned on the bell. There was no point in pretending Becca's distress hadn't affected him, and he'd grown used to being honest with his own soul even when he couldn't be honest with anyone else. He was still in love with Becca, and whenever he thought he'd conquered his feelings, something caused them to flare up. That was why his relationship with Ashleigh would ultimately go nowhere, and the only reason it continued was because she was in exactly the same situation as regarded Scott. Neither of them ever mentioned it, but they both knew.

Mikey answered the door. Out of the loop, Jude never knew whether to expect his brother or not, but it seemed as if Mikey's recent silence was casual rather than aggrieved, because his demeanour was cheerful enough. 'Hey, Jude.' He grinned. 'I love the way you bring Becca's cat with you when you call.'

Looking down, Jude saw Holmes stalking past him into the Satterthwaite household as if he owned the place. That would irritate Becca, who resented the cat's fondness for him, but he wasn't about to take the animal home. Besides, he admired Holmes' independence of sprit. 'Good to see you. Are you back for long?'

'Studying.' Mikey made a face. 'My last exam is next week and my flatmates have all finished and are on the lash. There's no way I'd ever get anything done if I was there.'

'Sensible man.' Jude followed Holmes through to the kitchen, where Mikey had spread his books and folders out over the kitchen table.

'Up to a point. The last week before the last exam in my last year of uni is probably leaving it a bit late to see sense.'

Jude snatched a look through the kitchen window at the green brow of Lowther Fell. If he and Ashleigh had got moving five minutes earlier they'd have been away from George's cottage before Becca got there. Not only would he have avoided the whole drama that had played out and been spared the awkward scene he'd just had with Becca, but he and Ashleigh would have had a whole day to walk and talk and look down on Ullswater and over to High Street, breathe in the fresh air and get away from the stresses of work. God knew he'd have welcomed that. 'Better late than never.' Mikey was smart and probably protested too much. Not a book learner, Jude couldn't help envying his capacity to absorb so much dull information in phenomenal detail and retain it for just long enough to regurgitate it in an exam.

'Well.' Mikey sat down at the table and reached for the bar of chocolate sitting there. 'I'm about due a break. Mum's out, if you're looking for her.' He snapped off two squares and offered them to Jude.

'I wasn't looking for anyone. Just waiting for Ashleigh.'

'Why wait for her here?'

Jude slipped a square of Dairy Milk into his mouth and allowed it to melt before he answered. 'She's got my car.' And then it was off onto the explanation of what had happened and how, and why, although Mikey stopped listening once the dramatic fact of George's collapse and death was over and done with so he was spared having to go into detail about Becca's uncharacteristic breakdown.

'How long are you hanging around?' Mikey seemed to remember his manners. 'Long enough for some lunch? It's must be about that time.'

'I expect we'll go out for a pub lunch somewhere. Ashleigh won't be long. She can't have been far behind us.'

Holmes jumped up onto the table and padded along it as if it were a catwalk, picking his way delicately through Mikey's papers to nudge his head against Jude's elbow.

Mikey swiped him aside. 'That animal's a pest. It's good that you got a day off, anyway. You work too hard.'

Everyone said that, and at least George's collapse wasn't suspicious and there would be no need to get involved, but even the thought of such a thing sent his mind back to the old man's death. He shook his head in irritation at Becca's irrational accusation that he, through the investigation into Summer's accident, was somehow responsible for what had happened to George.

It reminded him. There were questions it could do no harm to ask. 'You don't know Luke Helmsley, do you?'

'Only vaguely. He's a few years older than me. I know him well enough to keep out of his way if I'm ever in the same pub as him and never to look at a girl he's with, but that's about it. Why?'

'I wondered.' With a measure of relief, Jude heard the thrum of the engine of his Mercedes. 'That's Ashleigh. I'll leave you to get on. Work hard.'

'Oh, okay. Well that was short but sweet. Nice to see you.'

'When are you heading back to Newcastle?' Jude moved towards the door. 'Give me a shout before you do. We could go out for a drink some time. Have a chat.'

'I'll take the drink but you can stuff the chat. I don't need any of that *in loco parentis* stuff. Too awkward.'

'See you.'

'See you, bro.'

Holmes trotted out behind him, exactly as he'd trotted in, and shot up the path to Becca's front door, which opened. Walking to the car and assuming the driver's seat which Ashleigh vacated for him, Jude pretended not to notice either Becca in the living room dabbing at her eyes with a tissue, or the rather more deliberate presence of

Adam Fleetwood, standing on her front step with his arms folded.

'Well, that wasn't how the day was meant to go.' He started the engine, turned the Mercedes and headed back up towards Askham.

'No. What a terrible thing to happen.' Ashleigh was looking thoughtful. 'Poor George.'

She relied heavily on instinct and he dealt only in fact, but today he knew what she was thinking and felt the same. 'It didn't ring true, did it?'

'You thought that too?'

'Yes, but I don't know why. Probably because Becca was blaming it on everyone else when it was so obviously a stroke.'

'I can see why, though. Becca was really upset.'

He sensed the sideways look she gave him but they were approaching the village of Askham and he had an excuse to ignore it, negotiating his way past the cars parked along the village green. 'She mentioned Ryan. That's her cousin. He's over from Australia. Maybe he and George didn't get on. George is a great guy but he could be a bit bumptious.' Though he never was with Becca. 'She was very fond of him.'

'At ninety five you'd think his death was natural, wouldn't you?'

'You're going to tell me you think it isn't.' He turned at the bottom of the village without really thinking where he was going. Away from Ullswater anyway, and into the Eden Valley, where they had half a chance of a pub lunch without running into someone he couldn't be bothered talking to.

'I'm not going to say that. But he was so obviously trying to tell her something, but her being so upset was stressing him out.'

'She didn't come across as upset. I thought she was really professional in dealing with him.'

'She did all the right things, but she was upset, and he would know. I thought he was angry. Furious, in fact. Something had upset him, and it wasn't the stroke. And he was definitely trying to talk. What was so urgent?'

Jude thought of George and his titanic struggle to speak. 'Good question.'

'I had a quick look round the house, and I didn't see anything obviously wrong. And I know there's no evidence, and I know there never will be any evidence, but that doesn't stop me feeling there's something not right about it.'

'I couldn't agree more.' He turned the car off the A6 and into the network of country roads where the land flattened out towards the Pennines. 'Let's go and get some lunch and see if we can salvage something from the day. Though there was one good thing about it. That's the most civil conversation I've had with Mikey in years.'

FOURTEEN

'You know what? It's irrational, but I'm still worried about Summer Raine.'

Faye raised an eyebrow. 'Well, you know what? I think am, too.'

'It's the clothes.' Jude had been sitting at his desk thinking about the girl when he should have been thinking about something else, and when Faye had dropped in on her way back from the coffee machine to find out if the toxicology report had come in, he was glad of the chance to discuss it. 'Ashleigh made that point. If you're out of your head on drink—'

'And drugs.' Faye scowled and pulled up a chair. The report had indicated quantities of both alcohol and cocaine, the drug of choice for the rich, in Summer's body. While that simplified the case considerably in terms of supporting accidental drowning while impaired, it left the thorny issue of illegal drugs on the Neilson property.

'Yes. Drugs, too.' That was a matter Jude wasn't touching if he could avoid it. 'But you don't fold and hide your clothes. I had a look back through the files. When some of the guys went down to Summer's lodging early on to see if there were any clues as to where she might be, the place was in a mess. Her housemates said that was typical. She never folded anything.'

'You can't make a case for murder on uncharacteristic neatness. Not on its own.'

'No, but it doesn't sit right. And there's another thing. Just a tiny one. The clothes were hidden so you couldn't see them from the path. Why the hell would she do that?'

'Who knows why anyone does anything when they're high?' A deep sigh suggested Faye was as troubled about it, and as powerless, as he was. They both knew it was often the tiny things that caught criminals. 'This is the problem, as I see it. If it was murder — if — then whoever did it is extremely clever.'

'I know there's no obvious motive, but is it worth looking a little deeper? Especially if there's some potential connection with Robert Neilson. Had you thought of that?'

'Thought of it?' She rolled her eyes. 'I've spent half the night lying awake and worrying about it. We know Robert Neilson is up to something. So yes, I'm thinking the same as I suspect you are — that she may have found out something she wasn't meant to know, either in the house or from one of the twins, and that either she threatened to reveal it and had to be silenced or she had to be killed before she realised how important it was.' At the end of such a long sentence, she paused for breath and took a long sip of cold coffee.

'And we could look into that, perhaps.'

'You think so? The problem as I see it, apart from the fact that I've been warned again, in the strongest of terms, about attracting the wrong sort of attention, is that Robert Neilson is an extremely clever man. When clever people commit murder, or arrange to have it committed on their behalf, they do it very well.'

This was true. If Robert Neilson was a criminal he was the kind Jude feared most — the kind that got away with it. He'd take as long as he needed and spend as much as was necessary to cover his tracks. 'Yes. If he wanted it done he'd be nowhere near it.'

'As was the case. He was in Frankfurt at the time, very obviously so. He flew out on the Sunday morning for a Monday morning meeting. That rings an alarm bell, in its way, but being prepared isn't any more criminal than folding your clothes. If he wanted Summer killed, it will have been done by someone else, someone with no obvious connection to him, and that person will have cleared off and will never be seen anywhere near the Lakes again.'

It was the old problem. There wasn't enough initial evidence to justify the resources which might uncover the real evidence. 'If he paid—'

'His finances are already trying the patience of the experts. He's perfectly capable of laundering a hit man's fees.'

'Or hit woman.'

'Exactly. I can ask others to look into that for me, but it won't be a priority. So until you come up with something else, it rests.'

'Okay.' Jude turned his pen over in his fingers. Faye wasn't the only one who'd been spending more time than was good for her worrying over it. 'Then there's something Luke Helmsley said. He said Summer had said she was going to talk to Miranda about her masters dissertation.'

'She wasn't due to start her course until the autumn.'

'No, but she'd signed up for it and she seems to have been passionate about her subject, which was feminist politics. It's reasonable to suppose she was thinking ahead. I got Chris to have a quick look at her academic interests. Her undergraduate dissertation was on the subject of women who kill manipulative partners and whether it should be considered murder.'

Faye nodded, intently. 'Go on.'

'There was case study in that about a woman called Elizabeth Bell.'

Understanding dawned on Faye's face. 'Ah yes. I remember that one. What was it, ten years ago? Upper-class woman killed manipulative upper-class boyfriend and was cleared of murder. There was quite a lot of chat about that one in the press, wasn't there? It was a bit of a cause célèbre, as I recall.'

'I don't know if you know it had an unhappy ending. Elizabeth became the target of the wrong sort of attention and after a year or so she'd had enough. She emigrated to Australia, to Melbourne. Three years ago she died in a car crash.'

'Was it an accident?'

'Apparently.' Jude doodled a tangled spider's web on his pad. 'Back to the present. Summer had messaged Miranda asking if she could talk to her, though she didn't say what about. The text was sent on the morning of the Sunday and Miranda says she didn't open it until the evening. She didn't reply, possibly because she was angry with Summer over what happened on the *Seven of Swords* and she may have blamed her for leading the twins astray.'

Faye harrumphed. 'And what would Miranda Neilson know about feminist politics?'

'I suspect it was to do with the Elizabeth Bell case. Miranda was Elizabeth's flatmate and best friend. It was her evidence — very detailed, and challenged by the prosecution at every step — that cleared Elizabeth of murder.'

Faye liked that. He could tell by the way she sat and

thought it through with a little smile on her lips. 'Okay. You've made a neat connection. But Miranda wasn't in the dale at the time. The boys confirm she didn't return until an hour after they'd thought Summer had gone home. And why would she be worried about talking to Summer, even if she knew what it was about?'

'Maybe she wanted to put the past behind her.' Jude shrugged. 'I think I'd like to ask her about it.'

Faye thought about it a moment longer. 'I don't imagine it'll do any harm. But don't do it yourself. Get someone junior to call and pretend they're just tying up some loose ends.'

'Fine. I'll do that.'

'I'll get on then.'

'One other thing.' Jude half turned away from her, because he knew what she'd say. 'There's an old man who lived up at Martindale. George Barrett. He died of a stroke at the weekend. Ashleigh and I happened to be there just after he was found.'

'And?'

'It was almost certainly natural causes, but I've got a suspicious mind. There's a post-mortem due and I've noted that he seemed unusually distressed. No more. But given the context of two deaths so close together I put a note about it on the file on Summer's case. '

'Jude. Really. I know you have to consider everything, but you surely aren't suggesting we spend precious time and resources on—'

'Just a note on the file,' he hastened to reassure her. 'It was to cover all bases. Because you never know.'

'Hmm. I'd better let you get on.' She swung out of her seat. 'Let me know what Mrs Neilson says. And let me repeat. Don't do anything up at the Neilsons' place without running it past me first.'

As she left, Doddsy slipped in. 'Thank God. That was a narrow escape,' he said, as the door closed behind him.

'What from Faye?'

'Oh, God, no. Far worse than that.' And there was a tap on the door, which swung open before either could reply. 'Too late,' he said, under his voice. 'Morning, Lorraine.'

Lorraine Broadbent was one of their former close colleagues, a detective sergeant Jude had worked with when he was a mere constable but who'd never really had the taste for long hours when they conflicted too much with the demands of single parenthood and elderly parents. Since those days she'd shuffled sideways from one desk job to another until she'd landed up working her way to retirement in the backwater of the Professional Standards department.

Professional Standards meant trouble. A call from Lorraine could be like a knock on the door from the Grim Reaper for your career. Jude sat back and looked across at Doddsy, who seemed equally apprehensive, and the image of Adam Fleetwood swam into his mind and out of it again. Adam had a grudge but everyone knew it. He didn't anticipate much trouble from Lorraine. 'Morning.'

'I love the way everyone looks terrified when I come into the room.' She glanced from one to the other. 'Don't look like that, Doddsy. I'd expected you to have a clear conscience. But it's not you I'm after.'

'Glad to hear it. I'll head down and get coffee then. Leave the two of you to it.'

She waited until he'd left the room. 'I was passing, so I thought I'd save myself an email.'

And enjoy the sense of power, no doubt. 'Who's got it in for me this time?'

'I won't sit down,' said Lorraine, as though he'd asked

her. 'I don't have the time. Too bloody busy clearing up other people's messes.' She peered at him over her glasses. Lorraine was one of those people who did their best to pretend they had more important things to do than anyone else. Fair enough: keeping the law accountable was a justifiable end. 'I'll come straight to the point. I've had a complaint.'

'I bet you have.' He sat back.

'Oh, are you expecting one? That doesn't look good.'

'Everyone who's ever sent anyone down is expecting a complaint. You ought to know that. Is it serious?'

'It depends what you mean by serious. From your point of view, Jude, the good news is that it's anonymous, so we won't be able to go back to the complainant for details. Even if we can work out who it is, and I suspect you'll know straight away, by going out of their way not to provide contact details, the complainant has expressed a wish to remain anonymous and therefore we are unable to contact them unless they come back to us. The data protection laws may turn out to have done some good after all, if only to you.'

'Right.' She was enjoying herself a sight too much for Jude's liking. There was no need to speak to him directly about an allegation that couldn't proceed. 'So someone's making up stories and you've no proof. We've been here before.' Everybody had.

'If you don't want my help and support, fine. It's not an official notification but I thought you'd like to know. In case it gets nasty.'

He should let it go, but he couldn't. 'What am I supposed to have done?'

'Do you want to take a guess?'

'What, and incriminate myself? No thanks.'

'Fine. It came by post this morning. If they'd sent it

online they'd have had to say who they are, but oh.' She rolled her eyes. 'Some people think they're smart. It's assault, and inappropriate contact with the vulnerable member of the public.'

'What? When?'

'I don't know. You're the one who was there. Allegedly.' Lorraine had always found it easier to meet her targets inside the organisation for minor misdemeanours than outside for serious crimes.

'I was there.' There could be only one thing she was talking about. 'But I don't recognise this description of events.' Fury rose within him, with Lorraine, with Becca, wth himself. He should have sent Ashleigh back with Becca and stayed behind himself. Becca might have got just as angry but at least she couldn't have accused Ashleigh of behaving inappropriately. 'This has to be from my ex-girlfriend.'

'Oh, very tricky for you, then.' Lorraine's delight was obvious.

'There's nothing tricky about it. She found her uncle dying and Ashleigh and I were around so we went to help.'

'Right. So she'll be able to back up what you say.'

'No. Because Becca — my ex — was upset so I took her home. That's when she got mad with me and attacked me. I held her off, that was all. '

'Uh-huh. Hence the bruising she claims to have sustained on the wrists.' At least Lorraine sounded a little more sympathetic about that. She should be. She must have been in situations where sudden grief manifested itself in fury at the nearest person, and that person was often a police officer. 'What about the inappropriate contact?'

'That was her, not me. She apologised and gave me a hug and that was it. Or I thought it was.'

'She gave you a hug. Okay. That doesn't sound great, either, if I'm honest.'

'What's wrong with that?' It didn't matter whether it was Lorraine's smugness or Becca's contempt for him that made him angry, but something did. 'I've known her since she was a kid. We were neighbours. I thought we were friends. And I wasn't even on duty.'

'And that makes everything okay?' Lorraine shook her head at him. 'You don't need me to tell you the *trust-me-I'm-a-policeman* line is no excuse. I'm sure you meant well, but hey. Sometimes you have to learn to let your exes go. You know?'

'I've let her go. I was being neighbourly, Next time she calls me for help — and she did call me — she can just keep calling. I'll walk away.'

'Maybe you should have walked away this time, too.' Lorraine turned towards the door. 'I'll leave you with that, but we won't pursue it. We can't, unless our complainant gets back to us with their contact details. It'll stay on file. So in the meantime, think yourself lucky.' She paused. 'Just as well we can't act on it, eh? But you might want to watch your step with ex-girlfriends in future.'

FIFTEEN

'The police called me again this afternoon.'

Aida's little red hire car had barely left the driveway of Waterside Lodge, the day's work done, before Miranda appeared in the hall beside Robert.

'Oh?' He turned to her, his thin face sharp with suspicion.

'Yes.' She lifted a hand to calm him. 'It's nothing serious. It was just something they were checking up on, a tiny detail. But it bothered me and now…' She steeled herself to do something she should have done years before. 'Now I feel I should make a confession.'

One of the most comforting things about Robert was that he never jumped to a conclusion and therefore rarely reached the wrong one, and though he was notoriously tough in business, he was anything but at home. Even his bouts of fury with Ollie and Will were nothing more than a game he felt he had to play out, a curb chain on their rush to manhood, a constant check on their wilder impulses. 'Intriguing. Shall we go and get a drink?'

'Don't you have any work to finish?'

'No. I sent Aida away early because I'm tired of her

company and far more interested in spending some time with you. I haven't forgotten you were the one who had to pick up the pieces those boys left behind and that I wasn't there to help you. I owe you a lot for that, and my time and a sympathetic ear are the least I can give you in return.'

Ollie and Will were playing some loud video game in the family room, where at least there were limited opportunities for mischief, so Robert and Miranda drifted by mutual agreement into the dining room. From there, armed with a gin and tonic apiece, they went out onto the terrace and settled side by side in two wicker chairs. The warmth had gone from the sun and the lights had come on on the other side of the lake, streaming out towards them from the houses and hotels. A few birds rode the roller-coaster wind for one last time before settling down to roost in the rustling trees. With a shiver, Miranda pulled her cardigan around her.

'So,' Robert prompted her, shifting his chair a few inches closer to hers so he could reach out to her hand if he needed to. She knew that was what he was planning because he stretched out his hand a fraction as if to judge the distance and then he let it rest. But that was Robert. He planned everything, even his apparently spontaneous gestures, in the most minute detail and as a result everything was always perfect. 'Your confession.'

'Yes.' She placed her hand exactly where his eye had rested, to see how long it would take him to follow up. The sooner he did it the more sympathetic he would be. In the slipping sun, her diamond engagement ring picked up the sunlight and flung it back up into the air with the sparkle of a mighty star. 'Summer Raine texted me on the morning of the day she died. She said she wanted to talk to me.'

'What about?' His expression gave nothing away.

'She didn't say, and I didn't open the message until after she'd...after she must have died. But when she — the policewoman who called me. Ashleigh O'Halloran, a detective.' She was stumbling over her words now, even without the gin and tonic. 'She called me as a matter of routine, she said. Because they'd found the text on Summer's phone.'

Robert's sympathy unfolded sooner than she'd ever imagined. His warm hand over hers indicated that he'd help her. 'Go on.'

'Of course, I told them. I have nothing to hide. They said Summer was interested in feminist politics and they think she wanted to talk to me about someone I once knew.' She sipped her gin. His silence was comforting. 'I've never told you my whole story, though it happened not long before we first met.'

She paused to remember that first meeting with Robert, the moment of eye contact across a smart bar near her flat in Canary Wharf, the smile she'd come to know so well. He'd been waiting for a friend who'd been kept late at work, and she'd been drinking alone. 'Perhaps you remember. There was a woman named Elizabeth Bell who was arrested for killing her boyfriend. His name was Drew Anderson. I was Elizabeth's best friend and I gave evidence on her behalf in court.'

Those warm fingers tightened over hers. When she looked at her husband, his lips had curved upwards in what was almost pleasure. 'I know.'

'You do?'

'Yes. I knew before I asked you to marry me. The whole story. I'm glad you've found the courage to tell me and I'm only sorry you couldn't tell me before. But I knew you would, in the end.'

With her free hand, she lifted the glass to her lips. 'Now

I want to tell you everything. You know that. About what it was like.' About how she'd come to be alone in that bar, because she'd attracted so much hatred she'd become toxic and no-one was prepared to take on the burden of her friendship. After everything she'd done for Elizabeth.

'Standing up to speak out for your friend was a wonderful and courageous thing to do. I know you were made to suffer for it.'

He couldn't know how much. 'Drew's family tried to intimidate me. They told lies about me. His friends threatened me. I reported them to the police and it didn't stop them. I didn't sleep for weeks when the trial came up and I almost didn't give evidence, but I knew I had to do it. If I didn't, Elizabeth would go to jail. He'd treated her shockingly, appallingly. He was violent and controlling.' She heard her voice shake.

He leaned in towards her and brushed her cheek with his lips. 'I know what he was like, too.'

'There was no-one else who would speak up for her because he was so powerful and charismatic and charming, in that way that sociopaths have. No-one would believe the things he did and no-one else would speak out against him, speak up for her.'

'Except you.'

The sun had dropped a little further, plunging the slopes of Gowbarrow Fell into darkness. Down on the lake, a fish popped up to snatch at a fly and descend into the depths with its prey. A present relief mingled with a past fear. 'Yes. And that's why I was so scared when I thought Summer might want to talk to me. It brought it all back.'

'But everything you've told me is a matter of public record. Anyone can find you. You aren't pretending to be who you aren't.'

'I've never done that.' Sometimes she wished she had.

He looked down at his glass. 'I should confess, too. I knew who you were the first time we met. I recognised you across the bar, from the news coverage, and I was drawn to you straight away. You looked so vulnerable, almost hunted. I wanted to protect you then, Miranda, and I want to protect you now.'

Her heart warmed. It would be all right. 'I've never forgotten the threats. I've never forgotten how they told me I'd never be free of what I did. I've been waiting, ever since then, for someone to come after me and make me pay for saving Elizabeth. And three years ago Elizabeth died.' She'd nearly told him then but her courage had failed her once again.

He knew that, too. 'In a car accident. I read about it.'

'I don't believe it was an accident.'

'Oh, Miranda!' He laughed, a soft laugh full of love, even of joy. 'Is that what scares you? You told the truth. No-one should come after you for telling the truth. And I'll make sure they don't. I'll keep you safe.'

Miranda's heart lifted. Why had she ever doubted him? She'd be able to walk the fells without fear, without wondering where death might be lying in wait. She could leave her paranoia behind and know that if a stranger was shadowing her on the hillside it would be someone Robert had put there to protect her. She should have told him the whole story much sooner. 'Yes. But this is the real confession.' She drew a long deep breath, would have turned to the gin but somehow her glass was already empty. 'My testimony at the trial. I made it up.'

'What,' he said, at last startled, 'all of it?'

'No. Everything I said was something Elizabeth had told me and I believed her. But no-one else would. If I corroborated her evidence, he wasn't there to deny it, so I told them I'd seen things I hadn't seen. Things Elizabeth told me he'd done.'

'You lied in court?' he asked, his tone light, as if perjury were no worse than the smallest white lie.

'Not about what he did — I do believe he did it all — but that I'd seen him, or heard him. It was the only way to prove she was innocent.'

'Not innocent,' he observed, lifting his gin and turning the glass against the setting sun. 'But not guilty of murder.'

'Exactly.' She looked at him, anxiously. 'You don't mind that I gave false evidence?'

He considered, then laughed. 'Why would I? If, as you say, your friend was abused, I think you did something heroic.' He paused. 'You were on the wrong side of powerful people then, my darling, but you have an even more powerful man by your side now. Me. And who knows? Maybe one day I might ask you to give false evidence again. But this time it would be for me.'

SIXTEEN

'George has died,' Becca said, shouting into the phone though it was more in hope than expectation. The signal was fine down in Wasby but God knew what it was like up in the wilds. 'Where are you?'

'Does it matter?' Ryan bellowed back at her. 'I'm up in the Pennines somewhere. I'm having a blast. I just keep walking with the sun in front of me in the mornings and behind me in the evenings. Eventually I'll get to the sea.'

Sometimes Becca thought Ryan's easy-come-easy-go attitude was fake, put on to make himself seem more charming than he actually was. He'd hardly have got anywhere in the army without being able to know exactly where he was with a map and have a pretty good idea how to get somewhere he recognised without one. At that moment she was only surprised he'd bothered checking his messages and using his limited battery on calling her back. 'How soon can you get here?'

'Do I need to get back? Has something happened?'

'Yes. Didn't you hear me? I said George has died.'

'Oh, died! I thought you said… well, I don't know what I think you said. Geez. Hope I didn't frighten him to death. Your mum would never forgive me.'

Becca thought that crass. 'He had a stroke. At least, I'm pretty certain he did, but we don't know for certain yet. The police haven't come back about the post-mortem yet.'

'The police? I thought you said it was a stroke.'

'Yes but…oh I don't know.' It all came down to Jude again, and his inability to ascribe anything to accident or natural causes when sometimes they should be left well alone. That was what came of believing the worst of human nature. 'There has to be a post-mortem because he wasn't under medical care when he died. So we're waiting on the PM, but I expect it's straightforward.'

'Why is it a police matter?'

'It's just routine. It's an unexplained death. They're always involved.' Jude clothed everything in the drab uniform of routine. That hadn't endeared him to Becca's mother, who'd always thought him a little over-zealous. *Why can't they let the poor man rest in peace*, she'd said, though she knew well enough what the procedure was. Regardless of Jude's presence there would have to be a post-mortem. 'I called because I thought you might want to come through for his funeral.'

'You think he'd want me there? He wasn't exactly charm itself.'

It was a matter of respect. Once more Becca found herself irritated by Ryan's clumsiness. 'Bluntly, I don't think he'd care one way or another. But since you've come all the way across the world to see him and visit the old homestead, I imagined you might want to come.'

'Might be a chance to catch up with all sorts of rellies I've never met, I suppose. See if any of them have a good word for me.' There was crackling sound that might have been Ryan laughing or might have been the wind catching his words. 'When is it?'

'Sooner rather than later. Mum's had a word with the undertakers and they think they can find a slot for him on Saturday morning. We'll confirm it as soon as we get the death certificate. So it'll probably be then.'

'I'll get back as soon as I can.'

'If you're struggling, call me or Mum. We'll find someone to get over and pick you up, assuming you can get to a road.'

'I'll hike it back. It'll only take me a few days. I don't want to trouble you.'

That would be a change. Ryan hadn't shown any previous signs of such consideration. 'Right. I'll let you save your batteries, and I'll text you once I know the time.'

'Cheers. I'll see you at the church, then. I wouldn't mind the use of your washing machine. I got washed off the hills in a rainstorm the other night. Had to break into a barn for shelter. But I don't imagine anyone will mind if I look a bit scruffy.'

'Just give them your cheeky smile and they'll forgive you anything.' Becca ended the call.

Jude would almost certainly turn up at the funeral, because he was meticulous in that sort of social obligation and would have felt he had to appear even if he hadn't got on so well with the old man. George had a long-ingrained sense of justice which chimed exactly with Jude's and the two of them seemed to understand one another. The necessary fuss over the post-mortem report, which would have amused George, annoyed her, but she thought she could trust her ex to act like a friend of the family and not draw any attention to his job. He'd appear, sit at the back of the church and if he stayed for the interment he'd be away well before anyone had the chance to talk to him, and he'd certainly be too busy to turn up at the wake.

If and when he did appear, she'd do her best to avoid him. Her cheeks flamed with embarrassment when she thought of how she'd reacted to George's death, and the worst of it — the very worst of it — was that he'd understood why she'd behaved as she did and wouldn't hold it against her. She couldn't afford to be so morally and emotionally obliged to someone in whom she had no part of her future invested.

I don't break down, she told herself, knowing her fury with him, and the moment that immediately followed it when she'd turned instinctively to him for comfort, were both the result of what had happened to George, *or I shouldn't.* Day after day she went into the homes of the old and the sick and the dying, day after day she sat with patients as they slipped slowly away. It was by no means unusual for her to turn up in the aftermath of death, or do exactly as she'd done with George, sit holding a hand when all was lost and there was nothing to do but wait for an ambulance that had no need to hurry.

But with George it had been different. His death had been so sudden and so unexpected, even though at his age she should never have assumed, when she visited, that she'd find him alive. But at least, she consoled herself as she dashed the back of her hand across her eyes, he'd had his wish and passed away in the house he'd chosen as his place to die.

Ashleigh walked through the centre of Penrith in the late evening sunlight, brisk and businesslike, on a mission that could have waited. Everything about her life seemed, at that moment, to be profoundly unsatisfactory. Naturally she hadn't expected the highs of her relationship with Jude to last for ever — she was far too pragmatic for that — but nevertheless the creeping realisation that nothing lasted for ever got her down. Maybe that was the shadow of Scott, sounding so cheerful without her, as if he'd learned to live in a way she couldn't. Or maybe it was the frustration of work, knowing the accidental death of Summer Raine and the natural passing of George Barrett both seemed like pieces of a jigsaw everyone else wanted to see put back in its box, unfinished.

It was easiest to concentrate on work. Summer's clothes. The way George had struggled so hard to tell them something and failed. The fact he knew everything that went on in the dale and yet no-one seemed to have seen Summer walking along the path to her death.

She'd been working at home, and it was the last of the work emails she'd looked at before shutting down her laptop that had prompted her to head out. Regardless of how her relationship with Jude would eventually pan out, he was the person she wanted to see at that moment.

'Well, hello,' he greeted her as he answered the door. 'Come on in and have a seat. I was just thinking about you.'

'That's good to hear.' She stepped into the narrow hallway, slipped off her jacket and hung it up, then followed him into the living room, where he was taking one last quick look at the cricket before he turned the telly off. There was a table in one corner and he had his laptop propped up on it. He, like her, must have been spending the evening catching up. 'Sorry to interrupt. But I wanted to run something past you.'

'You aren't interrupting. I'm always glad to see you.'

Thank God in this modern, practical world you weren't

tied to to one perfect relationship, that it was acceptable to move from one to the other and to make what you could with a person who wasn't, in the end, the great love of your life. If it wasn't for that she'd have gone mad, because she hated to live, or sleep, alone. She walked over to him to hug him and he held her close, invitingly, and kissed her. 'If I wasn't busy working I might suggest something we could do.'

She decoded the message correctly. 'It's work I came over to see you about, as it happens.' Releasing him, she sat down on the sofa, leaving him plenty of space beside her while he stepped into the kitchen

'Maybe it won't take long and we'll be bored,' he called through with a wink, as he flicked the buttons on the coffee machine.

She hadn't intended to stay overnight, but she probably would. 'The work bit won't take long. I was just catching up on my emails and there was something I thought you might be interested in.' Of course she could have phoned him, or forwarded the email, but where was the fun in that? 'It was a nice evening and not much of a walk, so I thought I'd pop over.'

'You know I always like to see you.' He came back through and handed her the mug before sitting down beside her. 'Decaff, of course.'

'Thank God for that. My brain's been buzzing like crazy all day and now I know something I wish I didn't.'

'And that is?'

'George Barrett died of natural causes. A stroke.' The very naturalness of it irritated her and she could see by the frown on his face that she wasn't alone. 'I can't help it. I can't let go of the idea there's someone out there who's much cleverer than us. I have this terrible sense that the cosmos is laughing at us.'

'The cosmos can laugh all it likes. It's when the criminals have fun at my expense that it gets to me. You must have seen the PM results, then.'

'Yes, and they were everything they should have been. Straightforward. Severe stroke.'

'Dammit. I don't know there's anything more we can do about it. Faye was annoyed enough when I told her I'd made a note of my concerns. Even if somebody did literally frighten him to death, we won't be able to learn anything from the body. The family will want him buried as soon as possible.'

'Did Becca tell you that?'

She thought he tensed at the mention of Becca. 'No. I'm just assuming.'

'We should tell the family. They'll have seen the report, of course, but they'll want to know we won't be taking any action. I expect you want to do that.'

'No,' he said, far too sharply. 'Anyone else can do it. I won't. It's no big deal.'

Irked by something she couldn't identify, Ashleigh pulled at the end of her pony tail. 'Did something happen between you after George died?'

'Nothing.' He didn't look at her. 'Unless you count the fact she attacked me in a fit of sheer fury, then flung her arms around my neck in a fit of remorse, apologised profusely, and followed it up with an anonymous complaint about my inappropriate behaviour towards her.'

She caught her breath. 'Seriously?'

'Seriously.'

'But if it was anonymous then—'

'Lorraine bloody Broadbent took great pleasure in telling me all about it. They can't do anything. But yes. It happened.' He scowled. 'There was nobody there but Becca and me, and while I can't say my version of what happened is exactly the same as hers, I can recognise enough of it.'

No two people ever gave the same version of an event, or interpreted it in the same way. Becca had been distressed and Jude was always, unequivocally, professional, but the tiniest element of doubt lingered in Ashleigh's mind. She herself suffered from too much empathy with strangers, a constant weakness that influenced her career. Who would blame Jude for overstepping a line in a genuine attempt to comfort his ex? 'Did you hug her?'

'In the coldest way I could. Yes. I could hardly throw her off.'

'And that was all?'

'Yes. I know why she did it, of course. Adam must have seen it and he'll have put her up to it. I expect that's why she did it anonymously. She'll guess it can't go any further and he'll know I'll have heard about it. But it's on file.' He reached for his coffee. 'I should have told you at the time. I'm sorry. Let's not talk about it.'

He rarely showed hurt. She sensed it was the insult to his professionalism that outraged him, even more than the perceived betrayal. 'Not if you don't want to. There's plenty more to talk about. Two deaths with no evidence, for a start.'

'You know there's nothing new we can do about either.'

'I think that's a coward's answer.'

'I don't need insults from you, too.' A half-smile took the sting out of it. 'It's purely practical. It's about available resources and time and priorities. The minute you can come up with something more, or another person dies in an apparent accident in Martindale, I promise you I'll be crawling all over the place in full Sherlock Holmes gear with my magnifying glass. But until then, we do nothing.'

The reality was inescapable. 'I wonder how many criminals get away with it because we don't have the capability to follow up?'

'You know the answer. Too many.'

She stretched out a hand and placed it on his knee, receiving return a wry smile. 'Why don't I read the tarot for you?'

'You're a charlatan,' he grumbled. 'You know I don't believe in that garbage.' But he reached onto the side table where the deck of cards she'd brought back for him from a holiday in Sri Lanka had been sitting gathering dust and handed her the pack.

They were cheap cards, and had attracted her because of their garish colours and the grey cat that lurked in the corner of every one of them, yawning, stretching or toying with a mouse. They smelt faintly of incense, overtones of patchouli and some sort of spice, scents that ought by now to have faded. 'We'll just do something simple.'

'Tell the cards I want to know what happened to Summer. And if they come up with the right answer I'm prepared to concede the point.'

'They won't tell you. If you listen to them they'll help you think it through for yourself. But what we'll do is look at the problem, ask for a suggestion and then that will lead us to a solution.' That was a sensible way of approaching any problem, and one he could hardly object to. 'Pick three cards and lay them out.' She made space between them. 'Here. Here and here.'

'I don't know why I'm doing this.' He did as he was told.

'Humour me. Good. Now.' She laid her forefinger on the first card. The paper on the pack was already beginning to peel away. 'Turn it up and we'll see what our problem is.'

'I have too many problems.' He turned the card face upwards and looked at it. 'Do you know what, Ash? I don't need a pack of cards to tell me that my main problem is evil.'

'This isn't evil. You really ought to know better than to take things at face value. The card is the Devil.' With amusement, she noted that the little grey cat which lurked under the scowling shadow of the Devil wore a vicious expression of its own and had one paw, claws extended, clamped on the dead body of a small bird. 'All cards have positive and negative associations. In a positive sense this suggests we're all restricted by other people's expectations, which to an extent is true of all of us. But today we need to address a problem. And what this card says to me — and to you, if you'll listen — is that the problem we face is deceit and manipulation, and addictive behaviour.

'Yes, Madame Vera. But seriously — does that tell us anything we don't already know?'

'Fair point. If I was reading for myself I'd be looking to see what my own demons are, but in a reading like this it tells me I should be looking at the demons of others.' She thought, briefly, of the Neilson twins and their dabbling in cocaine. Who knew where that would lead? Not everyone was as lucky, or as soundly brought up, as Mikey Satterthwaite. 'Let's look at the next one. If you can approach this with an open mind, it'll help. This will suggest how you might approach the problem. Turn it over.'

When he turned over the Four of Swords he sat back, as if to indicate his disengagement. The battle between the two of them went on, she trying to persuade him of the benefits of alternative thinking, he resisting. 'Sit back and think,' she said, looking at the image of a god stretched out, eyes closed with the cat in contented slumber beside it. 'Don't rush anything. Let the answers come to you.'

'I wish it were that easy.' But he turned over the next card without any prompting. 'The Eight of Wands. And that tells us?'

Ashleigh frowned at it, though the cat in the corner, bemused by eight flies buzzing round its head, amused her. Sometimes the cards didn't deliver and this looked to be the case, but it was almost judgemental to say that. The whole objective, as she kept telling him, was to focus your thinking. 'This card tells you the importance of identifying the missing link, the key piece of information. It's about making the right choice of many.'

'That cat looks just like Holmes,' said Jude, with a chuckle.

'How does Holmes choose the right fly to snatch at?'

'The biggest and the loudest, usually. Though I grant you that isn't necessarily the right one. So maybe the cards are on the right track there.'

Ashleigh picked the cards up and shuffled them into the pack before fanning the whole lot out and sorting through. 'This one is the Seven of Swords.'

He looked at it, at the furtive young man scampering away with an armful of weapons. 'That's the name of the Neilsons' boat, isn't it?'

'Yes. Miranda Neilson said she got the idea from a fortune teller but I think it's a very strange card for someone to identify with. It's all about lies and deceit.'

'I remember you telling me once that you identify with the Fool, and I'd say you were anything but a fool.'

'Yes. But people choose a card and identify with it, and it isn't always the one that other people would choose for them, though it tells you a lot about the way they see themselves. You're right about me and the Fool. And I always think of Scott as the Three of Swords, which is about love and broken hearts and so on. But he would never in a million years see himself in that card.'

'So who does he think he is?'

'I don't know.' Jude, to Ashleigh's mind, was the Emperor, stern and just. Earlier, Becca had come into the conversation and now Ashleigh herself had, unintentionally, brought Scott in to join her. She wasn't surprised by his next question.

'Do you hear from him much?'

There was a reason Ashleigh hadn't been put out that Jude hadn't told her of his encounter with Becca. She'd kept things from him in her turn. Now was the time for them to come out. 'I spoke to him last week, and he called me again this evening. He's applied for Summer's job and he's coming up at the weekend for an interview.'

'Seriously?'

'Seriously that he's coming up for an interview, but do I think he'll take it if he gets it? No. He'd hate it.' Scott was born for the sun and the good life. She could only hope he had enough sense to remember that.

'Will you see him when he's here?'

'I've said I'll meet him for lunch, but only for old times' sake.'

'Right.'

The scepticism of that single word niggled at her. 'I know what you think.'

'I know you still have feelings for him. You told me.'

'You still have feelings for Becca.'

'Not right now, I don't. Not after what happened this morning.' He folded his lips into a thin line, took the cards and picked out the Seven of Swords. 'That's probably the one useful thing I've learned in all the times I've let you lead me astray. Subliminally or otherwise, Miranda Neilson sees herself as someone who's a deceiver and a manipulator, or else the victim of deceit and manipulation.'

She smiled as he slid the deck back into its box. 'You see? You're starting to see the way to enlightenment. And if you want me to lead you astray there are plenty of other ways I can do it.' And then she took the cards off him, slid her arms round him and leaned in to receive his offered kiss.

SEVENTEEN

Luke Helmsley had never loved Summer and lacked both emotional and academic intelligence, but he wasn't stupid. He had an animal cunning, an instinct for wrongdoing in others that was accompanied by a sneaking admiration, even envy, of it. He'd lived in Martindale all his life and had no desire to go anywhere else, and he saw its comings and goings just as George had, only without the level of open interest. Some things intrigued him, though, and the sudden death of the old man was one of them — so soon after Miranda Neilson had been in to see him, so soon after Luke himself had revealed to George that he'd seen her in the dale when she shouldn't have been there.

He topped out the piece of wall he'd been working on and stepped back to look at it. It was grand piece of work. Left to himself he'd spend his whole life dry stone walling, but at some stage his boss would decide that the job was done and there would be something less satisfying for him to do — fencing, or shifting stock from A to B and back again.

In the meantime, there was still the matter of Summer and the Neilsons. He wished he'd paid more attention when she'd wittered on about going to talk to Miranda about something. That would have put him in a position of greater strength than he thought he already was. But he knew enough to turn it to his benefit.

Miranda had been driving up the dale at a time when she said she wasn't, he was sure of that. If she denied it, it would come down to her word against his and nobody would believe him, but maybe it wouldn't come to that. If he thought she'd killed Summer it might have been worth taking it to the police, because after all he had a basic sense of justice and while a fight in a pub was something that should just be left to those involved, murder was different. He couldn't see how, or why, Miranda could have done it so there was no need to dirty his hands by turning her in to the police.

She didn't want people to know where she'd been, though. Maybe it was her husband she was worried about. He grinned. Miranda was a good-looking woman and Robert was away a lot, so a fancy man wasn't out of the question. That had to be worth a few grand for his silence and even if that wasn't the reason and she'd nothing to fear from her husband, the police wouldn't be happy she'd lied to them. Maybe he could short-circuit the whole process, avoid putting her through the hassle and feather his nest into the bargain.

It was almost noon and he'd seen Robert driving away down Martindale earlier that morning. It was a good opportunity to have a chat with Miranda. He crossed the bridge below St Peter's Church. The beck below it was full from the cloudbursts that had punctuated the week, foaming up to the banks as he headed towards Waterside Lodge.

The electric gates across the main drive were closed and, out of devilment, he ignored the latched pedestrian gate beside them and vaulted the low wall. It was badly built, and a few of the stones slithered out of it under his boot. Maybe if Miranda turned down his business proposal she'd let him rebuild it for her, for a fee of course.

The sun crept out, looked down on Martindale and crept back in again as the Ullswater steamer ploughed back from Glenridding, bumping over the choppy surface. On the doorstep, Luke paused in awe. He'd never had cause to come this near to the place before, never been invited, and the dealings he'd had with its residents had been distant, infrequent and always conducted off the premises. The picture windows, the neat lawns, the sleek silver bullet that Miranda drove and that was impossible to mistake for anything else, conspired to make him feel inferior.

Money didn't make you better than anyone else, he reminded himself; just more comfortable. With that thought to inspire him, he raised his hand to the doorbell.

There was no movement inside the glass door. He rang a second time, and a third, before his doubts overcame him. Miranda must be in, and the twins too, because their cars were there, and yet no-one was answering. After five minutes standing like a fool on the doorstep he gave up and crept away. They'd be laughing at him. That was the most bitter thought of all.

Emboldened by his determination not to feel inferior, he ambled across the wide paved forecourt to the the side of the house. The dinghy bobbed against the landing stage, the ornamental trees that dotted the lawn rustled in the rising wind, but no-one was in sight. 'Anyone there?' he called into the garden, but no-one answered and he dared go no further.

He'd come back. Luke was anything but a patient man, but there would be another time when Robert would be out. The police had passed Summer's death to the coroner and nothing more would be done about it, but what he knew of Miranda's lie would keep for as long as she was afraid of having it come out. He strolled back along the drive towards the crumbling wall, and the electric gates slid noiselessly open as he approached.

Luke was a man without imagination, but it made him jump. He looked around to the left and the right and saw no-one, but when he went through the gates they closed noiselessly behind him. Like a horror film, he said to himself.

Laughter interrupted him. He turned to the source of it and found himself face to face with the Neilson twins as they emerged from behind a bush vibrant with elderflower. 'Gotcha!' said one of them, and the other one, half a yard behind him, laughed.

'Looking for someone were you?' the second twin asked.

Luke would have hated the twins, if only because he never knew which was Will and which was Ollie, but there was plenty more reason than that to hate. It wasn't just the money but the casual way they treated it, and their failure to understand how hard the likes of him had to work to get a fraction of what they could put their hands in their pockets — or rather, their father's pockets — for, without having to get off their arses for a couple of hours' work. 'Nothing to do with you, kiddies. This is business for the grown ups.'

'It looks to me like you've done some damage to our wall,' one of them said.

'You might want to put it back,' the other echoed.

'Free of charge, eh, Will?'

'Oh, yeah. We definitely shouldn't have to pay him for fixing the damage he caused.'

He could smell the malty tang of beer on their breath. Reminding himself he shouldn't risk antagonising them until he'd spoken to Miranda, Luke dug his clenched fists into his pockets and contented himself with a muttered expletive as he walked past.

'Whoa.' One twin ran up to plant himself in the road in front of him. 'Did I hear what I thought I heard?'

'Want to say that again to our faces?' The other joined him and they stood side by side in the road.

Spoiled bastards that they were. Without a drink in him Luke was marginally more rational than otherwise, but no less angry. He marched on, aiming a shoulder at the gap between them, sure they'd give place when he reached them. When they didn't, the fists came out of his pockets and a wild haymaker of a punch sent one twin sprawling sideways into the road.

To his satisfaction the fight turned into a brawl, and there would only be one winner. As one twin got up, the other hit the deck. The two of them hadn't the wit to back off and coordinate a bit, and though one them got lucky and landed a punch it was the only damage Luke sustained, and he was more than happy to accept one black eye in payment for the punishment he was handing out.

'What's going on? Stop it! Stop it at once!' From nowhere, Miranda Neilson arrived on the scene, seizing whichever twin had been about to launch himself at Luke and pulling him away. She was in jeans and trainers, a quilted gilet and, he noticed, she had a bunch of cow parsley in her hand. 'Ollie. Whatever are you thinking?'

Luke, thank God, managed to hold back the right hook that would surely have sent Miranda into the ditch to join the other twin and probably landed him in a police cell. 'I'm just going about my business and your young thugs ambushed me, that's what.'

They hung behind their stepmother like a couple of jackals behind the pack leader, waiting for the order to pounce. 'That's not what happened, Miranda. We caught him creeping off the property. I think we'd better head up there and check there's nothing missing, don't you?'

'I went to the house because I wanted to talk to you.' He stuck his hands in his pockets again, fighting the temptation to keep at them and wipe the smirks off their faces.

She stared at him for a moment, twisting the stems of the cow parsley round her fingers. 'Will. Ollie. Go back to the house and clean yourselves up. And you can spend a few minutes thinking about how you're going to explain this to your father, because I don't intend to.'

'Dad'll back us up,' one of them said, though without as much confidence as Luke thought he might have intended.

'Yeah. He will.' The other twin dabbed at a split lip and looked down at the blood on his fingers with a look of awe, as if it was a badge of honour.

'Go,' Miranda instructed, with a scowl for them. 'Now.'

They went, and as she turned to watch as if making sure they were out of earshot, Luke began to regret the situation he'd got himself into. Robert, who was someone who would always back up his sons in public whether they were right or wrong, wouldn't give him any sort of a hearing; and though Miranda had shown her displeasure towards them he wasn't so stupid as to think it would translate into support for him.

'All right, Luke.' She turned back to him, scowling at him in exactly the same way she had at them, as if she had any authority over him. 'Fighting in the street? What's this all about?'

'None of your business.' He found the courage to spit, but she wasn't remotely perturbed. She was a tougher bird than he'd thought she was.

'Who started it?'

'Your kids started it. They jumped me when I was coming out of the drive.'

'And what were you doing in the drive?'

'I'd been up to the house. I said. I wanted to talk to you.'

Her expression wavered, as if it could go either way, as if she was choosing between standing up to him or placating him. She went tough. 'Fine. Here I am. If you have anything to say to me, you can say it to me now.'

His courage almost failed him. It was only the way she kept twisting the wild flowers in her fingers that gave away her nervousness. 'Them's protected. You're not supposed to pick them.'

She looked down at them with a frown. 'Oh, God knows there's enough of these. Is that really what you wanted to say to me? Because if so then I think you're being vexatious.'

He had no idea what that meant. 'Picking wild flowers is breaking the law. You don't want to go breaking the law.'

'I'm quite sure the police have more important things to do than worry about that, and of course we all know you regard the law as sacrosanct. But if it makes you feel any better…' She tossed them aside. 'Happy now?'

It was no wonder the twins had turned out the way they were, with a stuck-up bitch like Miranda to set them an example. 'Aye, that's how you people work, isn't it? You do something wrong and you ditch the evidence and you lie about it.'

'I have no idea what you're talking about.'

'On the day Summer died you came back before you said you did.'

'I promise you, you're mistaken. Will and Ollie saw me come back and they've already confirmed it to the police.'

'What if I go to the police and say differently?'

'What if you do? It won't make any difference. The matter is closed, and anyway it's irrelevant. Summer's death was an a accident. So please leave us in peace and don't assault my stepsons again, or I'll be the one calling the police.' She shrugged her way past him and stalked through the now-open gates.

'You want to be found drowned too, Mrs?' he called after her. 'You're going the right way about it.' But she carried on walking, and it wasn't until she was out of sight that he realised he'd forgotten to ask her for money.

Back at Waterside Lodge, the first thing Miranda did was call Robert. The encounter with Luke had been a chastening one, but her earlier confession and Robert's unconditionally positive reaction to it had been a game-changer. Fear flew from her heart like darkness ahead of light and the stroll she'd taken through the dale before stumbling upon the brawl in the road had been the first walk she'd had where fear hadn't stalked her.

'Luke threatened me,' she told him.

'Young hothead,' he said, when she'd outlined what had happened. 'He thinks with his fists. All the Helmsleys do. It'll just be the boys putting his back up. Nothing to do with the other thing.'

Even at a distance, his voice was reassuring. He was in Newcastle that day, not too far away. Some investment banker had been dispatched up to a regional office at Robert's behest, to save him from a trip to London. She smiled. 'When will you be home?'

'I'll pick up a sandwich and head straight back. Don't worry. I can see how it alarmed you, but I'll go down and speak to him this evening. It won't happen again.'

'I'll see you later on.'

'Goodbye, darling.'

When she ended the call, comforted by the unfamiliar luxury of being able to tell him anything, there was silence inside the house. The twins had gone to ground, and she had no stomach for chasing them and demanding an explanation. That was something for Robert to do when he came home, because at some stage in the previous month or so playing the stern parent with two such strong personalities had crept beyond her capabilities. She'd always known it would.

She helped herself to a sandwich lunch, looking out over the garden and the lake as she ate. In her heart she suspected a bit of a thrashing would do Ollie, in particular, no harm, but it was only part of a lesson they had to learn. And as for herself, well. She had the support of her husband and sharing her fears hadn't just halved them; it had caused them to melt away. A beautiful day called for the temptation of another carefree walk. Only now she was released from the prison of her fear did she realise how enclosed she'd been in it, how much more she could enjoy the open spaces of the Lakes.

When she'd cleared away her lunch things, she let herself out of the house and walked down the drive. To her left Hallin Fell rose up, pretending to be far more mighty than its height allowed. She liked it, the way it sat out in the middle of Ullswater's east shore and offered three hundred and sixty degree views. Today, perhaps, was a day to climb it.

Heading out of the gate, she hesitated for a moment before turning towards Sandwick. The alternative path was the one that took her along the water's edge, past Kailpot Crag, and though she'd never have described herself as a sentimental woman it was too soon to walk past the place where the police had found Summer's body.

Drowning was supposed to be peaceful. She bit her lip, wondering what she'd have done if the girl had approached her to talk about Elizabeth. Told her everything — or not all of it, not about the lies — probably, because there was so much already in the public domain. Something she could add to a body of research might, in the end, do justice to Elizabeth's memory. The only concern would be whether it might reawaken ideas of vengeance that should long since have died down, but who was going to pay any attention to a first-person account in a dissertation?

After all, Miranda told herself as she strode out along the road to where the road curved down into Martindale under George's cottage, looking somehow deserted even though no-one had been in to close the curtains, the fears that had trapped and troubled her for a decade were groundless and now she could start to live again.

The narrow banks of the beck pinched it into a gap where the bridge overstrode it, and she stopped to look over the parapet and back down towards the house. Below her, a figure in blue overalls sprawled in the beck, face down, the head tilted at an angle towards the bank.

As Miranda reached for her phone and dialled the police, the fear came flooding back.

EIGHTEEN

'Faye wants to show we mean business,' Jude explained to Doddsy as he swung his car down the ever-more familiar twisting lane past the Sharrow Bay hotel and into the the heart of nowhere. 'So make yourself obvious.'

Doddsy was unimpressed. 'We're the police. Who do we need to show off to?'

Jude slowed for a corner, and a Herdwick sheep stared back at him, reproachfully, from the middle of the road. He brought the Mercedes to a stop, waited a second and then nudged forward a foot to give the animal a hint. Faye's interest in Robert and his financial goings-on remained confidential but her determination was wavering. *Even if it turns out to be an accident*, she'd said, *it's probably time to let him know we're watching what happens on his turf.* 'The killer, I imagine. On the assumption that there is a killer, of course.'

'And why on this case more than any other?'

'Your guess is as good as mine.' No-one was going to escape by car, so in that sense there was no urgency, but the protection of the scene and the collection of evidence was a priority, and both of those degraded with time. Jude allowed himself to use the townie's trick of hooting the horn at the sheep, and it did the job, prompting the animal to shuffle off and slither up the bank and under a wire fence. He put his foot on the accelerator and the car slid off.

'Then I'll guess.' Doddsy, Jude could tell, was frustrated. 'Maybe she thinks there's something else going on, and maybe she's trying to panic someone.'

'Such as?'

'Such as someone who might have thought they got away with killing someone. And you know who I'm talking about.'

The case of Summer Raine had been shunted off to the coroner and once it had gone, Jude had had no time to discuss it with Doddsy — something he would have done, even six months before, over one of their regular pints of a weekday evening. Since Ashleigh had arrived on the scene, and since Doddsy had found himself a partner in the rather surprising shape of Tyrone Garner, the regular drinks had become highly infrequent and the exchange of information they'd facilitated was confined to office hours. Jude made a mental note to do something about it in future. 'You think somebody did?'

'Don't you?'

'Yes, as a matter of fact. And so does Ashleigh.'

'And you told Faye. And she must agree with you, or we wouldn't both be here.'

'She didn't to begin with, but she may do now.' Jude slowed again, for the hairpin bends at the Hause, where the road scaled the steep lower slopes of Hallin Fell. 'This may be unconnected, of course.'

'The call said it looked suspicious.'

'And on further questioning said it looked like a broken neck. But it was Miranda Neilson who found him, and although we don't yet have a positive identification, the first indication is that it's Summer's boyfriend who's dead.'

'Ah,' said Doddsy, and descended into a moment of reflection.

'My first reaction,' Jude continued as they topped the hill past the new church and looked down towards the old, where a police car blocked the way, 'is to wonder why she immediately assumed he was murdered and called the police, rather than assume it was an accident and call an ambulance. Then I wondered whether it's significant that it was Miranda who found the body.'

'Probably not.' Doddsy unclipped his seatbelt as Jude parked the car in the car park at the bottom of the fell. 'There's a limited selection of people who live down here, and it's only a few hundred yards from her front gate.'

'A walker might have stumbled on it, but you're right. They tend to take the shore road, or go up the fell.'

'Old George would have seen it.' Doddsy looked at George's empty cottage. 'He saw everything. It's a shame he's gone.'

'Ashleigh thinks there's something odd about that, too.'

Normally Doddsy respected Ashleigh's instinct, but this seemed to stretch his credulity too far. He shook his head and said nothing.

They descended the slope. The first car on the scene contained a police constable and a PCSO, one of whom was taping off the scene and the other taking photographs. The first of the locals, alerted by the blue flashing lights, was striding up from the farm to see what was going on. A quick scan of the tarmac told Jude there was unlikely to be much gained from a search of it. It was the quickest and most sensible way to approach the scene and he was keen — more than keen — for a word with Miranda.

'Where's Mrs Neilson?' he asked the PCSO.

'She went back to the house. We took a statement from her.'

Jude cursed, inwardly. Waterside Lodge was on the other side of the bridge, which carried the road over the beck and so controlled the only vehicular route in and out of the dale. Now it was a crime scene and no-one, not even he, could cross it until it had been released. He walked back down the road and looked over the scene from a secure distance. The body lay with the head downstream, and there was no sign of damage on the banks. He turned and looked upstream. Even from a distance, trampled vegetation and a boot-mark in the mud told a tale. However Luke Helmsley had been killed, his body had been neatly tipped down the bank and thrust under the bridge.

'No way that's a fall,' Doddsy said to him.

'No way at all.' Jude straightened up and looked back up the road. The next in what would be a lot of police cars was on its way. 'I'm going to leave you in charge here. I'm going to talk to Miranda.'

'Right. So I'm the one who has to explain to the parents they can't get their kids from school and the walkers they'll have a three-mile detour to get to their cars.'

'Don't say I never give you the glamour jobs. Tell them we're doing our best to speed things up.' Jude grinned at him. Tammy would appreciate the need to get the scene released as soon as possible. 'And you're good at controlling chaos.'

Leaving Doddsy in charge, he doubled back and cut off along the footpath along the base of Hallin Fell. As he walked he cast a long glance back towards the bridge. There was a smattering of cottages around it, almost all of them holiday cottages. Someone might have seen something, but the lack of civilian activity around suggested not. And George's cottage, the one place where, just a week before, he could have almost guaranteed he'd have a witness, stood empty.

Waterside Lodge was quiet when he strode up the drive, but there was a sudden, swift movement behind the kitchen window as he approached and Miranda appeared on the step, her finger raised to her lips. 'Are you the police? I knew you'd come. But can we be discreet? I haven't said anything to Ollie and Will, yet.' She offered him her hand.

'Jude Satterthwaite. DCI.' Her fingers were cold, even in the balmy May sun.

Letting go, she tucked a strand of hair behind her ear. 'This is so awful. Is it murder?'

'We won't know until we get the post-mortem results.' It could hardly be anything else, but there were times when it was convenient to hide behind the shields of evidence, fact and confirmation.

'Seriously, Chief Inspector.' Miranda looked at him with scorn. 'Do you think I'm an idiot?'

One look told him that wasn't the case, even if he hadn't taken the trouble to read up about her as background to Summer's death. 'Shall we go inside? I'd like to ask you a little about how you came to find the body.'

Miranda, he was sure, had intended to keep him on the doorstep, but she shrugged and led the way into the kitchen. 'I'm sorry. My manners deserted me. I've already told your call handler and given a statement to the police constable over there. It isn't difficult. I was coming out for a walk and I stopped to look over the bridge. And I saw…'

her lip quivered a little. 'Well. You've seen it, no doubt. And I called 999.'

'Okay.' He'd get the details from the PC, or from Doddsy, on his way back. 'Then let me ask you something. Did you try and get him out of the water?'

'No. Why would I? I mean, you aren't meant to touch a body, are you?'

'No. You aren't. But I wondered what made you think he was dead.'

'Oh.' Doubt ran through that single syllable. 'Do you mean he might not have been? But he must be.'

'It certainly looks like it now. But I wondered why you thought he was at the time.'

'But he just…he just looked dead. His face was in the water. Jesus.' She put her hands to her mouth, and subsided gently onto one of the kitchen chairs. 'I never thought. Poor Luke.'

'And what made you sure it was Luke Helmsley?' He tried to be gentle with her, not just because she was so clearly in shock but because he sensed she was the sort of witness who would close up on principle if someone put her back up.

'Of course I assumed it must be. Because of the overalls. And the hair colour. And because…well.' She looked down at her feet and then back up. 'You'll have to know, I suppose. Luke was around here at lunchtime. I'm afraid he had a bit of a run-in with my stepsons.'

'Oh?'

'I don't know what it was about. Only that they fell out and they came to blows. Of course, Luke was more than capable of looking after himself, and the fight broke up when I came out. The twins sustained more damage than he did, I think. Luke was rather abusive to me and threatened me when I tried to smooth things over.'

'In what way?'

She twisted her fingers together. 'He said that if I wasn't careful, Summer wouldn't be the only person to be found floating in the lake. But then he left — back to work, I thought — and I went back into the house. The twins went back before me, and they were in the house from then on. They're here now, playing some video game, I think. I had a cup of coffee and came out afterwards for a walk and I came to the bridge and I—' Words failed her. She nodded towards the bridge.

'Then I think the obvious thing for me to do is talk to your stepsons.' He paused. 'I'm guessing Mr Neilson isn't home?'

'No. He had business in Newcastle today and left earlier on, about nine o'clock I think. I called him immediately after I'd dialled 999 and he's already on his way back.'

Robert Neilson, out of the dale again at the crucial time. Faye would be interested in that. Though of course you could turn that around and argue that whoever had killed Luke — and in his mind there was no doubt that it was no accident — had made sure Robert was elsewhere before they did so. 'Right. Then I'll talk to the two boys, if I may.'

Miranda bounced to her feet and went into the hall, with Jude following her. 'Ollie! Will! Can you come down here, please?'

A head appeared at the top of the stairs, swiftly followed by a second. 'Everything okay, Miranda?'

'Everything is not okay. The police are here and they want to talk to you.'

The two of them came skidding down the stairs at that, like a pair of five year olds, wide-eyed. One of them had a swelling bruise under his right eye, the other a split lip from which blood still trickled. 'We haven't done anything. Jeez, Luke didn't call the police did he? It was only a joke. It was him who started it.'

'No,' Miranda said, sounding suddenly weary, 'he didn't call them. I did. Because,' (she gave Jude a quick look as if challenging him to stop her) 'when I was out for my walk I came across Luke—'

'We don't know what happened.' Jude decided to cut her off before she used the word *murder* and freaked them out. 'We found his body underneath the bridge at the entrance to Boredale. I'm just asking around to find out if anyone saw anything. Nothing more, at this stage.'

'Like you did with Summer?' one of the boys asked, and the other nudged him rather too obviously. From outside the sound of a distant siren split the air, some emergency vehicle coming late to the party, and they exchanged glances again.

'Yes.' Jude introduced himself, and caught the look that flicked between them as they registered his rank. Twins. If they had anything to do with it they'd have sorted their stories beforehand, just as they so obviously had done over Summer. For a moment he was tempted to interview the two of them together, just so he could try and read their interaction, intercept the secret signals they were bound to have, but in the end he decided against it. The chances were that they'd be able to read one another's minds, pick up on each other's cues, without him seeing anything though it was right under his nose. It was better to take them separately, to see if there were any differences. 'I'd like a quick word with you, a witness statement. You know the drill by now, I expect.'

'Shall I start? I'm Ollie.' The one with the bruised cheek put himself forward with the sort of grim determination you might see on a family trip to the dentist, the child who always goes first to get the misery out of the way. 'We'll go to the kitchen. That's where we were before.'

They went through to the kitchen and sat down, Jude making notes while Ollie rattled through an account of his and his twin's actions. 'It was childish, I know. But Will and I had had a couple of beers and we thought it would be funny to hang around in the lane and see if anyone came along that we could jump out on. Miranda said we were immature and I suppose you think she's right.'

Jude declined to comment. 'Go on. What happened?'

'We saw Luke come along, but before he got to us he turned up to the house. The main gates were locked, so he jumped over the wall and went up to the house. There was no-one in, and we reckoned if he was there for a long time he'd have broken in to see what he could get, so we hung around to see. But he was back down the drive straight away.' There was almost a trace of disappointment in his voice.

'Any reason why you supposed Mr Helmsley was going to break into the house?'

Ollie had the grace to look ashamed. 'No, not really. Except he obviously hates us, and I think the only reason for that is because we've got so much and he's got so little. But Dad started off here just the same as everyone else. It's not our fault he made so much money.'

'I see.' Luke's record of violence was unblemished by greed but driven, by all accounts, by jealousy. It was possible the one might spill over into the other but, in the context of the case, irrelevant. 'And so you jumped out on him.'

'Yeah. We played with the gates a bit, and he looked confused. And them we jumped out and he got angry and went after us. And of course we didn't run away.' Ollie fingered the bruise. 'He has a devil of a temper.'

'And then what happened? How did the fight end?'

'Miranda came along and interrupted it. She sent us back into the house, and we stayed there.' Ollie met his gaze with impudence. 'Getting our story straight, as it happens. For Dad, not for you. Because we weren't expecting anything to happen to Luke and we didn't think the police would come.'

If their father was the martinet Faye seemed to think, the boys would do well to find some way to appease him. 'Did you overhear any conversation between Mrs Neilson and Mr Helmsley?'

Ollie shook his head. 'We were just glad to get out of it. Ran back to the house like a pair of rats and stayed there. He can pack a punch, Luke.'

'Okay. Let's go over it once more to make sure there's nothing I've missed. And then I'll let you go and I'll have a chat with your brother.'

'Inevitably,' Jude said to Doddsy as they stood a little way up the hill and waited for the doctor to certify Luke Helmsley as dead, 'the twins had identical stories. But that's not really surprising. I suspect it would have happened even if they hadn't had time to agree something. And although I'm prepared to be wrong, I'm inclined to think it wasn't them.'

Doddsy nodded, looking in deep thought at the scene below the bridge. 'It's handy for someone that George Barrett died, isn't it? He'd have seen something.'

'I thought that. And are we sure no-one else did?'

'We haven't done the door-to-doors yet. Ashleigh will come down and take charge of that. But it won't take long.' There were only half a dozen houses in Martindale and

Boredale combined, plus the hamlet of Sandwick. 'We'll do the houses all the way up to Pooley Bridge, and see if there's anyone in the campsite who saw anything but I doubt it, unless there was someone up on Hallin Fell.'

'Even then, the path goes the other way round. I wouldn't swear to it but I reckon you can't see the bridge from most of it.' The killer, then, was clever. 'Did you speak to anyone?'

'The farmer came down. Luke's employer. He was out looking for him because he hadn't come back from his lunch break. I'd be surprised if it was him. I've never seen a man go grey so quickly when he heard what had happened.' Doddsy slid his hand into his pocket and extracted a lighter and a packet of cigarettes, then slid them back again when the doctor stood up and stretched himself, then turned and scanned the assortment of police personnel for them.

They went down the hill towards him. 'Dead, of course?' said Jude, as a conversation starter. It had been obvious.

'Well and truly.' The doctor was new to both of them, round and pink-faced, young enough to relish the excitement of certifying a body dead in the street. A tweed jacket and matching tie marked him out as a young fogey. 'Difficult to say for how long. The water would affect the body temperature.'

'And the cause of death? Obviously we need to wait for the PM for a final verdict, but do you have any ideas?'

'Broken neck,' the doctor said, without hesitation. 'Not just broken. Snapped. You may find the post-mortem shows water in the lungs and so technically he might be said to have drowned. But if the neck injury didn't actually kill him, it would have done within minutes. Bloody neat job, too. Almost certainly not accidental. In my view.' He glanced at his watch, glanced at his car. 'You can do as you wish with the body, now.'

'Thanks.' Jude saw him off while Doddsy gave the go-ahead to Tammy and her CSI team. At the place where the road was now closed, a Range Rover, new and top-of-the-range, pulled up and a man got out. Robert Neilson.

'Ey up,' Doddsy said, under his breath. 'Who's this?' He'd got the cigarettes out again and in the name of professionalism was forced to put them back again, but he kept his fingers tapping on his jacket pocket.

'I need to get home,' Robert was saying to the PCSO. He had his back to them and his tone was polite, but icy. 'My wife and sons are on their own in the house—'

The twins were more than capable of looking after themselves, and Jude thought Miranda was a tougher nut than she wanted them to think. He watched with interest.

'I'm sorry, sir. This is a crime scene. We'll clear it as soon as we can.'

'Officer. That isn't good enough. People live in this place. They have responsibilities. I insist you allow me access to my home.'

'Do we intervene?' asked Doddsy, under his breath.

Jude shook his head. 'Not unless we have to.' Not, at least, until he could justify it to Faye.

'I can promise you, sir, I understand. Being a local lad myself. It's a crime scene—'

'So you said. And I'm a local resident.'

The PCSO looked back over his shoulder towards them. 'If you need to talk to the detective in charge…'

'That'll be you,' said Jude, under his voice. 'I'm having nothing to do with it.'

But Neilson, turning, took a long look at them and backed down. 'No. That won't be necessary. I suppose I'll have to go and find myself a hotel for the night.'

'I very much hope you'll be back in your home later on this evening.'

'Okay,' said Jude to Doddsy. 'I'm out of here.' Discretion was the better part of valour, especially knowing Faye's opinion on the matter. Something told him there would be plenty of opportunity to speak to Robert Neilson in the future.

NINETEEN

Tammy and her team had put in a superhuman effort to get the road reopened, even though work continued around the bridge. The dale's children slept in their own beds on Friday night and Robert Neilson was able to return to the bosom of his family; but that was only the beginning of it. Inevitably, Jude took the flak for the ongoing disruption and the effect it had on George Barrett's funeral.

He'd been tempted to give it a miss and get on with the more immediate problem of what had happened to Luke, but there was only a limited amount he could do without the post mortem and the full results of the crime scene investigation, and anyway it was important to keep himself connected to convention. Missing funerals was a level of casual disrespect his mother would never have stood for, and he was in bad enough odour with Becca as it was. And he'd liked George. That, above all, counted for something.

The family could have delayed the funeral if they wanted, and he understood why they hadn't, but the irritation he'd observed from the mourners as they'd passed the uniformed police officer guarding the bridge had struck him as flimsy at best.

'And now we have to walk back past the whole thing again,' a woman in the row in front of him said to her neighbour as George's coffin was lifted by a collection of his distant male relatives at the conclusion of the service. 'You'd think they could have stood their men down, just for an hour. And taken away that white tent, for heaven's sake.'

He shook his head at that, hoping Tyrone, the officer on duty, had had the sense to show the coffin a little respect as it had been taken in to the church. The final leg of George's life journey, from the church to his interment, was a matter of yards. Thank goodness that, at least, was out of sight of the crime scene.

The coffin passed down the aisle and he looked away as Becca, her sister and her mother walked after it, at the head of the mourners. George had been well-known if not enormously popular, and the place was packed. He recognised plenty of faces, though it seemed most of them shared the prevailing view, that the taint of murder that lingered in the dale was his fault. Few of them spared him a smile.

It was as well he hadn't come to the church in the hope of increasing his approval rating. Fretting a little, he looked down at his watch. There would be time to attend the burial but he was keen to get back to the office to see what new information had come in. And there had been a message from Faye, the last one he'd had before he'd entered the church and turned off his phone, asking to be kept updated as a matter of priority.

As if he could forget. But he wouldn't be going to the wake and he was mighty glad to have an excuse not to.

He waited in his pew for the church to empty, so that

he could be at the back of the collection at the graveside just as he'd been in the back row of the congregation, scanning the mourners as they left. Miranda and Robert were there, she in a neat black silk suit and tiny black hat, walking down the aisle with her hand tucked through her husband's arm. She didn't look at Jude. There was no sign of the twins. In disgrace, or just not trusted out in public wearing the visible signs of a violent altercation with a man who'd been murdered barely an hour later?

Outside in the dale a soft summer breeze tickled the long grass in the churchyard and rippled the fresh ferns on the slopes of Hallin Fell and Steel Knotts as the mourners gathered for the committal. At the western wall of the graveyard, a pile of earth lay on a tarpaulin by the empty grave. When the short service of burial concluded with an *amen* that disappeared to heaven on the wind, the pall bearers lowered the coffin into the grave; Becca's mother laid an arrangement of flowers on the ground beside it; and as the mourners headed through the gate the undertakers moved in to shovel in the earth and smooth out the wrinkles in three rolls of turf they laid on top. And that was that, the end of George Barrett. *Earth to earth, ashes to ashes, dust to dust.*

Jude hung back once again as the line of mourners funnelled towards the bridge and their parked cars, and that somehow brought him closer than he'd ever intended to Becca. She was groping in her handbag, clearly fruitlessly, and couldn't have seen him for the tears that shone in her eyes.

No-one else had noticed, so in the end he gave in to gallantry he didn't feel.'Do you need a hanky?'

She took the one he offered without a word, dabbed at her eyes, blew her nose and only then seemed to realise who her knight in shining armour was. 'Oh, Jude. I didn't think you'd come. I told Mum you'd be too busy.'

The dig annoyed him. 'I wouldn't have missed it for the world. George was a great guy. Which isn't to say I'm not busy. Just that he was worth it.'

She blew her nose again. 'Did we have to have all these police around? On a Saturday, and at a funeral? And that horrid tent under the bridge? Couldn't you have stood them all down?'

She should know better than that: they'd been together long enough. 'The tent's a crime scene. The officers are protecting it. We went all out to get the bridge clear for the locals, but we still need to do a full investigation.' Briefly, as they walked along the lane below George's cottage up on the bank, he remembered Ashleigh's contention, and his own, that George might equally be the victim of a lucky, or a stunningly clever, crime.

'I suppose so.'

Tyrone, who was guarding the bridge, had taken his hat off as the mourners passed, something he saw was being greeted with approval even though the coffin was no longer there. Jude nodded to him, then carried on at Becca's side.

'Jude,' she said, looking away from him, 'can I ask you something?'

'Of course.'

She put his handkerchief into her pocket. He expected she'd return it, washed and pressed, via his mother, in due course. 'I'm worried about Ryan.'

'That's your cousin from Australia, right?' Jude had a clear memory of him from the time when they'd passed on the street between Becca's house and his mother's. What he remembered most immediately was the surliness of both his tone and his words.

'Yes. He isn't here.'

'Were you expecting him?'

'Yes. He's gone off wild camping for a bit, but I spoke to him after George died and told him when and where the funeral was, and he said he'd come along.' She hesitated. 'I don't really think he's got into any trouble. He's not a rookie. He's in the army so he's done a whole lot of survival stuff. But it doesn't matter how experienced you are. You can still have an accident.'

'In which case it's the mountain rescue people you should be speaking to.'

'Yes, but I don't know exactly where he is. Last time I spoke to him he said he was somewhere in the Pennines, but that could mean anything and anywhere.' She fussed at the hanky again. 'I don't know why I'm even asking you. There's nothing you can do, and even if there was you'd be far too busy. As usual.'

That stung. 'I'm not too busy to take half a day to turn up at George's funeral when there's a murder investigation on.'

'That's different.' She scowled back at Tyrone, in total contrast to her usual sunny nature.

It was a struggle to be dispassionate at the best of times with Becca, and Jude could see she was upset, but he wouldn't allow himself to respond to it. Since she'd started dating Adam he'd seen more signs of discontent and less evidence of her open and honest heart, as if his former friend's bitterness had spread to her.

Recognising the signs of the way she responded to distress — and hadn't he seen that same thing on the day of George's death? — he plunged his hands into his trouser pockets and waited for the storm to break. He was bitter, too, and between them she and Adam had given him plenty to be bitter about. 'Different? Why?'

'It just is. I don't know why you came here but you obviously didn't come here to support me.'

His patience ran out. 'Why the hell would I? Adam's the one who should be supporting you.' But he wasn't surprised Adam wasn't there. George hadn't liked him, and Adam had a flexible social conscience. 'After the way you've behaved to me recently, it's in my own interests to be very careful where you're concerned.'

Her scowl deepened. 'What's that supposed to mean?'

'I did everything I could to help you on the day George died, and so did Ashleigh. God knows I'm not looking for gratitude, but I don't need my good nature thrown back in my face, either.'

She stopped just before they reached her car, and glared at him. 'Okay, I shouldn't have flown at you, but I was upset, and I apologised. It was trivial. I'll apologise again if it makes you feel better. Don't tell me you're going to hold that against me. It's not like you to be so petty. Maybe you need to take a long hard look at yourself.'

Funeral or not, in full view of a selection of his colleagues or not, Jude wasn't putting up with that. 'You think it's petty? You put my career at risk over something you've just described as trivial and apologised for and you tell me I need to look at myself? Jesus, Becca. What kind of satisfaction do you get out of it? What kind of pleasure does that give you?'

'I don't get any pleasure out of it. I don't like being angry with anyone. I don't like anyone being angry with me. And I don't think I've done anything to deserve that.'

'Then why go out of your way to make my life difficult?'

'What are you taking about?'

'The complaint. What do you think?'

'Complaint?' She pulled out the hanky again and

dabbed at her eyes. A streak of mascara transferred itself from her eyelashes to the hanky, leaving a bruising blur on her cheekbone.

Even in his fury, he had to stop himself reaching out in a futile attempt to wipe it away. 'Yes. The complaint you put in about what happened last Saturday.'

'I didn't complain.'

'Don't insult my intelligence by lying to me. There was no-one but you and me there. Okay, so I can guess Adam will have put you up to it, but you did it.'

For a second they stood and stared at each other. A sudden breath of wind tweaked her hair across her face and she flicked it away. 'What you did was totally inappropriate.'

'What I did? I didn't do anything. For Christ's sake, Becca. I thought we were friends.'

Becca, breaking free, got into her car, slammed the door and drove away.

TWENTY

'There's no need to look so thoughtful.' Scott bounced in through the back entrance to the cafe, when Ashleigh had been looking out for him at the front. She didn't normally allow anyone to surprise her like that, but she'd been trying her best to be casual and not stare out for him like a teenager terrified of being stood up. 'Unless someone's died. But someone probably has, of course. Someone always does, in your line of work.'

She jumped, more than she should have done given she was expecting him, and scrambled to her feet in unusual confusion. 'There you are.'

'Obviously.' Scott swooped in on her, swallowed her up in a bear hug and kissed her.

Familiarity overwhelmed her. It was funny how, after so long apart, she remembered the good things better than the bad; but the bad things were still there. Even if she'd wanted to forget them she couldn't, with Lisa carping on at her in the evenings and Jude's thoughtful but silent appraisal whenever the mention of Scott came up between them. 'You're late. I thought you weren't coming.'

'The interviews were running late. Thank God, because the taxi driver took me all round the houses on the way.'

'The road's closed up at Tirril. That's why.'

'Wherever that is. But the person before me got held up behind a hearse. That's what made me think of death. And when I was done, the funeral party was passing. There would be something weird about tagging along with someone else's funeral, so I waited and chatted with the guy on the desk.'

'Was she pretty?' Ashleigh could read him like a book, and was pleased to see that he coloured slightly in response.

'Yeah, she was okay. A bit old for me, but you know.'

She saved that bit up as reassurance for when Lisa challenged her on every twist and turn their meeting had taken. 'Never mind. You're here now. But I can't stay long. I need to get back to the office.'

'I thought you were on a day off.'

'Supposedly. But we're investigating a nasty homicide. I only just managed to sneak out to see you.' She'd felt guilty about clinging onto those few hours of her supposed rest day when there was work to be done, but Scott was an obligation she couldn't shake off. Anyway, it was important for the two of them to meet without expectation and without rancour, another step on the road to friendship. Jude had lifted an eyebrow when she'd told him, but he hadn't said anything. 'You're lucky to get me at all.'

'Right. But you can run me into town on your way back, at least. And I'm going to have some lunch. How quickly do you think they can rustle me up a sandwich?' And he turned his charm on the waitress.

While he was cajoling her into prioritising him over the customer who'd been in before them, Ashleigh looked out of the window. George's funeral must be over: a collection of people dressed in black were parking their cars on the street and ambling towards the pub where the wake was being held. The solemnity had been broken, now, as always happened after the tears of a funeral, and they were laughing and chatting as they walked. Becca was among them, but her face bore a stormy expression and she was walking alone.

In a moment, as Ashleigh had expected, Jude drove past. Skipping the wake to get straight back to the office and try and work out who'd killed Luke Helmsley, no doubt, and cursing the traffic delay that would add ten minutes each way to the journey.

'You're such a star,' Scott said to the waitress as she whisked away with every sign of urgency, and then he turned back to her. 'How's it going?'

She tore her eyes from Jude, who was sitting in his car at the lights, fingers drumming on the steering wheel as he waited for them to change. He was looking particularly moody today, but maybe wearing black, or attending funerals, did that to people. Or maybe, knowing Jude, he was turning over the list of things to do, people who could be killers, who had means, motive and opportunity.

Scott saw the look. 'Is that the new boyfriend?'

'Yes.' Already on the defensive, she nevertheless gave him the chance to offer his blessing.

'Everything you're looking for in a man?'

Scott was a reminder that the down side of a dream was a nightmare. 'There's no such thing as a perfect man, Scotty. But to answer your first question, it's going really well. I'm settling in nicely.'

'Do you miss me?'

'No.' She'd promised Lisa she'd be robust in the face of his inevitable attempts to sweet-talk her. 'In one way, of course. You're good company. And that's how we'll keep it.'

'Did I suggest anything else?'

His whole demeanour suggested something a lot more intense than friendship, but it always did. That was how he kept getting himself in trouble. Women heard promises of fidelity he swore he'd never made. She'd fallen for it herself. 'I'm just warning you.'

'I hope you aren't going to cut me adrift. If I get this job, I'll be relying on you to help me settle in.'

The nightmare of having Scott permanently around was one she didn't want to think about, but it was by no means a done deal. 'If you get it, you'll have plenty of other people to see you right. They're a friendly bunch up at the watersports centre.'

'You know them?'

'I came across them through work recently.'

'Oh, of course. They were talking about the girl who drowned. Fate, eh? It's meant to be.' His sandwich arrived, alongside pint-sized mugs of coffee for each of them, and he spared a moment to thank the waitress before he tucked in.

Meant to be had been his favourite chat up line, and he'd delivered it so convincingly Ashleigh had overlooked the warning signs that flashed up as they'd approached the crossing point from lovers to marriage. 'I can't see you fitting in up here.'

'That's hurtful.' He winked across a slab of bread and cheese. 'You know I'm outdoorsy.'

'I meant it in a good way. Of course you're outdoorsy.' He was lean and fit and had the right amount of muscle in the places where muscles looked good, and he liked to show them off. 'But in a Mediterranean way, not a Cumbrian one.'

'Cold water,' he agreed with his mouth full, sending cheese crumbs flying in all directions.

An inveterate fidget, Ashleigh began gathering them up. 'You'll need a full dry suit with thermals underneath. Gloves and woolly hats when you're standing on the shore tutoring the beginners. Even in July.'

'God, no. Spare me the woolly hat. It would ruin my hair.' He was laughing at himself. 'Nah, you're right. I certainly wouldn't last up here for ever. I find my balls far too useful to have them frozen off up here all year round. And I never thought I'd say it, but I'm getting a bit fed up of the sun.'

He looked her in the eye as he said it and she was almost convinced, but all the time she'd known Scott he'd been a man who thrived on warmth and sunshine, on hot days and balmy evenings. He lived in shorts and sandals, sank shiploads of Spanish beer, and sported a tan that turned deep bronze over time. He was like a creature from a Greek myth, who came back to his country, and his wife for a season only, but had to return to the sun when the colour faded from his skin. 'Rubbish.'

'Well, maybe not fed up. But it's time for a change, perhaps. Maybe a summer somewhere else would be enough for me to learn to appreciate it. I could go to the Caribbean in the autumn. Call this idea wanderlust, if you like.'

Only Scott could satisfy his wanderlust by coming home. 'You're one of a kind,' she said and relaxed. Because it was only a couple of hours in his company and even if he was offered the job she was confident the privations of the Lakes would be too much for him and he'd refuse.

TWENTY-ONE

It was warm, and Jude's first action had been to open the windows and let in some fresh air. It was going to be a long day in the office for a lot of people as they picked over the bones of Luke Helmsley's murder. Now, with the initial briefing over and the team of officers he'd called in allocated to their various roles on the case, he could sit down in the incident room with those who chimed closest with his thinking and hammer out possibilities.

'Like a military killing, the doctor said.' Chris Marshall's talents lay inside the office and Jude included him in any general discussion where it was possible, because he could think outside the box — not so much in terms of the killer or any hypothesis about why and how a crime had occurred, but because he knew the best places to find information, and his instincts for an online trail were unerring. And he never gave up. His prize was the result, the piece of information which would confirm or deny the theories concocted by minds that worked in different ways to his. 'Do we have the PM report?'

'We do.' Jude tapped his fingers on the desk and listened to the bells of St Andrew's church, calling the faithful to Sunday service. Doddsy was listening to them, too, with a sigh, because he was the only one of them who was a regular churchgoer and somehow always seemed to end up working on Sundays. 'It confirms the cause of death as a broken neck. Death was instantaneous. There was no water in the lungs and no other signs of immediate violence.' Luke had had his share of bruises, some of them no doubt the result of brawling and others from a life of physical exertion, lifting rocks and manhandling livestock, but none was recent and there was nothing from the moment before he'd died. 'He hadn't picked up anything from his fight with the Neilson boys apart from a grazed knuckle and a black eye.'

'Military style.' Chris referred to his notes. 'That's what the doctor said.'

'Yes. The report isn't explicit as far as that goes, but it was a single, clean break consistent with his head being snapped backwards with considerable force.' Matt Cork, the pathologist, was a friend of Jude's and though he was overcautious and refused to commit himself, Jude had judged from his tone that he thought the crime had an element of professionalism about it. 'It may have been lucky, but I'm inclined to think not.'

'Time of death?' Doddsy asked. He was looking particularly world-weary.

'He can't say for certain. Luke met the twins at one and parted from Miranda almost immediately after that. Miranda found him at quarter past two. On the basis of that, Matt reckons he must have been killed almost immediately before she found him.'

The fourth member of the team, Ashleigh, had been silent up to that point, but at that she sat forward. 'Are you seriously suggesting Miranda is capable of carrying out that kind of killing?'

'No. Not at all. But if she narrowly missed seeing the murder, I think she's lucky to be alive.'

In the expectant silence, he got up and turned to the white board on the wall behind him. On the day of Luke's's murder it had sprung into being, with photographs, queries, maps all jostling for position on it. Jude unpinned a couple of pictures of Luke's broken body and dropped them on the desk, then stood looking down on them, hands in his pockets. 'Before we get to the why and the who, I think we can be fairly clear about what happened. I've spoken to Tammy and she's built up a picture of a neat, clean killing. It looks as if Luke may have been on the road, possibly on his way back up to work. He may have met his killer or he may have been attacked from behind, but death was instant. He may never even have hit the ground.' In his mind the killer caught Luke before he fell and tipped him neatly over the parapet in one smooth move. The crime scene had been spectacularly clean. 'There's just one footmark on the bank, where someone must have braced themselves against it, possibly with the other foot in the water. It's either a wellington boot or a walking boot or a Doc Marten. That sort, though the mark isn't clear enough to distinguish between them. In Tammy's reconstruction, the killer braced himself — or herself — like that while shoving the body under the bridge, jumped up onto the road and made off. As an aside, when I saw Miranda she was wearing trainers but she could have changed. And her feet are way smaller than the print.'

'Size 12,' noted Doddsy.

'Yes. And now we need to think about why he was killed, and that will help us work out who.' He picked up a black marker from the table and took off the cap. 'This is where I want to add something else into this equation. Ashleigh and I were talking about this the other day. About the coincidence of an accidental death — Summer — and a sudden death from natural causes — George Barrett — within such a small area. She had suspicions about both.' He gave her a half-smile. 'I said if there was a third death I'd bring both of those two back into consideration, and that's what I want to do.'

Turning back to the board, he wrote Summer's name in capitals, then George's beneath it, a question mark beside each.

'I want us to think about where there's something linking those three. There may not be. It may be there's a clear and separate motive for Luke's murder.'

'A lot of people disliked him,' Chris said, running his hand through his fair hair. 'But as far as I can gather the more aggressive ones were pretty much the same kind of people as he was. The sort who'd lose their temper and throw a punch and then run off leaving the body in the middle of the road, or hand themselves in. Whoever did this was clever.'

'Yes. And if Summer was murdered then that person was also clever. Which makes me think that Luke stumbled across something — or someone — he wasn't supposed to know about, and that meant he had to be removed instantly.'

'It can't have been planned. If it was, they'd have hidden the body.'

'Unless they wanted someone else to get the blame. My guess is whoever it was who killed him saw Miranda coming and had just seconds to hide the body and themselves.'

'Military killing, eh?' Chris had his thinking face on.

'Military style, at least.'

'Didn't I hear something locally about some army guy hanging around?'

'You did. George Barrett's great-nephew is a soldier in the Australian army and is over in the UK on leave.'

'He didn't get on with George,' noted Ashleigh. 'I'm sure I heard that somewhere.'

'Yes, from me. A lot of people didn't, including Luke, I believe. But I don't know that this guy — his name is Ryan Goodall — was in the dale when Summer died, and to the best of my knowledge he isn't around now. The last I heard of him, he was floating about in some unspecified place in the Pennines.'

'And that was when?'

'A couple of days after George's death. I heard that from Becca, but she hasn't heard anything since then. He said he'd be back for George's funeral but he never turned up.' Becca had been worried about him; but Becca worried about everyone. From what he knew of Ryan Goodall from Mikey, whom he'd grilled on the subject, he was the type of man to change his plans with no regard for others. 'I don't know if that's significant. It would probably have been more so if he'd been around.' Nevertheless, he wrote Ryan's name down on the board, too.

'There are the twins,' Ashleigh said, with a frown of doubt, 'and there's Miranda. The boys went to a good school and they may have been in the cadet corps or whatever.'

'I'd like to think they don't teach kids that age to kill.'

'I'd like to think so, too, but you never know. Miranda says they were in the house, but I suppose it's not impossible they carried on the row and she's covering for them. Or sneaked out and she didn't see them.'

'It's not impossible,' Jude allowed, with some reluctance, 'but they'd both been drinking and my guess is the person who killed Luke had his wits about him. And I can't see how he'd have let them get close enough to surprise him like that.' He pushed his chair back. 'We'll get on. Ashleigh, you can go down and see how the door-to-door stuff is going. Chris, I'd like you to try and track down Ryan Goodall. Ask Becca if she's got a number, though he probably won't answer it. We may be able to trace the phone.'

When they'd gone he stood up and crossed to the window, where he stared down on the scattering of cars in the car park. As he'd expected, Faye's was among them, and he was only surprised she hadn't drifted down to see what was going on. 'I'll leave you to it just now,' he said to Doddsy. It was time to go up and have a chat with Faye.

She'd been sitting making notes on a pad, but when he came into her office she flipped the cover closed. He came straight to the point. 'I think I'd like the Neilsons' property searched.'

'Yes, I'm sure you would.' She shuffled her coffee mug on top of the pad for extra security, guilty as a teenage boy caught writing poetry, then took it off again and flipped the pad open. 'I'd love to, as well, and I was just working through the arguments for and against it. I won't go through them with you. Some of them are things you don't need to know and I'll be putting this through the shredder when I'm done.'

'Then you'll authorise me to apply for a warrant?'

She shook her head. 'I'm surprised at you. I'm as keen to go ahead with it as you are, but you should engage your common sense. Softly softly, and so on.'

'I think the case is rock solid. A young man has a fight with two other young men who have been drinking and threatens their stepmother when she intervenes. Less than two hours later she finds him murdered and there's no sign of anyone else around. How much more reason do you need?'

'Jude.' Like a schoolteacher with a particularly slow child, she shook her head at him. 'Do I really need to remind you how clever Neilson is?'

'You keep telling me he's clever. I don't know the man and I haven't seen any evidence for it. I'm not suggesting he killed Luke Helmsley. In fact, we know he didn't because he wasn't there. We have his word for it. We have his PA's word for it. And just in case she's up to her eyes in some unspecified, well-concealed crime to go with it, we have CCTV of the two of them picking up a coffee at a petrol station on the A69. He was exactly where he says he was when he said he was there.'

'Is that right? Though I expected nothing less.'

'Yes. Someone dug it up for me yesterday afternoon.' In fact Robert had gone out of his way to identify his whereabouts and the confirmation of it had been obtained within an hour, with suspicious ease. 'But as I say, on those grounds I'm not suggesting he did it, but I am suggesting one of his family might have done it. Or the killer might have hidden on the Neilson property, or escaped through it.'

'I wonder if they have CCTV footage,' she mused.

'They had cameras installed last week.' Too late to be of any use in the investigation into Summer's death. 'I haven't reviewed the footage myself, but Chris had a quick look and it didn't show anything. But if there was something — if it shows the twins leaving the place when they said they hadn't, for example — it might have been doctored, or we might find that a bit of it had gone missing.'

'Were they difficult about handing it over?'

'Slow, I'd say.' Usually people were only too keen to provide any evidence to the police, and in this case it had been forthcoming, though not immediately, as if there had been a short delay to ascertain whether there was anything incriminating.

'How very interesting,' said Faye, as if it weren't interesting in the least.

He waited for a moment, testing her out. After all, he didn't need her authority and he was only seeking it because of her earlier warning about handling the Neilsons with care. 'Supposing I were to approach the magistrate—'

'You might get a warrant or you might not. But if you do that, and if that jeopardises any other line of investigation, then someone senior to me will kick me into the middle of next week, and when I get back I'll give you your bits to play with. Understand?'

He stiffened. 'Three people have died and at least one of them was murdered.'

'I've told you before. There is a very serious money-laundering investigation under way and a lot at stake.'

'Murder trumps fraud, Faye. Every time. In my book, at least.'

'I don't deny it, but we don't have to choose between them. As far as I'm concerned, this case will remain very much live. If Robert Neilson has anything to do with it, we'll get him for it in the end. Never forget Al Capone.'

And by then the person who did his bidding, the actual killer, would be out of the country, if they weren't already. 'If we don't look for the evidence we may never secure a conviction.'

She spread her hands in a gesture of resignation. 'There's nothing I can do about it. I'm sorry.'

He left her to her paperwork, to her pointless thinking,

and strode back down the corridor towards the incident room, racking his brain for an alternative, for inspiration. In his mind he saw Luke Helmsley's face, lying in the mortuary, a face that had been so full of life and emotion, but had ended as a cold mask that showed nothing but shock.

TWENTY-TWO

Sometimes Becca worked on a Sunday morning, and sometimes she helped out at the Sunday school in Askham. Over the past month or so she'd mangled to wrangle both into passable excuses not to spend a Saturday night at Adam's, and today she'd managed to extend avoiding action right into the Sunday afternoon by virtue of the son of an old friend of George's having come up for the funeral and been invited to her parents' for Sunday lunch. But eventually that drew to an end, and it was some time after four o'clock that she headed to Adam's flat.

As she drove, she found herself reflecting uncomfortably on the funeral. It wasn't Jude's fault she'd been so upset. It wasn't his fault that whenever she met him she couldn't control her bad temper and ending up abusing him in a way she'd never dream of doing to anyone else. It wasn't his fault she'd made a fool of herself when he'd taken her home, either.

Now, at least, she knew his patience had an end. She could hardly blame him for losing his temper with her on the way back from George's grave. He was a good man, one of the better ones. It was just a pity that his goodness and his attention were focussed on other people, on the never-ending pursuit of what he thought of as justice, rather than looking out for those who were close to him. You couldn't live like that.

She wasn't prepared to admit she'd been wrong about Adam, though she allowed that Jude's motivation, which had been Mikey's welfare, had been a noble one. She knew he wouldn't give an inch on the morality of it, but he didn't have to. She'd let it go.

Jude lived on the same street, half a dozen doors up and on the other side of the road, and the closest parking space she found was always outside his house. Sometimes it struck her as vaguely sinister, that Adam took so much pleasure in being so very visible to his former friend, though at other times, most notably when she herself was feeling particularly inferior under the shadow of Jude's high-mindedness, she understood it a little better. It took a moment before she nerved herself to get out of the car, as if she was afraid of being spotted, but the house looked well and truly empty.

It was a Sunday afternoon. Jude would be at work. He always was, even without the additional stresses of a murder to deal with. She'd always pressed him to lighten up, to try a little self-care, but in vain.

Adam's house fronted the street and through the bay window she could see the telly on. He'd been watching golf. She could have stood and watched him for ages without being seen, just as he must have watched her before he'd called at the cottage after George's death. Now the source of Jude's accusation, which had struck her as unjust, became clear. She walked briskly up to Adam's doorstep and rang the bell.

'Hey, Chica.' He opened the door and kissed her when she stepped over the threshold. 'I thought you weren't going to come by.'

'I nearly didn't. Lunch went on a long time.'

'I had a narrow escape then.' He grinned at her. He'd been invited and had excused himself, on no real grounds whatsoever, but no-one minded. He had no obligation to spend a Sunday afternoon with her family.

'I think so. It turned into a second wake for poor old George, as if we hadn't had had enough of that yesterday.'

'Give the old boy his due.' Adam snapped the telly off and flopped back down in his armchair. 'He's that old, you'd never have got through all the stories about his life in a couple of hours. Have a seat. I'd offer you a beer, but I know you'll want to drive. Unless you'd rather stay.' He winked.

Turning down the beer, she sat down, ticking off the things she liked about him, as if she needed to justify having chosen him as her boyfriend. Adam was good fun, undemanding, and ready enough to make time for her. In this respect, he far outscored Jude. He wasn't intellectually challenging and he knew the value of a companionable silence. And, rather more to the point, he wasn't burdened by a dysfunctional family or the impulse to take on other people's problems.

He had his faults, too. Right at that moment the one that troubled her most was his tenacity for a grievance, his inability to let an old sin die. In her own way, Becca had as strong a sense of justice as Jude, and her conscience was troubling her. 'Adam. Do you mind if ask you something?'

'Ask away.'

'After George died.'

'What about it?' His look was challenging.

'Someone complained to the police about Jude. He

thinks it's me. Because it was about what happened when he brought me back home. Was it you?'

He stiffened, but he didn't look away. 'You weren't going to.'

She drew in a long, furious breath. 'Right. I don't know what you think you saw, but whatever it was you were wrong. He didn't do anything.'

'I trust my own eyes. You were in a distressed state and he tried to take advantage of you.'

It was never a good move to lose your temper with Adam. 'Stop talking about me as if I'm a teenager who's been drinking too much. I was upset. I tried to hit him. I'm in the wrong. Not him.'

'You wouldn't have tried to hit him if he hadn't done something to upset you.'

She thought back to the moment, to the upwelling of fury that had almost drowned her at the loss of George, at her failure to help him. Her feelings, she was sure, were mostly directed at herself, but she didn't think she'd have hurled herself at Adam in the way she'd tried to vent her anger on Jude. 'I was upset and he was there. That was all.'

'When I walked in it didn't look like he was fending you off. Far from it. That's not okay.'

'I hugged him, too.' A deep flush crept upon her. She had a vague memory of kissing Jude at Mikey's party a couple of months before, when she'd had a drink or two too many. He'd been more receptive to that kiss than to the hug. 'It wasn't him who started it. And do you know what? Even it had been him, even if he did behave inappropriately, it's none of your business. It's for me to decide whether to report him.'

A vein of old, vengeful fury beat at this temple. 'I thought you'd understand.'

'I do. You haven't forgiven Jude for what he did. I get

that. But it was over three years ago and it's done. And he was only doing his job.' She'd always believed that Adam had no-one to blame but himself. No-one had made him shift drugs, or resist arrest and end up with a longer sentence than he would have done as result. At the time she thought — still did think — that Jude should have dealt with Mikey differently, but that was nothing to do with Adam. 'You've redeemed yourself. Let it go.'

'He put me in prison.'

'He didn't know you were involved. He turned in Mikey, that was all.' Mikey had got away with a slap on the wrist, because of his age, because his crime had been possession rather than supply and because he'd expressed public remorse, though she knew there was no remorse in private. 'You need to let it go, and you need to stop harassing him.'

It was impossible to have a row sitting down, so she stood up. but as soon as she did so she knew it was a mistake. He bounced to his feet as well, and that was when she remembered he'd broken a policewoman's collarbone in his struggle to escape from the law. Adam was no respecter of anyone, regardless of gender, regardless of the relationship. She picked up her bag and headed for the door.

He came after her, clamping a hand on her shoulder. 'Right. Now I'll tell you something. Something you might not want to hear. Prison's hell. Do you want to know what hell it is?'

'No.' Shaking him off, she made for the door, wrenched it open and stepped out into the fading sunshine. Thank God. 'I'm not Jude's biggest fan. You know that. But you've got to take responsibility for your own actions and you can leave me to take responsibility for mine.'

'I've done that. I've done my time. You said. I'm rehabilitated. But don't think I'm ever going to forgive him for what I went through.'

She'd thought he was he redeemed, but maybe not. Drugs ruined people's lives, sometimes killed them, tortured and tormented their loved ones. 'I don't want to see you again. I can't trust you.' Worse than that: suddenly, he scared her.

He leaned on the door frame and laughed. 'He won't take you back, if that's what you're thinking. He's got someone a whole lot better than you, now. Better looking. Hot as hell, too. Someone who speaks his language the way us ordinary people never will.'

'I don't want him back.' She turned her back and stalked up the street to her car, her heart beating faster than it ought to. God knew she wasn't an idiot. She'd always suspected Adam's interest was more to do with Jude than herself and that the relationship would fade into insignificance as it had just done, an unofficial ending after which the two would barely speak. Adam's deliberate choice to rent a flat opposite Jude's house now looked creepy and his determination to achieve some kind of satisfaction seemed downright sinister.

She got into the car and watched as Jude's Mercedes drew up opposite. She should apologise for Adam's actions, tell him she'd contact the Professional Services department and withdraw the allegation she hadn't made.

The time for an apology had been at George's funeral when he'd told her about the complaint, but he'd caught her by surprise and so she'd missed the opportunity. She looked across the road. Jude got out of the driver's seat and Ashleigh out of the passenger side. Both of them were in their work suits, dark and sober, but his expression was one of lurking amusement and she was obviously giggling. So he'd managed to do what he so rarely did and leave the job to someone else for a few hours. Now he'd be looking forward to a cosy evening in with Ashleigh O'Halloran, no doubt. She watched as he unlocked the door, as she very obviously pinched his backside and he pulled her inside and snapped the door shut like a prim novelist ending a chapter to spare a reader's blushes.

When she'd told him he should allow himself a little more self-care, that hadn't been what she meant. She sighed and dialled Doddsy's number instead. 'Doddsy, it's Becca. Can I have a word?'

'Yeah, sure.'

There was a muffled sound. In the background, a male voice called out something and Doddsy called back. 'Just a second. I need to deal with this. Sorry, Becca. What can I do for you?'

Even the long-celibate Doddsy had finally found love. Suddenly she felt very alone. 'It's just a quick call. Someone made an anonymous complaint about Jude on my behalf. I want it withdrawn. What do I do?'

In the silence, she imagined him crinkling his brows as if it were a trick question. 'Just email. It's pretty straight-forward.'

'Thanks. I'll do that. See you sometime.'

Doddsy would think her a fool, but anything she said to him would get back to Jude sooner rather than later. It saved her the embarrassment of approaching her ex directly, and it was important to her he only thought badly of her for the things she'd done to hurt him. She sat for a while, until an unseen hand whisked the bedroom curtains closed in the house over the road. Feeling too much like a voyeur, she started the engine and drove off.

TWENTY-THREE

Aida turned up at Waterside Lodge at nine on Monday morning and she and Robert retreated into his study. The twins had been up at a reasonable hour and headed out for a brisk walk, more to get away from their father's scowling fury than because of any sudden enthusiasm for the outdoors, or so Miranda thought. After that, silence enveloped the house.

Miranda had made chicken pie and had just covered it with foil when Aida popped her head round the door. 'Mr Neilson has asked me to go down to the post office in Penrith, Mrs Neilson. Is there anything I can get you while I'm out?'

Miranda sighed. Aida was as bad as Luke had been, refusing to accept any kind of familiarity and instead treating her with a rigid formality which made her feel subtly marginalised in a place where she had every right to be. With Aida it was worse, because this was her own home. 'No, thank you.' She opened the fridge and slid the pie inside it.

'I expect I'll be about an hour.'

'That's fine.' Her phone pinged. She looked down at it. A message from Ollie. *Miranda, we need to talk to you. Don't tell Dad.*

Not again. Surely they hadn't got themselves into yet more trouble? Conscious of Aida's presence, she reached for her phone.

In the few seconds between Aida leaving and Robert emerging from the study, Miranda managed to flip a text back to Ollie. *Will it do later?*. 'Robert. Would you like a coffee? I was just going for a walk, but it can wait.'

Soon! Ollie pleaded.

Jesus. Her heart raced. What was it now? Were they going to tell her that somehow, after all, it was they who'd killed Luke? Or Summer? She turned her back on her husband, pretending to watch Aida's car heading down the drive and disappearing into the green dale and using that as a shield to cover her texting. *Where?*

Old George's house. As soon as you can.

'A walk? I'll come with you,' said Robert, cheerfully. 'Just for ten minutes, to clear my head. Aida found a mistake in some numbers, and thank God she did, but I think we've sorted it. I have time. And I daresay you'll be much happier with some company.'

Normally she'd have treasured a moment like that, because they were so rare, but today the last thing she needed was his presence as she set out to handle the twins. Since confession of her fears to Robert, he'd been carefully solicitous of her, looking out for her wherever she went. This was ironic, because telling him of her fears had liberated her from them in a way she didn't understand. 'Are you sure you have time? I thought I'd take a walk up Martindale.'

'I can come with you as far as the bridge, at least.'

The police had finished there. Luke's body had been taken away, the threatening white tent had been removed and you'd never know it had been the scene of so violent a death. 'I'll be all right. You know I will.'

'Call me over-cautious, but I'm still a bit uncomfortable about you being out. Things being what they are.'

'You mean Luke? It'll have been to do with his private life.' Summer's death, not just unexplained but somehow inexplicable, troubled her more than Luke's. She'd seen for herself how quick Luke had been to anger, and his reputation went before him. There were plenty of people in Pooley Bridge who didn't like him, and you never knew how long or how deeply people could bear a grudge. 'His former girlfriend's new partner is ex-army I think. There's more than a bit of needle there. I imagine that's where the police are looking.' Though she vaguely recalled hearing someone in the post office saying that the man was working out on what was left of the oil rigs and so in the clear.

'I still don't like the idea of you being on your own.'

'I won't be. I'm going to walk up and meet the boys. They were out early.'

A shadow passed over Robert's face. 'I hope they've had enough sense not to do something else stupid. They're getting out of hand. Their mother spoils them. I'll have to get more involved.'

They let themselves out of the house and walked down the drive, hand in hand, past the newly-installed CCTV cameras. It had been another rainy night and a dull morning but the May sun had crawled out from its nest in the clouds and gathered strength. Steam rose from the wet tarmac and the smell of the countryside, fresh and clean, lifted her optimism. Of course Ollie and Will wouldn't be in any more trouble. They'd just be wanting her help to get Robert to relax his attitude.

'The trouble with Luke,' said Robert, as they approached the bridge, 'is that he antagonised everyone.'

'Yes.' Miranda hesitated. She knew she'd have to cross it at some point, but she wouldn't look down. Not this time. 'It was horrible finding him, but do you know the strange thing?'

'What?'

'I wasn't afraid. Even though I could see he was dead and I could tell that it had happened so recently and it was so obviously deliberate, I never felt in any danger. It made me think. If someone wanted to kill me they'd have done it by now. They've had so many opportunities.'

'Yes. And now you've told me I'll make damned certain you're looked after. You're safe enough here. We've got the CCTV. But even in London, or anywhere else. You'll be safe. And anyway the police are floating around. Up at Howtown, I think, still asking questions about what someone might have seen. So if you need any help, all you need to do is shout and they'll come running.'

'Oh, Robert. I wish I'd told you the truth years ago.'

They stood on the bridge and kissed like teenagers, and after a moment he stepped back. 'I'd better get back. I don't want Aida to find out I've been playing truant.'

'I don't expect I'll be long.'

Leaving him behind her, she summoned her courage to cross the bridge and walked past George's house and up to the church, where she stood beside the rolls of turf that barely covered George's two-day-old grave, and stood there paying silent respects until she was sure her husband was out of sight. Then it was time to sort out whatever mess the twins had got into.

Robert was right. They were getting out of hand.

Going into George's house was too bad, and even if they didn't want to be seen they could surely have found somewhere a little more respectful. She supposed she'd have to try and reason with them and hope they listened, because if their father decided to come down hard on them there would be trouble and misery all around. She'd no doubt he'd take the fight all the way if he had to, cutting off their allowances and only breeding resentment. She wanted neither to take the blame nor to be too obviously on their side. Tricky, but something she was confident she could solve.

They wouldn't have forced entry to the cottage. Everybody in the dale knew under exactly which loose flagstone George kept his spare key. Miranda went up the path and put her hand to the door, opened it and stepped inside. She closed it carefully behind her so as not to attract attention. She, too, was trespassing. Someone — one of the family, presumably — had been in and closed the curtains as a mark of respect for the funeral and had yet to come in and open them. The place was oppressively dim and smelt of plain food and stale tobacco. 'Ollie? Will?'

There was silence, absolute stillness. She must have arrived before them; but if so, who had unlocked the door? 'Ollie?'

A movement behind her, the sharp click as if a safety catch were being released on a gun. She turned and saw only a black shadow among the greyness. 'Ollie?' she whispered.

And a voice. 'Goodbye, Miranda.' And then the shot.

Jude's car chased the shadow of a cloud down the Ullswater shore, catching up with its fading remnants in the shape of a rainbow hovering over Howtown pier. He pulled up beside the patrol car parked up by the pier, where Ashleigh was deep in conversation with two uniformed police officers, and wound the window down. 'Any joy?'

Ashleigh lowered the clipboard. 'None.' She ended the discussion with the two officers and drifted over to Jude while they returned to their patrol car. 'I think we're just about finished here. We've spoken to everyone we know was here, and I've put out an appeal for anyone who was walking up there yesterday, but I'll be surprised if we find anything, to be honest.'

'No, I think you're right. All the signs point to it being a very smart piece of work. So smart I almost wonder if it was a professional hit.'

'On Luke? You really think that?'

'I do. Hop in and we'll have a chat about it. I want to go down there and have another look around in case I can find any more inspiration, and I'd also like to talk to Robert Neilson about it.' Faye hadn't liked that idea but it had become increasingly difficult for her to argue. They were at the point where not speaking to him would look suspicious. 'He's bound to have crossed the wrong sort of people at some stage.'

'I'm done here anyway, so I can spare you some time before I head back to the office.' She got into the car and clipped on her seatbelt. A red car, driven by a grey-haired woman who he recognised as Neilson's PA, drove past and headed up the steep hill, very slowly, as if the driver wasn't used to the sequence of hairpin bends.

'Good. I've been scratching my head over this and it infuriates me. It's so neat, so tidy. A murder committed on a public road with no evidence left behind. It can only have taken seconds. I can't imagine it was somebody with a personal grudge who met up with Luke on the road. It's far too professional for that.'

They followed the red car, catching up with it at the bridge where Luke had died, and there Jude turned off while the car continued on its sedate way towards Waterside Lodge.

'Is it possible someone could have paid a hitman to take out Luke?' asked Ashleigh.

'Oh yes.' Jude stopped the car on the grass verge just beyond the bridge, outside George's cottage where he'd pulled up on the day the old man died. 'I want to satisfy myself as to where you can see the bridge from. I don't think you can see it from the church.'

'Nobody saw anyone going down the dale,' said Ashleigh, flicking through the papers on her folder as he stared down the road. 'There's a chance whoever it was got away through Boredale and down to Patterdale, but Tyrone spoke to a witness at one of the farms down there who's adamant that no-one went down the road.'

'I was wondering if they'd cut up behind the church and headed up into the hills that way.'

'You wouldn't have to be a serious walker to do that, but you would if you wanted to make a clear getaway. But you've already thought about that, haven't you?'

Jude got out of the car and she followed him. 'Yes.'

'So let me guess. You suspect Ryan Goodall.'

He walked down towards the church, hands in his pockets. 'It makes sense. He'll have all the skills he needs to do the job, he'll blow through and disappear. If you're an opportunist — whether you're someone who wants to take out Luke Helmsley or whether you have a grudge against Robert Neilson — then he's ideal, and he had every reason to be about in the dale if anyone saw him.'

'But he wasn't here.'

'He told Becca he wasn't here. That's not the same thing.' Jude frowned. It had never occurred to him to question Becca's version of events. Maybe Ryan had guessed that. 'I know it's improbable but I wonder if he was here all the time. Waiting. And he did the job and disappeared.'

They stood and scanned the dale. There were a dozen escape routes if you wanted them, if you knew your territory. Jude himself knew this section of the eastern fells as well as most other people, and the terrain was rough but by no means as unforgiving as some of the fells further west. Given a good start — a few minutes would be enough — all you had to do was make the cover of the rising bracken. From there, especially if you were dressed in the greens and greys and browns of the hillsides, you could pick your way to the skyline, choose your moment to get over it, and then you were out of sight and away. 'If you pick your route, you're only twelve miles or so from Penrith and no-one's going to look twice at a guy with a rucksack there, are they?'

'There's CCTV at the station, isn't there?'

'Yes. I've already got Chris looking at that. But it occurs to me. Luke might not have been the man he was after, but just the man in the way. In which case, maybe he's still here.' It wouldn't be the first time a criminal had hidden in plain sight. 'Let's head up the hill and have a look.'

'We're hardly dressed for it.' Ashleigh looked at his suit and brogues, then down at her own flat shoes.

'We won't go far. You don't have to go far up there before you get a really good view. And I suspect he won't have gone far, either. He'd need to be able to drop down into the dale and out again pretty quickly as soon as he saw his opportunity.'

Despite her reluctance, despite the poor grip of his smart shoes on the muddy grass, he headed off along what passed for the path up the side of the fell. It petered out rapidly, obviously rarely used, and the bright green fronds of the ferns rippled in the breeze. A gut feeling drove him. He could see exactly how Ryan might have staked out the dale, how he might have perched up there expending a week's worth of patience, watching and waiting for his intended victim — whoever that victim was.

But surely not Luke. Who, then? Robert had been out of the dale but perhaps that was what suited him. With Miranda and the boys out of the house, maybe that was his opportunity to get into Waterside Lodge. And then he'd met Luke.

A ripple of self-preservation took him. He'd back himself in a fight with most people, if it came to it, but maybe not on a windswept hillside with a trained assassin. He slowed down. 'We'd best ca' canny, as my old granny used to say.'

'I was about to suggest we get someone out to search the fellside,' said Ashleigh. She stopped for a moment to disentangle herself from a strand of heather that had caught itself up in her trousers. 'But I don't think we need to. Look.'

She was looking away from him, at a wall about four feet high that marked the lower end of an old sheep fold. On the upslope side of it was a tent. A cooking stove was set to one side of it.

Jude crashed his way through the heather. God knew who was in there, if it was Ryan Goodall or someone else. But he wouldn't have lasted long in the police by being faint-hearted. 'Morning! Anyone there?'

No answer. The wind rippled the green nylon of the tent.

He headed up the path for a few yards to where the

wall had fallen, and scrambled over it. 'Anyone there?' he called again.

'Jude,' said Ashleigh, agonised. 'Take care.'

He could bluff it out, if he had to. 'Hello!' he called again, but the silence was resolute. He ducked down and lifted the flap of the tent. Empty. The he reached down to touch the kettle that sat by the camping stove. There was still warmth in it. At the back of the tent was a bowl with the remains of a breakfast, cereal barely congealed. At the front, tucked under the flap, was a pair of high-spec binoculars. 'There you go. He's been keeping an eye on what's going on, and he's around here somewhere. If it's our man, and I think it is.'

She was aghast, and he could see why. 'We need to get someone up here as soon as we can.'

He thought about it for a moment. There was little justification for flooding the dale with police when the tent could belong to any old camper. 'You reckon? I think right now I'd rather keep an eye on this place. He's obviously using it as a base. He'll have to come back. I might get someone to get a drone up and see if there's anything going on, and I'll make damn sure there's someone keeping an eye out down in the dale. When we know more we can ask him a few questions. But yes. Let's get back down to the car and start looking innocent. We don't want him to know we've found him and we don't want to look any more suspicious than we already do.' He got out his phone and checked it. 'No signal, dammit. Sometimes you get it and sometimes you don't.'

They slipped and slithered their way down the slope. 'So if he's hanging around,' said Ashleigh, after a furtive look about to make sure there was no-one listening, 'that means there's unfinished business.'

'It looks like it.' Jude scanned the dale. They should

have searched it. If they had, and the camp site hadn't been there immediately after Luke's murder, that definitely suggested that the camper — whether Ryan or someone else — had moved back in for the kill.

He paused for a moment longer, as if something was off, something not quite right. 'Let's go and have a look at old George, shall we?'

'Why on earth would we do it now?'

'No-one uses the church. Maybe there's a crypt. It would be an excellent place to hide, wouldn't you say?'

He pushed open the gate to the churchyard and held it open for her, letting it swing back. The gate was self-closing, controlled by a weight on a chain that pulled it closed and as they went through, a black cloud of flies rose from it.

Eternally curious, Jude gave the contraption a second look, and it didn't disappoint. 'Ashleigh.'

'What?'

'Look.'

She bent down towards it as the flies settled back, took a look and stood up again. The look she gave him was troubled. 'That's blood.'

'Yes.' He stood and surveyed the churchyard. The long grass was still trampled from George's funeral two days before and the police search the day before that.

'What the...?' Ashleigh saw, at the same time as he did, the mess of soil next to the grave and piled below the neighbouring yew tree. Dry soil, when the grass under their feet was wet. And the roughed-up turf that overlaid the grave, and the family's arrangement of flowers, perched askew upon the grave.

He'd stood at the back of the crowd during the funeral, ready to make his escape, but he'd have sworn that the soil had been piled on a tarpaulin so as not to spoil the grass of the churchyard and make it easier to fill in the grave when all was over. He strode over to the grave and looked over the wall. A substantial quantity of dry soil lay scattered on the thick grass and on the leaves of the overhanging yew tree outside.

Dry soil, he said to himself again. *Dry soil.* He dropped to his knees by the grave, moved the flower arrangement, and unrolled the turf that had been laid upon it.

''What are you doing?' said Ashleigh behind him, scandalised. 'You can't dig up George!'

If he was wrong, he wouldn't find anything. He'd dig down a couple of inches, realise the effort was futile, replace the soil and the turf and leave the graveyard with no-one but Ashleigh and himself aware of how he'd desecrated George's grave. If he was right, he'd be disturbing the crime scene.

But if he was right whatever — whoever — was in there might not have been there long and so, if it was human, might still be alive. He thrust both hands into one end of the loosely packed soil and his fingers touched something solid, a bare few inches below the surface. 'Ash. Call for help.'

Down in the dale there was a signal and she was already on her phone, calling in to Doddsy as Jude kept on, turning the soil, scraping it away with little care for anything other than speed. But he was too late. He knew he was too late but still he kept scraping the earth away until the shape of a face emerged. 'Ah, hell.'

'Jude's found a body,' Ashleigh reported, 'in the graveyard up at Martindale. In George Barrett's grave. I don't know. Hold on a minute.'

'No rigor,' Jude reported, his voice terse. 'It hasn't been here long.' His fingers closed on something hard and cold. 'Bloody hell. It's a gun.' And then, scooping away soil by the handful, he revealed a head, the skull marked with a bloody mess of soil, blood, matted hair. But beneath all that, a recognisable face.

He sat back on his heels. 'It's Ryan Goodall.'

Whatever he'd been expecting, it hadn't been that.

TWENTY-FOUR

The patrol car from Martindale had reached them in minutes, and it was another half an hour before the CSI team rolled in. 'I should just set up camp in this place,' Tammy had said to them, in passing. 'And I hear you've contaminated the scene, too. Can't trust you clodhoppers.'

Jude had shrugged the objection aside. She might joke about it, and he'd unquestionably made her job more difficult than it needed to be, but she'd know as well as he did that he'd had to be sure the man couldn't be saved.

'He can't have been there very long,' he said to Ashleigh as they left the scene to the experts and more cars poured down the dale.

'No. And that's the puzzle. If you're right and he killed Luke, then who the hell killed Ryan? Or are we on the wrong track altogether?'

Instinct and experience told him not. Luke's death bore the hallmarks of a killing of which Ryan was eminently capable, while Ryan's own murder looked messy and opportunistic. 'We'll find out. Eventually.'

'Here's Doddsy.' Ashleigh made a general wave in the direction to accompany her statement of the obvious. She was frowning, as though something troubled her about it as much as it troubled him. He strode away towards his friend's car. 'Good to see you. All we need — another dead body. Charlie Fry will fill you in on the detail, but I think you might want to get a drone up and see if there's anything untoward. He can't have gone far.'

'I don't know how it can have happened,' Ashleigh said, her voice rich with frustration. 'He's barely dead. How didn't we see anything?'

Jude thought back. They hadn't looked in on the churchyard on the way, and when they'd been scrambling up the fellside and down again they'd been paying more attention to where they were going than to any activity below. And there were blind patches, hidden by a wall or a clump of trees or the solid bluff of Winter Crag. The killing could have taken place almost under their noses or, at the very least, immediately before they arrived. 'I don't know. But he sure as hell didn't do it himself. We'll stop any cars leaving the dale, of course.'

'I've got a couple of uniforms stopping people at the footpaths at the Pooley Bridge end,' said Doddsy, scratching his head. 'But yeah, a drone would help.'

'I'll leave you to sort all that.'

'Does that mean you've got something more important to do?' Doddsy put his head to one side and gave his friend a quizzical look.

'Possibly. I want to get down to Waterside Lodge and see what kind of response this news gets. And I'd like to get there before the gossip mill.'

The police cars had come without sirens but some of the locals had already spotted that something was up. Luke's boss was looking from the cab of his tractor, as if he didn't quite dare ask what was going on, and was already picking at his phone. The Neilsons might not be locked into the heart of the local news network, but it was only a matter of time before Robert's PA headed out again, or someone from the hamlet of Sandwick came past, and then the news would spread. 'Then I'll need to get back into town and have a word with Faye.'

'Ah. Yeah, leave it with me, then.' Doddsy drifted off, his brow crinkling as he in his turn took in the scene.

Jude and Ashleigh drove the three quarters of a mile to Waterside Lodge, but he pulled up in a lay-by just before it. The gates were open. 'That's handy,' he said. 'I like a bit of a surprise. We'll walk the rest.'

They got out of the car and he turned to look back. You couldn't see the church from the gates, nor the entire length of the winding road, but you could just see George's cottage and the point on the hill where the tent crouched behind the wall. Interesting. 'Right. Let's see what the Neilsons have to say.'

They approached the front door, and he paused before he raised a hand to the bell. There were muffled voices from somewhere that sounded as if it was the garden on the other side of the house. But he never got to the bell, because the door opened and Robert's PA answered, her face a mask of neutrality but her eyes narrow with suspicion. To her, it was clear, they were nothing but a nuisance 'Yes? Can I help you?'

Jude flashed his warrant card and Ashleigh did likewise. 'Jude Satterthwaite and Ashleigh O'Halloran. We'd like a word with Mr and Mrs Neilson.'

'Mr and Mrs Neilson, or Mr or Mrs?' She gave them both a cool glance. Her eyes were as steel-grey as her hair and as the neat business suit.

'Both of them, if that's all right.'

'Come into the living room. I'll fetch them.'

The French windows from the living room were open and Miranda and the twins were on the patio, engaged in a heated discussion. One of the twins looked cowed, Jude thought, and was staring in silence at his shoes. The other was putting up an argument, but Miranda, uncharacteristically, was furious. Her voice carried clearly towards them. 'For God's sake, Ollie. What were you thinking of? What do you mean, you lost your phone?'

'For Christ's sake.' The second twin, who must be Ollie, clearly thought she was over-reacting. 'What's wrong with you? I mean, I lost my phone. It'll be around here somewhere. I haven't been anywhere to lose it. And supposing I did drop it somewhere and it's in a ditch or in the lake or something. We can get a new one.'

'What if someone had needed to contact you?'

'They'd have called Will. Does it really matter? Nobody died.'

'Someone did die, Ollie. Do you have such a short memory?'

Aida coughed.

'Yeah, but not because of my phone.' Ollie was the one to respond to the cough, looked up, looked over Miranda's shoulder and saw them. 'Aida wants you,' he said, tonelessly. It seemed that the goings-on in the dale had knocked most of the stuffing out of him.

Miranda turned towards them. She was already pale, but what was left of the colour drained away. 'Chief Inspector. What is it now?'

That was a slip for the normally impeccable Miranda.

'The chief inspector would like a word with you and Mr Neilson,' said Aida, as though the situation was perfectly normal. 'I'll just go and get him.'

'We'll head off, then.' Ollie was looking for an escape.

'It's okay,' Jude said, as affably as possible with the touch of a man's newly-dead body still shivering at this fingertips. 'I'd quite like to have a word with you as well.'

Miranda shooed the twins into the living room, where they sat side-by-side on the sofa at the far side of the room, their faces wearing matching sullen expressions. She seemed to have recovered herself. 'Do sit down.'

'We won't be long, Mrs Neilson.' Jude sat, and Ashleigh followed his example, only for both to bounce up as Robert Neilson came in.

It was the first time they'd come face to face, such had been Robert's ability to be out of the dale when anything untoward had occurred. Until that moment there had been no need for Jude, or anyone else, to approach him for so much as a witness statement, even if Faye's instruction to keep at arm's length hadn't been in play. That being the case, Jude's impression of this kingpin financier, this clever man suspected of involvement in massive fraud, had been one drawn from documented research rather than observation. The photographs he'd seen showed Robert to be a man slight in build, a thin face, fair hair that might already be fading to grey without anyone noticing, but in his presence there seemed a strong sense of purpose. He was a man you looked at with respect. It was clearly Robert from whom the twins got both their looks, though those were coloured by the invigorating freshness of youth, and their attitude. Jude stretched out a hand in response to the man's gesture of welcome, fascinated. 'DCI Jude Satterthwaite. We haven't met.'

'No, but I've heard all about you.' Robert met his gaze, full on, a searching look. 'What brings you down here?'

'Some more bad news, I'm afraid.' Robert didn't sit, so Jude remained standing too, and the conversation narrowed to the pair of them in the centre of the room, like two boxers in a ring. 'I'm sorry to say there's been another unfortunate incident just down the road.'

Miranda, he noticed, could go no paler. The twins perked up, interested in a degree that suggested innocence.

'Really?' Robert sighed, with a trace of irritation.

'Yes. Someone's been found dead down in Martindale.'

Miranda moaned, but stopped when Robert darted a glance at her. 'Who?'

'We've yet to identify the body. But I thought I'd let you know there may be some disruption around the place. I also want to ask if you've seen anything unusual.'

'Unusual? No, not really. Miranda and I walked up the road to the churchyard in the middle of the morning. I wouldn't normally do that, but Aida — you've met Aida, my PA — went down into Penrith on an errand, so I took the chance of a break. But that was all. I have a lot to do, so even that was a luxury. We walked as far as the church, stopped at the gate and came back again.'

'Did you see anything? Anybody?'

'Nothing and no-one.' Robert's voice was firm and Miranda, when her husband looked across at her, shook her head in obedient confirmation.

'And what about your sons?' Jude turned away from Robert and looked at them, crouched on the sofa as if they'd been penned there by an enemy.

'We were here all morning, weren't we, Ollie?'

'Yeah. We daren't go out of the place for fear of being accused of killing someone.'

'That's enough, Ollie.' There was warning in Robert's voice.

'Okay, thank you.' Jude backed away from any further conversation. He'd got what he came for. 'Thanks. We need to go back to the scene now, but I wanted to let you know. Someone will be round a little later on to take proper witness statements from you all. Thanks for your time.'

Ashleigh got to her feet and Aida, fulfilling the function of footman, saw them off the premises. As they headed through the gate and back towards the bridge, the graveyard was abuzz with activity.

Keeping in step with him, Ashleigh stopped to flick a look back towards Waterside Lodge. 'What did you think?' she asked.

'I wish I'd had the chance to give them a full cross-examination before they had a chance to cook up some kind of story. Miranda knows something, doesn't she?'

'It might just be that what's happening around here is getting to her. My money says her stepsons are giving her all sorts of grief, so she'll have that on her mind as well.'

'You say that, but I bet you think the same as I do. She knows something about what happened, and so does Robert, and their stories will tally in every possible way.'

'But could she have killed Ryan?' Ashleigh shook her head. 'Surely not.'

'It seems bizarre.' Jude opened the door of his Mercedes and slid into the driver's seat, thinking of Miranda and Summer and George, and of the muscular, army-trained Ryan. 'But no. Surely not.'

TWENTY-FIVE

Faye appeared at the door to the incident room, and Jude's heart sank. He'd been at his desk a long time with no break, and he wasn't in the mood for her directness.

She strode across to where he was sitting, at a desk close to the whiteboard. 'Any update?' she asked, coming to a halt beside him.

'Not yet. I'm waiting for Doddsy to come in.'

'When are you expecting him?' She glanced at the clock. It was after eight.

'Any minute. It depends how long the queue is at the pizza place.'

Faye never had much of a sense of humour, and what little she had evaporated under the slightest pressure. 'I hope that's a joke.'

'No. A man's got to eat. I'll be here a while. I asked him to pick me up a pizza.'

She shrugged that off. 'You're going to have to speak to the media about this fiasco. The media team have arranged a press conference for tomorrow morning, so you'll have plenty of time to think about what to say.' Her irritation was unusual, obvious and intense. 'We can't go on pretending there's no connection between these three deaths, although I'd very much like you to keep the line that Summer Raine died by accident.'

At least no-one but Ashleigh and Jude himself had any suspicion about George's death. That would have whipped up a national level media storm. 'Fine. I can come up with something bland and uninteresting. But do you want to know my take on the matter?'

'I think I'd rather not.' Faye's expression was grim. She knew how the plot was unfolding and it was at odds with the line she was trying so hard to hold to, that the deaths in Martindale might implicate Robert Neilson in murder before the law had a chance to catch him and a dozen others for fraud.

There was no-one within earshot, but nevertheless Jude lowered his voice. 'It's looking ever more like something that involves Robert. But perhaps not in the way I'd thought.'

'Let's keep this quiet, shall we?' Faye motioned him to the door and he followed her out into the empty corridor. 'Really?'

'Yes. I know you disagree, but I still think there's something suspicious about Summer's death. I still think it's likely she knew something she shouldn't, or that someone — Robert or Miranda — misinterpreted what she wanted to speak to Miranda about and thought it might be blackmail. But we'll leave that aside for the minute.'

'Even if I accept that, you need to explain to me why Robert Neilson would murder Luke Helmsley.'

'I don't think he did.'

'Oh?'

'It was a military-style execution.' Jude rubbed his chin with a forefinger as Doddsy so often did, thinking it through. 'Robert has no military training and that doesn't strike me as his style. He'd have to get his hands dirty. In any case, he wasn't there.'

'He's never there.' Faye's distrust of the cast-iron alibi mirrored his own. 'Always one hundred per cent provably somewhere else, what's more. But it might have been done on his say-so.'

'It might, but I don't think so. I think Ryan Goodall killed Luke Helmsley. He was certainly lying about his whereabouts, because he'd told his family that he was elsewhere and there's no proof of where he was.' Except the tent, and they'd know soon enough if that was his. 'He's in the army. There's a gun in the grave, although I don't yet know if it had been fired or where he might have got it. He had all the survival skills to make himself scarce in the hills for a long time, and he was well-equipped.' He thought, briefly, of how Becca would respond to the news. Judging by past experience, he'd get the blame for that, too, as if he could somehow have stopped it.

'All right. But why did he he kill Luke? I know the man was hardly an innocent, but his crimes aren't exactly complicated.'

'Because Luke came across him somewhere he shouldn't have been and he knew he'd have to stop him talking. Luke wasn't bright, in an academic way, but he wasn't stupid either. He'd know when something wasn't quite right. He'd have heard Goodall had left. Maybe he said something to him. Whatever. He was a risk, he had to be removed, and there was one chance to do it and no chance to dispose of the body.'

'So what was this man Goodall doing in Martindale anyway? Apart from visiting family, which looks like a smokescreen, if you're correct.'

'I don't know. But as you seem to suspect Robert Neilson of being up to his neck in very large-scale crime indeed—'

'I don't suspect anything. Other people suspect it and they're the ones looking for evidence. All I'm doing is trying to keep you from compromising their investigation.'

He waved the disclaimer away. 'Right. And had you thought it might be all about Robert Neilson?'

She stared at him for a moment. 'Well, if he's up to no good I imagine other people would know it, apart from us. Where there are winners in business there are losers, and losers make enemies. But that doesn't explain who killed Goodall.'

'For my money, almost certainly Robert.'

'That's very interesting,' she said, after a moment. 'But I need to know a lot more than that before you get me involved. Come back to me as soon as you've got something a bit more concrete.' She turned and headed back down the corridor.

Summarily dismissed, Jude went back into the incident room and turned his mind to a press statement. He'd camped out in his preferred place, in front of the white board in the incident room. It was late and the place was all but empty. Faye was right and there wasn't a lot he could do until they'd gleaned all the evidence they could from the scene, but he couldn't bring himself to leave. On the other side of the room, Chris Marshall was standing next to someone's desk in deep conversation. There would be witness statements to collect and collate, CCTV cameras to check from the station, an appeal for information from the public to see if anyone had seen anything suspicious, information from the grave and the area around it. And now he'd need to make sure there was a visible police presence in the dale long beyond the clearing of the crime scene, to reassure the local community.

He picked up a marker pen from the desk and added Ryan's name to the board. Two murder victims for certain, possibly more, and nothing to link them but the location in which they'd been found.

'Okay, Jude?' He'd been so deep in thought he hadn't noticed Doddsy coming in, carefully closing the door behind him. 'This'll keep you going for a while.' He unloaded a pizza box onto the desk. 'I'll be heading off shortly. I had an early start and I've another one tomorrow. What an unholy mess, eh?'

'It's all of that.' Jude took one last look at the board, and all it did was puzzle him more. He was sure, in his heart, that Robert Neilson was responsible, if he wasn't the actual killer, but he couldn't see how to make the leap from gut instinct to fact.

Instinct. He was getting as bad as Ashleigh. Next thing he'd be turning over the cards and looking for answers there. He flipped open the box and ripped into a slice of pizza. 'I take it there's nothing more to be done down in Martindale?' he said, with his mouth full.

'Not today.' Doddsy checked his watch. 'I'll pop back down tomorrow and see what's going on. The body's on its way to Carlisle now. PM tomorrow morning. I imagine you'll want to go.'

It was one of the least appealing parts of the job, but had to be done. 'Faye's arranged a press conference at eight. I'll go along after that.'

'Becca's parents are going up to the hospital tomorrow to give us a positive ID.'

'Okay. Thanks for the warning. I've spoken to the authorities in Australia and asked them to break it to his parents.' Strictly speaking they should wait for the official ID but there was no real doubt.

'And have you told Becca?'

There was a moment's silence. 'No.'

'Don't you think she'll expect you to?'

Becca expected a lot of him, even now he owed her nothing. 'Her parents can tell her, if they haven't already. I'll be here late tonight. I've other things to do. And no doubt she'd only accuse me of behaving inappropriately again.'

'She's going to be withdrawing that complaint, if she hasn't already.' Doddsy checked his watch. 'I'm going to head up and update Faye on my way out. I'll be in sharp tomorrow. I can head back past Becca's place, if you want.'

Jude felt a wave of relief. He should't feel any obligation to Becca after the way she'd treated him but he did. 'Thanks, mate. Yeah, you get on.'

'Fine. I'll be in sharp,' said Doddsy, for the third time.

'You can take the briefing meeting if I'm up at the PM.' Jude sighed, aware his bad temper was getting the better of him, that his frustrations with Faye's attitude and his anger at the way Becca seemed so suddenly to have turned on him, when the years should have put a gloss of distance on their relationship, were holding him back from what he was doing.

'I'll see you in the morning.'

Doddsy passed Tammy on the way out. She offered him the curtest of nods and came straight over to Jude. 'We're nowhere near finished down in Martindale, of course. I've left a couple of guys down there working on it under lights. But I wanted to pop by the office and pick some stuff up on my way home. I guessed you'd be here.'

'You know me. I never rest.' He tried to make light of it, but it was a struggle. Maybe, after all, Becca was right and he just gave the job more time than he could afford. He spent long enough checking the hours everyone else worked, for their own welfare as well as the cost implications, but he never bothered keeping a check on his own.

The look she gave him was sympathetic. 'Yeah, I know how it is. I thought since I was here I'd brief you on where we are so far. No forensics, of course. Not yet. We'll get those later. But I daresay you'll stay awake late fretting about it, or you might as well have all the information I've got to play with.'

'Go on.'

'I think you'll have seen the key thing. Whoever killed him had obviously disposed of the body in the only place they could think of — the grave.'

'I wonder if they meant to come back later and move him.'

'Maybe. There's blood on the stone that controls the gate, and on the grass. I'm not the one who makes hypotheses. That's your job. But it looks pretty clear to me.'

'Killed on the spot?'

'Probably. Though quite how someone like that would allow himself to be killed with a stone chained to a gate is beyond me. Maybe the post-mortem will give you an idea.' She shrugged. 'Anyway. The body was in the grave, but as you'll have found, not very deep. The gun — I'm not up on guns, but it looked a modern one, a handgun — was in there, too.'

'Thrown in to be retrieved later?'

'Possibly. It has all the hallmarks of a temporary disposal of the body for me. And there are a few interesting things, from your point of view at least. One's that the gun had been fired.'

Jude sat back and looked at her. He said nothing.

'It would be more accurate to say there was one bullet missing from the chamber. The PM will tell you how he died, but I didn't see any gunshot wounds. And we haven't found a bullet.'

'Okay. So we might be looking for a bullet, or an injured person.' More than ever he itched to search the Neilson property. Was it possible the missing bullet had been sent to Robert as a threat and so he'd been forced to strike first? 'What else?'

'He had two mobile phones on him. Doddsy's passed them on to the tech guys. We've taken dabs off them. I'll prioritise that for you, but I expect they'll have been Goodall's prints only.'

'And the tent? Was that his?'

'Maybe. There wasn't a lot in it. Not even a sleeping bag. Certainly no ID. Just binoculars and cooking gear. Almost as if he was only there for a day. He'll have dumped the rest of it somewhere I expect, and just done a lightning raid into the dale. For all the good it did the poor sod.'

Jude succumbed to black humour. Becca had wasted time worrying about Ryan not being there for George's funeral. He'd probably been up on the fellside the whole time, watching the proceedings. 'Well, well. That's fascinating.'

'I thought you'd think so. It'll be interesting to see what else comes up.' She turned towards the door. 'I've emailed you some of the pictures we took. See if those offer you any inspiration.' She whisked out.

Jude sat down for a moment, and thought about it, then got up. 'Chris. Get home. There won't be a lot more for you to do tonight.' Then he headed up to Faye's office. She, in her turn, was clearing and locking her desk. 'Can you do one thing for me before you go?'

'I imagine so.'

'Ryan Goodall had two phones on him. I need to know what's on them.'

'Isn't that already in hand?'

'I need it hurried along. I'd like to know what's on them by tomorrow morning. And you know how it works. The higher the rank the more weight you can bring to bear.' His relationship with the technical team was, at best, fraught.

'Okay,' she said with a sigh, 'leave it with me. You won't get anything tonight but I can get them onto it sharp.'

Jude went back to his office and sat down to scroll through his emails. Buried among them was one from Lorraine Broadbent, informing him that the anonymous complaint against him had been withdrawn by a person who preferred not to be identified and whose subsequent account of events had tallied more closely with his own. The tone of the email, he thought, lacked the relish with which she'd pounced on him originally.

He sighed, writing off the incident as an unnecessary distraction, and got on with his work.

When the doorbell went, very late in the evening as the May sunshine was fading into darkness and the very last stripe of sunlight touched the top of the Lowther escarpment and gave it an otherworldly look, Becca jumped to her feet and brushed Holmes off her lap and onto the floor. She wasn't expecting anyone but it was bound to be

Jude. She'd taken Doddsy's advice and contacted the police to withdraw the complaint Adam had made, and now she was ready for him to turn up and talk about it. And other things, of course. The village was buzzing with gossip about what had happened up in Martindale.

Composing her face into an expression of contrition and preparing to apologise for something she hadn't done, she strolled towards the door with exaggerated calm and opened the door. 'Hello. Oh.' She checked herself. 'Hi, Doddsy. Come on in.'

'I won't, if you don't mind.' He hovered on the step, his long shadow stretching behind him. In Linda Satterthwaite's cottage opposite, a lamp went on and Mikey's thin figure glided across the window.

'Is everything okay?'

He spread his hands out in a gesture of futility, and Becca felt ridiculous. Of course it wasn't all right. 'It's been a long day.'

'I thought you might be Jude.' She might as well be honest about it, since Doddsy was the one she'd trusted for advice.

'He's working late tonight. You'll have heard there's bad news from Martindale.'

'I know.' She gave him a troubled look. 'My dad called. Is it right they think they've found Ryan?'

'I'm afraid so.'

Death was something Jude kept close in his soul, had never shared with her during their relationship, though he dealt with it on daily basis. She did, too, though in a different way; slow decay of the living who were approaching their time to die, rather than the short shock of a violent and unexpected death. Perhaps, if they'd talked more, if she'd asked him to share and been able to bear it, they might still be together. 'What happened to him?'

'We don't know yet, but I think we can be pretty certain it wasn't an accident.'

Becca wasn't squeamish and she hadn't really liked Ryan that much, but he was family, and if he hadn't been he was still a human being. A tear gathered in her eye and rolled down her cheek. She ignored it and appreciated Doddsy pretending not to see it. 'Thanks for letting me know.'

'I think Jude would probably have come to tell you himself. If he—'

'If he wasn't busy. Yes, I know.' she paused. 'Good of you to come.' And then, as she thought once more about Ryan she hurried the conversation on before she could shed any more tears. She was anything but heartless, but on balance she preferred to grieve alone. 'You don't happen to know if anything came of my…um… complaint, do you?'

He shook his head. 'I expect it'll go through the system. I'm not in the loop, and Jude hasn't mentioned it to me.'

'It's just that I asked them to withdraw it.' Though quite why she hadn't named and blamed Adam she didn't know. Perhaps she was just too cowardly to make an enemy of him the way Jude had done.

'Then it'll be fine.' Doddsy hesitated, but only for a second. 'I'll be off, then. Tyrone will be wondering where the hell I've got to.'

'I'll see you.' She closed the door and heard his car engine start up, rev and then die away. In all the sadness, she managed to find a smile. It was about time Doddsy enjoyed a little happiness.

Essentially and unshakeably practical, Becca went back to the living room to repair relations with Holmes and think about what to do next. Move on, of course. She wasn't on shift until twelve, so she'd take the chance to do what she'd promised her mother she'd do, and go down to Martindale next morning to begin sorting through George's belongings.

TWENTY-SIX

The post-mortem was scheduled for eight o'clock in Carlisle and Jude was in the office to catch up before he headed out. Someone had been up before him, though, because as he headed past the security desk just after six, his phone rang. He answered it walking down the corridor to the incident room, not recognising the number. 'Jude Satterthwaite.' He stopped at the coffee machine in the empty corridor and threw a selection of coins down into the slot.

'Jude. It's Kelly McKay over in Adelaide. Wondered if you'd be up.'

'Hi.' Jude stifled a yawn. It was hard enough to function at this time of the morning anyway, but even harder without coffee. The last thing he needed was mockery from colleagues on the other side of the world. 'It's six am. Isn't everyone at work?'

Kelly laughed at him, in a manner far too jolly for someone used to dabbling in deceit and death. 'Sorry to call you so early, mate. But there's been a misunderstanding.'

'What sort of misunderstanding?' Jude picked the coffee out of the machine and carried it towards the incident room. Jamming the phone between his shoulder and his ear, he swiped his security card and opened the door.

'Mate.' Kelly laughed. 'He isn't dead.'

Jude put the coffee on the table and rolled his eyes. It was way too early for a joke and he was already too tired to appreciate it. 'Sorry?'

'What I say. He isn't dead. There's a case of mistaken identity at your end.'

'I saw him with my own eyes.' More than that, he'd brushed the dry soil from Ryan Goodman's face with his own fingers.

'Nope. Because when I went to confirm his whereabouts with his parents they said he wasn't in England, and never planned to go there. He'd never expressed any interest in his family over there. As far as they knew he was with his unit. I've spent all morning verifying his identity, and I'm happy with it. He's sitting in the office with me this very minute.'

The clock on the wall ticked through ten seconds. 'Okay,' Jude said, 'Thanks for that. I'd better get on and stop his relatives here doing the official ID, then, hadn't I?' And he rang off and called Faye.

Holmes woke Becca early, as he too often did in the summer. He was no respecter of a day off or a lie-in and the only authority he acknowledged was that of the weather and the seasons. After ten minutes she gave up trying to ignore him, got up, made a cup of tea and then headed down towards Martindale.

The police were still swarming over the churchyard.

Seeing the white tent over George's grave made her feel vaguely queasy, though she knew they'd have to treat the old man's coffin with appropriate respect. She parked at a respectable distance and walked along the dale. George had left the house to Becca and her sister, and she knew Kirsty would want to sell it, but she herself wasn't so sure. It needed a little bit of work, but it could easily be made liveable. Perhaps she could sell her cottage in Wasby and buy her sister out, and then she could settle in splendid isolation and enjoy looking at the world going past, just as he'd done.

It was a ridiculous fantasy. For one thing, it was inconveniently far from work, and while that might not be a problem on a glorious day like today's, the winter would be a different matter entirely.

She strolled up to it. The patch of green around it had begun to run wild in the ten days or so since George had died, and she stooped and pulled a young and enthusiastic dandelion from the ground. The rosette of leaves snapped off, the root stayed in the ground and Becca was left with damp soil beneath her fingernails, like a metaphor for her life.

She had a key but she was accustomed to walking in and calling out George's name, and so she fumbled with the lock. The key wouldn't turn, but when she twisted the handle it opened easily. Her mother, in her flying visit to empty the fridge after George's death and to close the curtains ahead of the funeral, must have forgotten to lock it.

She made her way briskly through into the kitchen and crossed to the window, flinging open the curtains to let the light in. The place was strangely silent, though the curtains stirred in a draught from underneath the warped window frame. If she did buy Kirsty out, the windows would be just the start of the repairs. She turned around, wondering where to start. In George's bedroom, perhaps, or the desk where he kept his few valuables and an old chocolate box filled photographs of people whose names he'd long forgotten.

She frowned as she turned. One of the kitchen chairs lay on its side, one leg cracked as if someone had smashed something against it. The photograph of George's parents on their wedding day lay on the floor, face downwards in a crystal halo of shattered glass.

That wasn't how she'd left the place, and she was sure her mother wouldn't have left it like that either. She picked up the frame. A perfect circle, blurred at the edges, punched a hole between bride and groom. With growing dread, she crossed the room. Above the sideboard, where the photograph had stood, a hole of the same size punctured the wall.

Becca had learned a lot from Jude, and not of all of it had turned to bitterness and regret when the relationship had failed. Touching nothing, she backed out of the house the way she'd come, opened the front door using her elbow rather than her fingers, and set off down the hill towards the police officers gathered around the church.

'Becca found that someone had been in the house,' Jude was saying to Doddsy when Ashleigh appeared in the incident room on her return from checking in with the house-to-house team in Martindale.

She paused to suss out the body language before she interrupted. He had a grim expression on his face, the look of a man who thought he'd seen the pieces of a puzzle forming a shape in front of him and saw, in a moment, that they were illusory.

That would be down to the news from Martindale, no doubt. Unless there was more bad news to come.

'Was she okay about it?'

'Oh, yes. I'm mightily glad she didn't go there at the wrong moment, though. God knows what she might have walked in on.' He looked up, saw Ashleigh and gave her the warmest of smiles, as if to compensate for the fact that he'd just been caught being solicitous about another woman. 'Good. You're back. Have you learned anything?'

'Up to a point.' She sat down and placed her iPad and notebook on the table. 'I know every detail of everyone's comings and goings. I know how old their kids are and who does what day on the school run, and why it was so much of a hassle when we had to close the bridge and Mrs McGinty couldn't get into Penrith to get her corns done.' She laid the folder of witness statements down on the desk with an exaggerated sigh. 'I swear I'm now so well-known in Martindale they'll be fighting to invite me round for Christmas dinner.' Everyone had an opinion — they always did — but nothing she'd heard shed any light on the mystery.

Jude took his usual seat at the table beneath the white-board, and motioned for Chris to join them. 'I'm reeling from all sorts of things coming at me today. I don't know where to start.'

'Ryan's maybe a good place,' observed Doddsy, as Chris left his desk, picked up his cup of coffee and his pad and came over to join them.

'Ah. Yes. Though obviously he isn't Ryan, and we don't yet know who he is, so we may as well keep calling him that until we hear something else. But we'll find out. I've asked for DNA and fingerprint tests to be run through as soon as possible, and I've asked our colleagues in Australia if, when they've finished falling about laughing, they wouldn't mind digging a bit further into who he might be and how he came to be impersonating the real Goodall. Though to be honest, I don't hold out any hope from that direction. Not immediately, at least.'

'In fairness.' Chris checked his watch. 'What time is it over there? Two in the morning or something?'

All of them saw two am more often than they'd like but, Ashleigh knew, none of them would have stayed up late for that if the request had been reversed. Chris's time check reminded her that she hadn't had any lunch. She reached into her bag for the sandwich and family-sized packet of crisps she'd picked up at the garage on the way back in. 'Don't mind me. I need food and coffee to function.'

'Before you get stuck in.' Over-familiar, Jude reached out and ripped into the packet of crisps. 'Run us through what you've got. No-one saw or heard anything. Right?'

'I'm afraid so. Whoever killed Ryan must have done it as quickly and as efficiently as whoever it was — possibly Ryan himself — did to Luke.'

'It's a bit early to get any responses from the press conference and TV appeal.' Doddsy followed Jude's lead, picking out a few crisps between his fingers. Before she knew it the packet would be gone. 'We've had a couple of calls after the lunchtime news, but not many and nothing too promising, though those are being followed up. But maybe there's someone out here who was up on the hills and saw something but didn't realise. Or heard something.'

'There has to be a chance.' Ashleigh looked at the map on the board. Jude's frustration showed in the web of lines he'd drawn on it, marking where the tent had been and what could be seen from it. 'The difficulty is the topography. George's cottage is on that wonderfully prominent spot, and you can see almost everything from there. But the church is down in a dip, a really beautifully sheltered spot, and the only place you can see it from is the farm. The farmer didn't see anything, but he was up on the hill with his dog for a lot of the time, and in any case their living space looks the other way. He says he saw Miranda and Robert walking out towards the bridge when they said they were there, but he never paid them much attention as he was on his way elsewhere, and he never saw them heading back.'

Jude's frown deepened. 'Right. And the CSI team didn't find anything outside the tent and the graveyard. Inside the graveyard is another matter. But we'll get to that in a minute.'

'What about the post-mortem results?' asked Chris 'Do they tell us anything? Was he shot?'

Jude's expression darkened even further. He'd been away at the post-mortem for most of the morning, and it always left him out of sorts. None of them enjoyed watching the pathologist slicing open the remains of a human being, picking them apart and exposing their innermost secrets. 'Two blows on the head. The first was on the temple, inflicted by some kind of blunt instrument. The skin isn't broken although we think we may have the weapon. I'll come to that later. That was sufficient to stun him. The second blow, to the back of his head, smashed his skull and killed him. He was dead when he was buried, and the time of death seems to be not long — maybe half an hour — before Ashleigh and I found him. The second blow was inflicted on him by the stone that controls the self-closing mechanism for the churchyard gate.'

Chris handed out some of the photos that Jude himself had taken in the churchyard. 'It must have been inflicted in situ. You can see how the chain is screwed into the stone via that hook, and the ends of the chain are attached to the gate and the wall. None of those fixings has been moved in years. They're rusted over.'

'So, he was stunned.' Ashleigh tapped fingers on the desk. She knew, from the find at the cottage, how it must have been done, and she could see that he did too. 'Time's of the essence. They've got their man, unconscious, but they need to kill him. For whatever reason they don't use the gun. Do they?' She looked at Jude.

'No. They don't. They may have been afraid of attracting attention.'

'Of course. So they look for the nearest weapon. For some reason they don't use whatever inflicted the first wound—'

'It wasn't heavy enough.'

'Yes. So they look around and they find the first large stone they can.'

'They have to stay in the graveyard,' Doddsy supplied, 'because if they get out of it they run the risk of being seen.'

'Yes. The stone sits on that chain and although it's heavy you can open the gate you can lift it off the ground and swing it. One good blow and the skull's fractured. Your unconscious man is a dead man. And then they shovel the earth out of the grave — at a guess with their hands, which will have taken a while and been a messy business — put the turf back and get rid of the rest of the earth over the wall in the hope it won't be spotted.'

'How long would that take?'

'Yes.' Jude tapped his pen on the pad in front of him. 'Is someone keeping a note of all these times? Because I think it's important. They must have had some time in hand, but they were in enough of a hurry not to go and find something easier to handle than the stone. They could have found something suitable lying around outside the graveyard, for example. But they had enough time to excavate the grave and get rid of the surplus soil, though not very tidily. And then they must have done a runner.'

Chris had been sketching out what passed for a timeline on the pad in front of him. 'Okay. So you and Ashleigh came down into the dale at about ten past eleven and Robert and Miranda say they were there at half ten, though neither of them could be specific about it. They say they walked down to the graveyard and although they didn't go in, they didn't notice anything out of the ordinary. There's a gap of about forty minutes between them leaving and you arriving, and in that time, if the post-mortem is correct, the person claiming to be Ryan must have been killed, buried, the grave refilled, the soil cleared, and then they made a clean escape.'

'Yes.'

'Not by car, though,' Ashleigh noted, 'because we didn't pass anyone coming out of the dale and we've accounted for every one of the cars that was in it. It's a dead end. The road forks before the bridge and you can go up Boredale or Martindale or into Sandwick, but everyone who has a vehicle there can account for where it was. The first thing we did was make sure anyone seen leaving the dale was intercepted and there was nobody suspicious.'

'Could they have made it to the steamer on foot?'

'Not without passing us. They'd have had to go right round the base of Hallin Fell. It's about two and a half miles, and by then we'd alerted the constables who were already in Howtown. So, no. Whoever did it was still in the dale.'

'And of course,' Jude said, reviewing all the evidence,

'it's obvious where they were. Where Ryan was all the time.'

'Up in the tent?' Chris gave him a quizzical look. That's not possible. You'd have seen them.'

Chris wasn't up on the latest development. Ashleigh had been in Martindale when Becca had come running down the hill, close to tears, to tell them what she'd found. Perhaps it was as well Jude hadn't been there. 'They must have been in George Barrett's cottage. Becca said it wasn't locked.'

'Yes.' Jude nodded. 'And to go back to the earlier question of the first weapon. That's answered there, too. What we found in the cottage — what Becca found — was that someone had been in there. There had been some kind of a struggle. A gun had been fired. The ballistics report isn't in yet, but it'll almost certainly be the gun that was found in the grave.'

'I don't suppose we have the forensics, either.' Chris sighed. 'Obviously we know Goodall was in there visiting the old guy, but that was a while ago. And Becca Reid, obviously. It'll be interesting to see who else had been in there.'

'Goodall was there all right,' said Ashleigh, 'and recently. The rest of his kit was upstairs. He'd made himself comfortable in there for a few days, by the look of it.' After George's death she'd taken a look upstairs in the cottage, just to reassure herself that her instinctive concerns about he case were false. She'd seen nothing untoward but one thing had struck her — the sweeping completeness of the view from the bedroom window.

'George didn't do stairs, as far as I'm aware,' said Jude, with a sigh. 'He hadn't done them for years. But it would make sense if fake Ryan, as I suppose we have to call him, had been in to the house. He could have crept in there when he needed something, helped himself to food, that sort of thing. There would be no problem if he didn't mind not having the lights on at night.' He paused. 'I'm kicking myself we never searched it, but why would we? It was locked. We can't go breaking down the doors of every empty house on the off chance there's murderer hiding in there.'

Ryan had had a key in his pocket, Tammy had said. A quick check would show whether it was the key to George's cottage. 'Do we have any idea yet who he is?'

'I've emailed the fingerprints through to Kelly in Adelaide, They'll run them through their database. If he's been ID'd Down Under that'll come up pretty quickly. DNA and dental records will take a bit longer, and I've sent them a photo.'

'How long do you think he'd been there. Do we have any idea?' Ashleigh asked.

Jude shook his head. 'Tammy can't tell. I know what you're thinking, though. About George.'

'Yes. I walked around the house, though I didn't see anything, but I wasn't looking for anything. Ryan certainly wasn't camped out there at the time. But he may have come in for shelter in that really heavy rain there was the night before George died, and George heard him. And perhaps then Ryan had the idea of coming back when the place was empty.' Even as she thought about it, she regretted how quickly she'd checked the place; but once George had gone she'd been keen to catch up with Jude. He wasn't the only one kicking himself over a small action not taken.

Jude considered. 'George always had a short fuse. I can see him getting so worked up his body couldn't take it.'

If that was the case, it was probably as well for him, given what they thought Ryan was capable of. At least it had been a relatively peaceful and natural death, and at least he'd had Becca with him. But still Ashleigh was frustrated at what she must have missed.

'What about his phone records?' Doddsy looked to Chris, who flipped up another note.

'Not a huge amount, but something. These came through quickly. Was it your charm, Jude? Made friends with the intelligence guys at last?'

Jude shook his head. 'I asked Faye. She must have leaned on them.'

All four of them shared a wry smile. The intelligence unit were never in a hurry at the best of times, let alone at weekends. There was a lot to said for labelling everything you did as secret so that no-one ever knew what was there that was more important.

'Go on then,' prompted Ashleigh. 'What do they say?'

'There are two phones. One's his personal phone, bought in the UK a couple of months ago and registered in the name of Ryan Goodall, probably using forged documents. It's the phone he used to contact his supposed family. The second is much more interesting. It's a burner phone.' He paused for a moment. 'When I was on the beat, we busted a guy who made a business out of these things. For drug dealers, mainly. A nice number that could be tracked to a place but never to a person. This one has been quiet for a while, so it looks as though someone has been waiting for a while to use it. One number, no name in the contacts. I expect that number goes to a similar phone, meant for one person and one only. There's an exchange of texts between them.'

'Is there a drug connection, do you think?' Jude leaned forward, alert. 'What did the messages say?'

'It might be drugs. They might just have picked up the trick from the county lines guys. That's for smarter people than me to work out. But whatever's at the root of it, the calls make it clear what Ryan was up to.'

'Go on.'

'There aren't many messages, and we've yet to trace exactly where Ryan was when he sent them, but it's pretty clear why he was there. There are references to a target. There are references to Robert's movements, when he'll be in the dale and when he'll be away. When Miranda will be there, when his PA will be there. When the twins will be there. They were tracking the movements of the people down at Waterside Lodge.'

Jude sat back. 'Is there anything there that indicates when Robert was on his own?'

'No. Miranda or the twins were always there with him. You reckon it's Robert they were after?'

'Could be.' Jude shook his head.

Ashleigh knew exactly what he was thinking. If Robert suspected anything, Ryan could have been waiting a long time to catch him alone. And had Robert turned the tables, lain in wait for Ryan and surprised him? Been cornered, perhaps? And had Miranda lied to protect him, and the two of them were sitting in Waterside Lodge knowing the threat to them was gone?

She checked her watch. 'We should go and talk to him.'

Again she sensed his hesitation, the reluctance to challenge Robert Neilson. It wasn't surprising. Robert was clever, not a man you'd want to approach unless you had your strategy clear. 'I might pop down and see him tomorrow. But I think I'd like to know who Ryan is before I do.'

TWENTY-SEVEN

'I should probably go home.' Ashleigh yawned.

'Probably,' Jude agreed, with a straight face that he managed to keep for about five seconds before he laughed. 'No. Why should you, if you don't want to? I'm not going to turn you out, as long as all you want to do is talk about work.'

They'd stayed in the office until past ten and now it was touching midnight, but she knew, by the hand he laid on her knee he was joking and work wasn't first on his mind. 'I'll get my union rep onto you. I work far too hard and you work me all the hours God sends.'

Her mind was moving the same way as his. It often did, after days like today — endless, relentless hours dealing with the damage left by sudden death. The man they'd known as Ryan Goodall would have people waiting to mourn him, as Luke Helmsley had done, and Summer, and even George, whose time on Earth had been well-lived. Sometimes nothing but the closeness of another human being could ease the pain.

'Glad we're in agreement,' he said, and shifted closer.

Getting into bed with Jude, which was where the evening would inevitably end, was the ideal antidote, if only for a moment. She was happy enough about it, though she'd been thinking too much about Scott recently, unnerved by his joking threat to take up Summer's job. Her move to Cumbria had been, in part, to escape the complications of loving the wrong man too much, and now her past was tracking her as relentlessly as she and her colleagues were closing in on the Martindale killer. First Faye had appeared, and now Scott, teasing her with the occasional message. *Haven't heard yet. Must be taking up my references*, his last text had said.

There was no-one more different to Scott's brand of selfish but irresistible charm than Jude. It would make her life so much easier if she could have fallen in love with him. To move the conversation on, she shifted it to something that kept it personal but made it a little less uncomfortable. 'Doddsy said Becca was going to withdraw her complaint.'

'She has.' He got to his feet, standing with the TV remote in his hand and shuffling through the rolling news channels for anything of local interest. She stifled a smile. He'd never change. 'Although in fairness, she told me she hadn't complained and I believe her. I had an email from Lorraine from Professional Standards and she seemed positively disappointed to tell me the matter's been dropped.'

'So it was Adam Fleetwood, then.'

'Must be.' Jude tossed the remote control down on the arm of the sofa and dropped back into the seat next to her.

'Will he ever let go?'

'I doubt it. He's a terrier when he has a grievance, and you know what people like that are like. But he won't get anywhere.' Jude spread a casual arm along the back of the chair as a local news bulletin kicked off with the latest on the discovery of Ryan's body. 'I'm wise to him, and every time he reports me for something I haven't done, Professional Standards get a little bit wiser to it, too.'

'The camera loves you,' Ashleigh said, nudging him as the film switched from long shots of the church and the white tent over George's grave to Jude himself, looking uncomfortable in a press conference, too obviously reading out a statement.

'That's one thing it doesn't do.' He always watched himself back with a rueful expression.

Seeing him on television was the only time Ashleigh felt sorry for him, the only time he ever showed any weakness. 'At least it shows you're human.'

'Oh, I'm all of that.' He'd been about to lean in towards her, ready to kiss her as the news moved to an item about sheep rustling, but his phone interrupted them. He sighed, but he answered it. 'If it wasn't for this whole shenanigans up in Martindale I'd switch this thing off in the evenings. Don't people know it's nearly midnight? Hello, Jude Satterthwaite.'

Perhaps one day he'd learn to do that. Ashleigh sat back and watched as he listened intently, but she was too much of the same mindset even to try and change him. There would come a point where he needed to switch off before the pressures of the job overtook him but this wasn't it. As long as there was justice to be served, his phone would be on and he'd always answer. She shifted a little closer, to hear the conversation.

'Okay. Karl Faulkner.' He nodded to Ashleigh, repeating the key points of the conversation for her benefit. 'From Melbourne. Okay. Ex-army. Yes. Bluntly, I don't know how much his background in Australia is going to help us, because I have a hunch his death is very much rooted in the here and now, but send me whatever you've got and I'll see what I can make of it. Right. You have it on file already, then? Right. Questioned over a car accident in Melbourne but no charges laid. Thanks. I appreciate everything you've done.'

Melbourne. Something flicked in Ashleigh's brain. She reached for a pen and an envelope which lay on the side table, the envelope covered with Jude's thoughtful doodles, an indication of the way his mind never left his work. *Ask him about Elizabeth Bell*, she wrote.

He looked down at the note, flicked a querying eyebrow. 'One last thing, which may or may not be connected. There's a woman called Elizabeth Bell.'

He rattled through the story of Elizabeth Bell, the back story to her emigration. 'No, I don't mind waiting while you see what you can find.' He put the phone down and turned back to Ashleigh. 'What's this about?'

'I'm surprised at you.' She shook her head. 'At me too. We should have made the connection when we knew Ryan came from Australia.'

'Australia's a huge place.'

'And Martindale is very small. So it's a bit of a coincidence if Ryan turns out to have been in the place where Elizabeth Bell died, and then shows up in Martindale where Miranda is, don't you think?'

Jude turned back to the phone. 'No, that's great. Ah, right.'

Ashleigh leaned right in so she could pick up the Australian voice at the other end of the line. 'Mate, you might be on to something. The accident he was questioned over. Elizabeth Bell died in it.'

'Right,' Jude said, his voice neutral as always, though surely he must feel the same rising excitement as Ashleigh did, over a hunch that now looked like inspiration. 'Questioned but not charged, you say?'

'Yep. The woman was doped up to the eyes with anti-depressants and God knows what else. She should never have been on the road. He said the car was all over the place and he couldn't avoid her. No witnesses. It was an open verdict. I can send the coroner's report over to you if you want.'

'That would be brilliant. Thanks. I do believe we've got something.'

'I'll get back to you if we can dig up anything else. Have a good evening.'

'I intend to.' Jude said, with a grin, and hung up.

Work waited, but only until the distraction of having Ashleigh O'Halloran in his bed when they were both in the mood for love had passed. Just before he reached out to switch off the light, Jude remembered the call, remembered the note. He grinned. He must be mellowing in his old age, if he was leaving his mind roaming loose while a woman got in the way. He rolled back onto his back and looked up at the ceiling. Luke. Ryan. Maybe Summer. There was an answer. 'Okay. Before you led me astray we were talking about Elizabeth Bell.'

'I led you astray?' she pretended to grumble, rolling in against him and resting her head on his shoulder. 'That's not how I remember it. But since you ask, shall I tell you what I think?'

'I think I know. I wondered briefly if Miranda might actually be Elizabeth, but I can't stretch my credibility to two fake identities in one case. It might be worth going back to check, I suppose, but in this day and age it's only worth trying to be someone else when you're alive. When you're dead, the science will get you.' As they'd discovered with Karl Faulkner.

'Yes. And then Ryan, or Karl, turns up in Martindale when Miranda's there. I knew there was something.'

'The messages on the phone specifically referred to Robert.' Jude inspected the shadows on the ceiling. 'They describe him as the target. They say when he's at the property.'

'But they say who else is at the property, too. And I can't remember them in detail, but I'm pretty certain you can work out who else is there. And that means that you'd have been able to tell not just when Robert was on his own but when Miranda was there by herself. And on the basis of those messages, I'm going to bet she never was. Because if she had been, she'd be dead.'

A fly beat its sluggish way across the room, through the dim circlet of the light the bedside lamp left on the ceiling. 'Miranda was on her own. She went out walking on her own. She was alone when she found Luke.'

'But Ryan didn't know that. My guess is that Miranda had a very lucky escape that day, and if Ryan hadn't bumped into Luke, realised the game was up and killed him, she'd have met him on the road and it would have been her who was found in the stream, not Luke.' Jude watched the fly again. There was something curiously therapeutic about it as it battled its way across the room. In the corner, a cobweb loitered, one he never had any time to remove. 'A trap. That's what it was.'

'Yes, but what—'

'Ollie's phone. When I went down there, after we found Luke dead, Miranda was shouting at Ollie for having lost his phone. She's a cool woman, and she doesn't lose her temper, but here she is shouting at some kid for being casual. Why did Miranda get so stressed? Maybe —

just maybe — it was because someone had messaged her on that phone. And maybe someone had tried to lure her into a trap.' He sat up.

'Jude.' Ashleigh sat up, too, pulling the duvet up in a pointless gesture to hide her modesty. 'This is speculation. You're not telling me Miranda went up to the house, was surprised by Ryan, stunned him, carried him down to the churchyard, buried him and went back home. All on her own.'

'No. She must have had help, and the help must have been Robert. I need to—'

'No.' Ashleigh lay back down, pulling him down, too, with a hand on his arm. 'Jude. You don't have to do anything right now. You need to go to sleep and in the morning we can start thinking about what happened. Because we still don't know who might have paid someone to kill Miranda, if they did.'

'And we don't know who was calling Ryan on that burner phone.'

'Surely not one of the twins?'

'I can't believe it was one of them. Eighteen's young to be luring their stepmother into a trap, and they're too smart to be conned into it. But someone did it.' A light flicked on in his brain. He understood, There was only one candidate. 'And I think I know who it was.' The greyest, plainest, least likely person on the planet. An efficient, low-profile, utterly unthreatening, middle-aged woman.

'It'll be the PA,' he said. 'Aida Collins.'

TWENTY-EIGHT

Faye was sitting with an expression of intense irritation on her face, a blank pad in front of her and both hands curled around a mug of coffee, when Jude made her office his first port of call.

'Faye. I need to talk to you about the Neilsons.'

She raised a hand to silence him. 'I'm sure you do. But this is difficult enough. I don't need you complicating things further. My colleagues are keener than ever that you keep your distance from Robert Neilson, which leads me to suppose they think they're onto something significant.'

'Did you see what I forwarded you? The Australian coroner's report?'

'I've seen it but I haven't had a chance to read it yet.'

'Then I'll summarise. You know Miranda gave evidence to clear Elizabeth Bell of murder. Elizabeth died in a car accident and the other vehicle involved was driven by the man we know as Ryan Goodall. He was cleared, on the basis that she was on some medication that may have affected her ability to drive. That's a hell of a coincidence. And you know what I think of coincidence.'

Faye, who never trusted coincidence either, pursed her lips. 'He'll have to have been very smart to have persuaded them he wasn't involved.'

But there was every chance that Ryan, or his sponsor, had been very smart indeed. 'And then he turns up dead less than a mile from Miranda's front door. Don't tell me she had nothing to do with it.'

'And don't tell me she's capable of killing him in the way he died.'

'Not without help.' Jude took a deep breath. 'Robert's help.'

She drummed her fingers on the desk. 'Well, do you know what, Jude? If that's correct then it's highly unlikely anyone else is going to die, and we can afford to wait a little while longer — and gather some more evidence — before we look at it.'

'Faye. For Christ's sake. Someone killed Ryan Goodall and buried him in George's grave. You can't just pass on that.'

'I don't want to pass on it. But I—'

'What if I tell you I think Aida Collins might have been involved in giving Goodall information on Miranda's whereabouts?'

She touched her forehead as if she were dealing with a particularly trying child. 'Jude. The last thing I can afford is to have you talking to Robert's PA and giving him a reason to think we're interested in his business affairs. I forbid you to speak to her without my express permission.'

He bristled. 'Two people have been murdered in Martindale. Maybe two more have been, too. And besides, do I have to remind you? We don't know who killed our fake Ryan Goodall.'

'We don't know, but if you're right and it's Miranda,

there's no immediate need to worry. We'll get her for it later. I can't see that she's a danger to anyone else.'

'What about Summer?'

'You've yet to provide me with any evidence what happened was anything other than an accident.'

If there was much about Faye and her way of working that Jude liked, he struggled against her blank resistance to what he was trying to tell her. 'This is your patch. If you want to move in and question Miranda about murder and Robert as an accessory, you can do that. If you want to search the property, you can do that.' But she wouldn't, because Faye was an ambitious woman and getting on the wrong side of anyone who might be in a position to review an application for promotion wasn't in her plan.

'I can. But I don't think either of those steps is necessary.'

'And have we made any progress on finding out where Summer got the drugs from? What if it was Robert?'

'Didn't you put Doddsy on to that? Maybe you should ask him.'

Doddsy was as frustrated about that element of the case as Jude himself. 'We haven't made any progress. That's rather my point.'

'Then maybe you should concentrate on that.'

'Okay.' He kept his temper anyway. 'Faye. I'm going to talk to Miranda. I believe she lied to us, even if she didn't kill Ryan. I won't go in hard, but I will go in.'

Faye considered. 'I suppose it'll look odd if you don't go down and talk to people, but really. I don't want you to let any of them think that we suspect them, seriously, of murder.'

None of the Neilsons was stupid. There would surely come a point where they'd start wondering why they hadn't been hauled in and interviewed under caution, and that might be the point at which Robert started wondering about the reason for the softly-softly approach. 'Okay. We'll go straight along.'

'Try not to surprise them too early in the morning. Most people keep more civilised hours than us.' There was a lurking humour in her face as he turned to the door but as he laid his hand on the handle, she called him back. 'Jude.'

'What?'

'I absolutely forbid you to mention Aida Collins in connection with this case, or to speak to her. Don't think I don't understand where you're coming from. But there are many ways to skin this particular cat. All right?'

He left the room with a sigh, collected Ashleigh from the incident room and, leaving Doddsy in temporary charge, they headed down towards Pooley Bridge and towards Howtown.

'Faye was adamant we don't rock the boat,' he said to her, as he squeezed into a gateway to let a tractor pass, 'but I tell you. If I think there's any immediate risk to Miranda, or anyone else, I'll do everything I can to intervene.'

'You really don't want to get on the wrong side of Faye,' warned Ashleigh. 'She won't forget.'

He smiled at her. 'I don't want to get on the wrong side of anyone. But I'll do it if it saves lives.' Or if it brought the guilty to justice.

'Hopefully she's right in what she said. If someone's after Miranda, they've surely been put off.'

'They won't be put off for ever, though.' There might already be someone moving in to take Ryan's place as an executioner.

'Poor Miranda. She did the right thing, speaking up for her friend. It's awful how she was hounded for it.'

'I don't disagree. But if she had to kill Ryan to save herself, she should have told us. Straight away.'

The car crawled up over the hairpin bends beyond Howtown and down past the Martindale turn. The electric gates to Waterside Lodge stood open, as though the Neilsons hadn't a care in the world — as if they knew any immediate threat had been eliminated. Jude drove through them and saw Aida's red car parked outside. 'Looks like we're not the only ones who start work early.'

'Maybe Robert's been on the phone to Australia, too.' Ashleigh stifled a yawn.

'There's always money to be made somewhere in the world.' Jude parked his Mercedes neatly next to Aida's car and got out. 'Let's go.'

It was Miranda who answered the door, apparently unsurprised to see them. 'Chief Inspector. Sergeant O'Halloran. I'm afraid I'm in the middle of breakfast, but come in and have coffee. Do you need to speak to Robert?'

'Just yourself right now, Mrs Neilson. Though I expect we'll need to talk to him later.'

'Who's that, Miranda?' Robert's voice burst out from distant part of the house.

'Just the police,' she shouted back. 'Routine. Nothing to worry about.' And she led them into the kitchen. 'Have a seat.'

They sat, while Miranda made them coffee and dealt the mugs out on the table with the skill of a saloon barmaid, then resumed her seat and looked down at the remnants of toast and honey on her plate. She was silent.

She hadn't slept well, Jude judged. There was tiredness in her eyes — more than that, resignation. 'Well, Chief Inspector. Please don't tell me you've come to say someone else has died.'

'I sincerely hope no-one else will die, Mrs Neilson. And I suspect no-one hopes that more than you do.'

Tears filled her eyes. Getting up, she tore a piece of kitchen paper off the roll on the kitchen unit and resumed her seat, dabbing at her eyes. 'I'm so glad you've come. I knew you'd find out about Elizabeth.'

'It would have been more helpful if you'd told us straight away.' He knew now that she must have killed Ryan, with or without her husband's help, but surely she'd try to plead self-defence. 'Begin at the beginning.'

'You know about Elizabeth, of course.' She began to pick the kitchen paper apart. 'Everybody does. Drew — her partner — was a violent, manipulative man, and no-one believed her when she said so. I was the only person who would stand up in court and speak up for her. No-one else dared. Yes, she killed him. She admitted it. But she did it to save her sanity, if not her life, and if she'd gone to prison it would have destroyed her after what he did to her. I believed, at the time, that I'd saved her by speaking up.'

'What you did was very brave,' said Ashleigh, quietly.

'I didn't think so. I just thought it was the decent thing to do. Afterwards, of course, there was a whole lot of media attention and then it became a social media thing.' She shook her head. 'It was horrible. Constant. I was baffled by it. People wrote books about it. I got a lot of support but there was a lot of negative attention, too. And it was nothing to what poor Beth had to deal with.'

'I believe that's why she left England.'

'Yes. I never heard from her after the trial.' Miranda shook her head. 'It was sad, but I'm not in any way bitter. She'd been through hell and she had to go somewhere where no-one knew her, or knew anything about her. But it left me isolated. I lost a lot of friends.'

Doing the right thing always did lose you friends. The

more Jude saw it happen, the more he wondered why anyone bothered. 'You bounced back.'

'Oh, yes.' Miranda placed the tissue on her plate, took a sip of coffee and looked at the two detectives in front of her. 'You don't have any choice in life, do you? You have to keep going or you go under, and you have to do it any way you can. I was sorry Beth felt she had to go, but I understood. I carried on. I went back to my job. I was still receiving a lot of the wrong sort of attention. Drew's family threatened to break me. His brother took to following me around and I had to take a restraining order out against him. I received death threats on social media. A couple of years later I met Robert and married him.'

'Did he know about Elizabeth?'

Her smile was tremulous. 'I told him a few days ago, but he already knew. He's a very thorough man, and he checks everything. He was very supportive, thank God. Because things changed for me, badly, three years ago. Beth died in an accident. They said she was on medication, but there was only one witness. Maybe that witness had caused the crash. Because she was in fear of her life.'

She picked up the tissue again. 'I couldn't sleep for worry. Maybe it was murder. I remembered a couple of the threats I'd had, before the fuss died down. One of them said: *bitch, never sleep. We'll come when we're ready, when you don't expect us*. I started to believe that they were coming after me.'

Ashleigh put her coffee mug down and looked across at her. 'That must have been hard.'

Once again, in some inexplicable way, a witness responded to her obvious sincerity and transferred her attention from the senior officer to the junior. 'Yes. Unbelievably. I became very tense. I won't say I was nervous. I'm too strong to be nervous. But I became aware of people around me. I noticed every stranger. I assessed every approach, every smile, every place for a potential threat.'

'And in Martindale?'

'I felt safer here than anywhere else. Not wholly safe, because people can always get you and I wasn't hiding. I would go out and wonder where they'd come for me from.' She bowed her head. 'And then one day something happened.'

There was a pause.

'Summer?' Ashleigh prompted.

Miranda nodded. 'She messaged me and asked to speak to me about Beth, and about the trial. I didn't know what to do. The boys must have given her my number. I wasn't afraid of the girl, or not at first. But I knew whoever came to kill me could be anybody. And it struck me that pretending to talk about Elizabeth would have been an elegant approach for an assassin.'

'Summer's interest was genuine,' observed Jude from the sidelines.

'Was it?' Miranda continued to address herself to Ashleigh. 'I wasn't sure, but even if it was, I didn't want the matter resurrected. If people had forgotten who I was, I didn't want them reminded. The afternoon she disappeared I knew the boys had invited her here, so I made sure I was out. But I couldn't settle, so I came back early. I decided I'd speak to her and get it over with, just do it, meet the challenge head on.'

Ashleigh folded both hands in front of her. Her sympathy was obvious. 'That isn't what you told the police.'

'No.'

'Did anyone see you?'

'Luke Helmsley. I didn't realise that until he threatened

me, on the day he died, but I didn't kill him.' She paused. 'I didn't kill Summer, either.'

'Then what happened to her?'

Miranda's look was agonised. 'God forgive me. I didn't do anything. Anything at all. When I got back I saw them fooling around on the *Seven of Swords*, her and Ollie and Will. They were obviously out of their minds on something and I didn't want to know what. I went back into the house, wondering what I'd say to Summer if she spoke to me, and when I looked out again a while later I saw her. Just her. The boys must have crashed out by then. She was stumbling about on the boat and she tripped and went over the side.' She put her head in her hands. 'I didn't do anything. I was so scared. I thought Fate was intervening to save me. Years ago, a fortune teller warned me I'd be in danger but the *Seven of Swords* would protect me, and that was what I thought of. That it was meant to be. Because that was why I'd named the boat.' Her hands shook. 'I must have gone a little mad.'

'And then?' Ashleigh, Jude could tell, was fighting to keep her tone nonjudgemental, but surely she must be thinking the same as he was, imagining poor Summer floundering in the cold waters of Ullswater, struggling to reach the shore or the safety of the boat and giving up, too soon.

'It was done. The boys woke up and found her dead and Ollie suggested they hide the body, so they did.'

'They confessed?'

'We struck a deal. We agreed that none of us saw anything. I saw nothing on the boat and they never saw I was back early. And it's true Summer's death was an accident. No-one killed her.'

Summer could have been saved, and the extended police operation had caused distress and used up resources that could have been deployed elsewhere. Her parents could have been spared those hours wondering what had become of their daughter. Opening his mouth to make that point, Jude saw Ashleigh's fierce frown in his direction and let her carry on. 'What happened after that, Mrs Neilson?'

'I was still very shaken.' Miranda looked at her, imploringly. 'When I found poor Luke dead, I didn't know what to do, or think.' She looked at Jude, reproachfully. 'You asked me why I'd assumed he'd been killed. Now you know. I was sure there was a killer in the dale and if I was right I knew I'd be the target.'

'You let Summer die—' Jude began.

'Because I was afraid. Because standing up in court to save my friend from prison had brought me threats, and she was dead, and suddenly this whole thing was on my doorstep. I did not *let Summer die*, as you put it. I just didn't do anything to save her, because I was paralysed with fear.'

No doubt that would be the line the defence counsel would take, and there was a reasonable chance that, with a sympathetic jury, it might come off. 'All right. Carry on.'

'I guessed Luke had stumbled upon something he shouldn't have seen. That's when I told Robert about it, and he promised he'd look after me.' She looked beyond them, through the open door of the kitchen to where Robert must be sitting in his office with the expressionless, and possibly complicit, Aida. 'I relaxed after that. I knew he'd have people watching me. I knew I'd be safe. But then I did the stupidest, stupidest thing. I trusted my good nature.' She shivered. 'I'll never do that again.'

'You get on well with your stepsons, don't you?' asked Jude.

'You know about the phone calls, then. You must do. How?'

'We heard you talking to Ollie about his phone.'

'Yes. He lost it. Now, of course, I see it must have been stolen and someone had used it to text me.'

Jude thought again of Aida, on the spot. Surely now Faye would let him haul her in for questioning. 'You didn't suspect?'

She shook her head. 'Not at all. I worry about them. Such bright boys, but no sense of restraint, and they have Robert's energy. They're always in trouble and what happened to Summer shook them. When I got a message from Ollie asking me to meet them up at George's house, I went straight away. I was terrified they'd got into trouble somehow. I even worried that they might somehow have killed Luke, although my head told me they couldn't have done. I went to the house. The place was dark.'

'The family hadn't been in since George died.'

'No. The door was open, but we all knew where he kept his key, so I assumed the boys were in there. When I went in I saw a shadow. A figure. And I knew. They'd come for me. I'd been right to be afraid and it was finally happening.' She bit her lip. 'I was sure I was going to die.'

The kitchen clock ticked. In the bowels of the house a mobile phone rang. Outside, a pair of jackdaws fretted their way across the lawn. 'So what happened then?' Ashleigh asked.

'It was Ryan Goodman, that man who had upset George. I knew about it through the local chat. I'd never met him. He had a gun but I moved very quickly. You don't know what you can do until you're scared for your life, do you?'

She lifted her coffee cup, but it never touched her lips and she set it down again. 'I lunged at him and the gun went off. I swear I felt the bullet go past, but it didn't hit me. I grabbed the chair and I must have got a lucky hit. He fell over. He must have hit his head on the table or something, because he didn't get up.'

'And then? What did you do?'

'I should have called 999.' Miranda inspected her fingernails. 'I don't know why I didn't. But then he came round and—'

'And?'

'I helped him up. He didn't know what had happened. He didn't know where he was, or who he was. I spoke to him and called him by his name and he just looked back at me. So I told him I'd take him back to the house and help him, and I took him along to the church. I hit him with the stone at the gate and then I buried him in poor George's grave.' At last she began to weep, silent tears that rolled down her cheek and dropped into the plate among the crumbs.

Ashleigh got up and fetched her a second piece of kitchen paper.

'I had no choice,' Miranda said to her, accepting it. 'At any moment he might have killed me.'

But she was lying. If Ryan had come to his senses he could still have carried out her execution and every moment she'd spent with him was a risk. She must have had help. Jude saw Ashleigh about to say something, probably the same thing, and shook his head at her. It would wait. 'Okay, Mrs Neilson. In the light of this confession, I'm going to take you back with me and ask you to repeat your statement in an interview room and in the presence of a lawyer. You're under arrest for the murder of Karl Faulkner, also known as Ryan Goodman. Further charges relating to the death of Summer Raine may follow. You aren't obliged to say anything further, and anything you do say will be taken down and may be used against you in court.'

Miranda dipped her head. They stood up and she piled the coffee cups and plates in the sink. 'I'd better tell Robert,' she said, as they went into the hall.

'Tell Robert what?' The man himself erupted from the distance. 'Miranda?' His face was concerned.

'I've told the police about Ryan.' She faced him. 'I told them I killed him. I told them how I took him to the churchyard. That I buried him.'

As clear as day, she was warning him. The game might be up but Miranda, it was clear, was still prepared to lie to protect those she cared for. Jude met Ashleigh's eye, and nodded. Best to leave Robert for someone else to pick up. There was nowhere he could run to.

'I'm calling my solicitor.' He dived back towards his office. 'I'll follow you up. Don't worry, Miranda. I'm in control of this situation. Do as they tell you just now. It'll all be sorted out.'

They headed out of the house, Aida hovering behind them. 'Mrs Neilson. If there's anything you need…'

'It's all right thank you, Aida. Everything will be fine. And at least I'll be safe.'

At Ashleigh's side, she moved towards the Mercedes while Jude, on the driver's side, called Doddsy. 'Get a couple of cars down to the Neilsons', would you? We're bringing in Miranda. She's got a confession for us. I want you to bring in Robert on suspicion of aiding and abetting, if not for murder itself.' It wouldn't take long to get the truth of what happened in the churchyard, even if Miranda thought her easy confession had worked. He closed down the call. 'Okay, Mrs Neilson. Let's go.'

Miranda went willingly. 'If I'm honest,' she said as Jude went round to the driver's seat of the Mercedes, 'it's a relief. In prison I'll be safe.'

Jude looked back at the house, directly at Robert who

was standing on the gravel with Aida a few yards behind him. Something about Robert's uncertainty held his attention and then he saw the financier reach into his pocket, saw the slight fumble that suggested he didn't quite know what to do, saw the flash of sunlight on the barrel of a compact hand gun.

Christ.

'Drop that!' he shouted, too late to stop Robert's finger on the trigger or the bullet that hissed along an impossibly fortunate line between Ashleigh, Miranda and himself and starred the two front windows of the Mercedes.

As Miranda screamed, Jude moved. Too late, too far away.

'Stop right there!' said Robert, his voice shaking. 'Everyone stay still.'

Jude stopped. Miranda had taken shelter behind Ashleigh, crouched against her body with her fingers digging into Ashleigh's arms, restraining her protector from taking on her attacker. The second bullet, which would surely have found Miranda's heart or her head, remained in the gun.

That shake of the hand. *He doesn't want to do it.* Jude's training kicked in. 'Put the gun down, Mr Neilson.'

Robert ignored him. 'Move out of the way, Sergeant. Let me treat my wife with the respect she deserves. Let me blow her brains out the way her friend beat my friend Drew to death.'

'This isn't doing any good to anyone.' Jude made his voice sound crisp and confident. Robert Neilson was a man who paid others to kill and the only thing Jude could do until he got closer was play on his weakness. 'Don't make things any worse for yourself.'

'You're a lying bitch, Miranda.' Neilson ignored him. 'You lied in court about Drew. It was your evidence that got that woman off. Well, she's paid for killing him and you're going to pay for protecting her. Sergeant O'Halloran. Stand aside or take the consequences.'

Ashleigh backed away from him and still Miranda clutched at her. She couldn't move if she'd wanted to. He bit back the command he knew he couldn't make, to tell her to stand aside and save herself. His heart raced. Hours before he'd cradled her in his arms in the warmth and security of his bed and now death stared her in the face.

But that failure to fire the second shot hinted at hope. If Robert was squeamish enough only to kill when he had no option, Jude had to make sure he thought he had a choice.

'Robert,' whimpered Miranda. 'What are you saying? What do you mean?'

'Drew was one of my best friends. You know me, Miranda. I'm like you. I'm loyal to my friends, to the death. You stood up for Elizabeth Bell. I'm here to stand up for the man she killed. You were warned.'

'I thought you understood,' she wailed. 'I told you the truth because I trusted you. And I lied to them, to protect you. I didn't tell them it was you who killed Ryan.'

'Your mistake, then. Sergeant O'Halloran. Move.' His tone had unmistakably sharpened.

Ashleigh took a step sideways and Miranda, still digging her fingers into her for grim death, moved, too. 'I'm sorry, Mr Neilson.' Even in the drama she kept her voice steady. 'As you see. I can't.'

Every second spent talking weakened Robert's resolve. Jude edged away from the others, trying to draw Robert's nervous gaze towards him and give Ashleigh a chance to get Miranda to some kind of safety. He'd have to deal with the gun himself but that was better than seeing one or both of them slaughtered in front of him. 'Let this go, Mr Neilson. Robert. It's done. Your wife has been punished enough.'

'We disagree. Miranda, you lying bitch. For the last time. Let go of Sergeant O'Halloran, or you'll have someone else's death on your conscience.'

'Drop the gun!' Jude was a step closer now, but still too far away. And now Aida — oh God, not her, too — was leaning forward with a look of determination on her face.

An upstairs window crashed open and a twin's voice cried out, incredulous: 'Dad?'

In that second of distraction, both Jude and Aida moved.

The second bullet exploded from the gun.

'Get down!' Ashleigh shouted but Aida had already sent the gun spinning across the gravel. In appalled horror, Robert turned on her and Jude, lunging forward, sent him crashing to the floor.

The man was easily subdued. Whatever his many qualities, he was no fighter. Jude had the cuffs on him in a moment and was back on his feet, looking around to see Miranda's face, grey and appalled, to make sure Ashleigh was safe. Only then did he turn his attention to Aida, standing over her employer in shock.

'I'm so sorry!' she wept. 'So sorry! But I couldn't do it, Robert. I couldn't let you kill Mrs Neilson.'

TWENTY-NINE

'All right.' Faye bounced into the incident room, and all eyes were on her. Ruefully, Jude reminded himself that she wasn't someone who cared too much about sparing someone else's public humiliation. She'd been out of the office all day and he was mightily grateful for that. 'As if I don't have enough to do. I get back in after a long day and find you've got yourself and another officer involved in a firearms incident. Explain yourself.'

'Read the debrief note.' He was tired and wound up, and he'd been proved right, though not in the way he'd expected. Faye's irritation was unjustified. 'It's all in there. We went to talk to Miranda and she confessed. And we know who wanted to kill her and why. I expect you know people who'll find that interesting reading.'

She stared at him with narrowed eyes, looked around her at Ashleigh's apprehensive gaze and Doddsy's intrigued one, and must have decided that private was better after all. 'All right. I take your point. Come along to my office and we'll discuss it in private.'

He followed her down the corridor, still simmering at her lack of respect for his professional dignity. 'Miranda Neilson killed someone, and allowed someone else to die. Okay, I hadn't guessed about Robert, but I'd got to the point where I felt I had to haul her in. Sorry if that's upset your standing with people more important than I am.'

'That's dangerously close to insubordination.' She slammed the door behind them. 'At least you're both unhurt. That's something.'

'There would have been a hell of a lot of paperwork if one of us had been killed, eh?'

Faye let that pass. High-handed behaviour on her part, backchat on his. Stress made the calmest of adults bicker like kids in a playground. 'Sit down. And tell me about Robert.'

'He was at school with Drew Anderson. The man Elizabeth Bell killed. The two of them were very close.'

'Did you know that when you went to Waterside Lodge this morning?'

'No. Chris just looked it up for me. If you'd allowed me to dig into Robert's background before, I might have found out earlier, and we could have saved a whole lot of trouble.'

'I thought you understood why I gave you those instructions.'

He had understood, though he'd disagreed. 'I've you to thank for it, as it happens. It was something you said about Robert never being there, being out of the way, that made me wonder. It was pretty obvious Miranda couldn't have killed Ryan on her own. It needed someone else to do it. She sticks to her story about having walked him to the churchyard, but she says she called Robert for help and he insisted they had to kill him. She wanted to call us.' Or so she'd said.

'He had his identity to protect. Ryan would have known who the paymaster was, perhaps. Or not, but either way he couldn't risk it.'

With distance, everything was clear. Robert had made sure he was out of the dale at crucial moments, but time must have over-run him. When criminals made mistakes it was because their plans didn't work and they couldn't adjust. 'I think I first suspected there was something about him when she said she hadn't told him about Elizabeth but he knew. That was odd. He must have planned it for a long time.'

'He must have had hundreds of opportunities. Why wait five years?' Faye fidgeted. she was still clearly irritated, but she must know Jude's position was defensible. If Miranda had been the victim of an accident while they were waiting for Robert to walk into some trap spun from years of paperwork, there would have been a lot of questions to answer.

'I can think of a couple of reasons. One is that the longer he left it, the less suspicion there would be. It took with years to kill Elizabeth, assuming she was actually murdered and assuming that the murderer was working on Robert's instructions. The second is that he might have enjoyed being married to her. She struck me as nice enough, she's a good looking woman, and she clearly loved and respected him.' He made a face. Maybe Robert had loved his wife, in his way, and it had taken five years for the balance of his feelings for her and his thirst for revenge to tip against her.

'I take it you have people trying to unpick the background to that?'

'Of course. It may take a while to find everything, but we have Miranda's confession and Robert's attempt at killing Miranda. That's enough to leave him locked up for a long time. In the meantime I expect we'll be able to fill in a lot of background. I imagine we'll find Robert knew George had a nephew he'd never seen, in Australia. He probably made inquiries over several years, in the guise of polite chat, and established no-one else knew him, either. He'll have recruited Kyle Falkland, had him kill Elizabeth — high risk, but he got away with it. Then he brought him over, had him hang around in the dale, and the idea was he'd do away with Miranda and disappear. If anyone saw him, they'd think nothing of it. I imagine the plan was that he'd stay with George and people would get used to seeing him around. But it all went wrong when George wouldn't play ball.' He frowned. George's death was certified as natural, but he was sure that Ryan, either accidentally or deliberately, had scared the old man into his fatal stroke. Some time, when he had a little more courage, he'd have to break that to Becca. 'We'll never know what happened between Ryan and Luke, but obviously Ryan felt he had no choice but to kill him, and after that Robert must have decided he couldn't afford to wait any longer. So Ryan had to move quickly if he was to kill Miranda and get away without anyone realising he was about.'

'Hmm. That sounds far-fetched.'

'You think so? I'll tell you what the clincher was, for me. Ollie's phone.'

'Oh?'

'Yes. According to Miranda, the calls that lured her into the trap were made from Ollie's phone, which he'd lost. Ryan wouldn't have risked going anywhere near the property. I thought Aida was involved.'

'So you did.' A smile played on Faye's lips.

'Yes. But no-one had a better opportunity to take it than someone in the family. Robert. He might even have sent the messages himself.' The phone would probably be at the bottom of the lake, alongside the other one on which Robert might have relayed to Ryan the details of his own, and his family's, movements.

Faye sat back and regarded him thoughtfully. 'It's fortunate for you Aida was there.'

'I'm amazed at what she did. Extraordinary. A PA. She acted like she was a police officer.'

'Jude.' Faye's expression had been irritated, then pensive, and suddenly became smug. 'Really? You hadn't guessed?'

'Guessed what?'

'Robert isn't the only person who takes a long view. Aida's a serving officer with the Met. She's been working with Robert for the past three years. I don't think she's blown her cover, although he's bound to sack her after this. But she's probably done enough already to implicate a lot of other people, along with Robert himself, in major fraud. But of course, I didn't tell you that.'

Jude felt suddenly light-hearted. There had been a moment when he'd feared for Ashleigh and he didn't know what he could have done for her if Robert had had the nerve of an executioner rather than an executive. Aida's intervention had been the difference and they all owed her a debt of gratitude, even if they'd never get the chance to repay it. 'Someone will be getting a bill for the damage to my car, that's for sure.'

'That's what your insurance is for.' She fidgeted a little. 'Off you go. You've got a hell of a lot of work to do on Robert Neilson, and I have a hell of a job to explain it. So let's just get on with it.'

'Are you all right?' Jude placed his empty glass on the table. Around them the group of detectives, who'd decided on an impromptu night out in unspoken celebration of a case solved, were laughing at some joke or other, but Ashleigh hadn't been listening.

'I'm a bit distracted, that's all.' She sighed.

'I know. It's been a hell of a day.'

The two of them had settled at the edge of the group in the first place, and neither had joined in the general conviviality. 'No doubt we'll have the health and safety people on our backs at some stage, making sure we're not too stressed. It would be too much to ask for three days off to recover, I suppose.' She forced a laugh. 'Not when there's all that work to be done.'

'I don't think we need to do much more to have Robert done up like a kipper, but there you go. It'll be good to get him for everything he's done.' Jude paused. 'Do you want another drink, or shall we just slip out unnoticed?'

Ashleigh picked up her almost-empty glass. It wasn't often she contemplated using alcohol as a crutch, but today was different. Common sense won out. She put the glass down. 'Better not. Let's go.'

'Are you sure you're all right?'

She shook her head without thinking about it. There had been other perilous situations in her time in the police. There had been drink or drug-crazed men with knives, furious women who'd kicked and punched her as she tried to help them. There had been a car driving at her one dark night on the beat, and a long fall into the freezing River Eden in a vain attempt to stop a suicide. All had shaken her, but she didn't think any of them had the effect on her that Robert had done as she'd stood as a human shield to the terrified Miranda. Every time she closed her eyes she'd see his shaking hand and the mean, menacing circle of the gun's deadly barrel, feel Miranda's desperate fingers digging into her shoulders. 'No, probably not. Let's go home.'

'Sure.'

He stood up and picked up her jacket, holding it for her to put on. This untypical, gentlemanly gesture comforted her a little. And anyway, it wasn't just the thought of how close she'd come to dying, of how the only things that had kept her alive were Robert's own lack of a killer instinct and the extraordinary instinctive courage of his PA, that worried her. 'Have you told Becca about Ryan?'

'No. I've left that for someone else. I don't know who. Doddsy will end up doing it, I expect.'

'You don't want to do it yourself?' She slipped his hand into his as they stepped out into the street.

'Do you want the honest answer? I think I probably ought to but no, I don't want to. Right now the less I have to do with Becca the better for everyone. I don't imagine I can avoid her altogether, but I don't feel I have to go out of my way to see her, either.'

Something told her this wasn't a lie, but nor was it the whole truth. Jude still had feelings for Becca and he was good-mannered enough not to act on them, but somehow the fact that he felt the need to distance himself from an old friend warned her that time wasn't the healer everyone promised it would be.

'I wanted to help you,' he said, out of the blue. 'This morning. I wanted to tell you to stand aside and let him do what the hell he wanted, as long as he didn't hurt you. But I couldn't do that. You know?'

He was right, but somehow she couldn't help seeing it as a betrayal. 'If it had been Becca—' she blurted out, before she could stop herself.

'Yeah. I know. I'd have put her safety ahead of Miranda's. But not because it's her. Because she's a member of the public and you aren't. That's all.'

Damn him. He was right. But she couldn't help comparing him with Scott who, driven by some false, chivalrous impulse, would have been sure to fling himself at Robert and risked all for death or glory. The pragmatic approach was the right one, but surely everyone yearned for someone who put them first, even before life itself. 'I understand.'

'I don't suppose it makes it any easier, but even if I did still care for her, it's gone. Done.'

Becca had hurt him before, and now he must feel she'd hurt him again. Even though it was Adam who'd put in the complaint and Becca who'd withdrawn it, she could tell he still placed the blame at his ex-girlfriend's door. Or his own. Jude was quite capable of blaming himself for not having been tougher on his wayward heart in the beginning, and that cut both ways. 'I had a text from Scott this evening.'

They walked side by side from the wine bar towards the point where they'd have to decide. Did they go to the same house for the evening, or did they sleep alone? 'Oh?'

'He's been offered Summer's job, and he's taken it. He texted me this morning but in the middle of everything I forgot to tell you.'

They walked another few steps in silence. 'That's going to make for an interesting summer.'

'Don't worry. I'll be far too busy to see him, even if he wants to.' Loving Scott was a fantasy and the reality was pain.

'He will want to, won't he? Isn't the whole reason he's coming because you're here?'

'The reason Scott's coming is nothing to do with me. If

he thinks I'm going to give up on the little free time I have with you, he can think again.'

They reached the Market Square. Jude's route home lay ahead of them, Ashleigh's to the left. 'What do you really think of him?'

They were still holding hands, standing in front of the Musgrave Monument. 'Now? I don't know. He was the love of my life, I suppose, and I'm never going to fall in love like that again.' Just as Jude, whether he admitted it or not, was never going to fall in love with anyone the way he had with Becca. 'You know that. I've told you.'

'Yes. That's true.' They'd always promised to be honest with one another, and somehow they'd kept to it. That was how you forged relationships, through fire. It was how you came out on the other side with something that was better than you had when you went in.

'I'll never get over the way he behaved, but I am moving on. You're moving on, too. I'm in a relationship with you, now, not him. Don't ever think anything else.'

Somehow they shuffled apart, though their fingers still touched. 'Okay. That's fair enough.' He smiled. 'I'd never have forgiven myself if something had happened to you today.'

'But nothing did.' She returned the smile, and thought they both meant it. 'Let's get home. My place or yours, then?'

'Mine.' And he tightened his fingers around hers and they set off together along the street.

THE END

MORE BY JO ALLEN

Death by Dark Waters

DCI Jude Satterthwaite #1

It's high summer, and the Lakes are in the midst of an unrelenting heatwave. Uncontrollable fell fires are breaking out across the moors faster than they can be extinguished. When firefighters uncover the body of a dead child at the heart of the latest blaze, Detective Chief Inspector Jude Satterthwaite's arson investigation turns to one of murder. Jude was born and bred in the Lake District. He knows everyone... and everyone knows him. Except his intriguing new Detective Sergeant, Ashleigh O'Halloran, who is running from a dangerous past and has secrets of her own to hide... Temperatures – and tensions – are increasing, and with the body count rising Jude and his team race against the clock to catch the killer before it's too late...

The first in the gripping, Lake District-set, DCI Jude Satterthwaite series.

Death at Eden's End

DCI Jude Satterthwaite #2

When one-hundred-year-old Violet Ross is found dead at Eden's End, a luxury care home hidden in a secluded nook of Cumbria's Eden Valley, it' not unexpected. Except for the instantly recognisable look in her lifeless eyes…that of pure terror. DCI Jude Satterthwaite heads up the investigation, but as the deaths start to mount up it's clear that he and DS Ashleigh O'Halloran need to uncover a long-buried secret before the killer strikes again…

The second in the unmissable, Lake District-set, DCI Jude Satterthwaite series.

Death on Coffin Lane

DCI Jude Satterthwaite #3

DCI Jude Satterthwaite doesn't get off to a great start with resentful Cody Wilder, who's visiting Grasmere to present her latest research on Wordsworth. With some of the villagers unhappy about her visit, it's up to DCI Satterthwaite to protect her – especially when her assistant is found hanging in the kitchen of their shared cottage.

With a constant flock of tourists and the local hippies welcoming in all who cross their paths, Jude's home in the Lake District isn't short of strangers. But with the ability to make enemies wherever she goes, the violence that follows in Cody's wake leads DCI Satterthwaite's investigation down the hidden paths of those he knows, and those he never knew even existed.

A third mystery for DCI Jude Satterthwaite to solve, in this gripping novel by best-seller Jo Allen.

Death at Rainbow Cottage

DCI Jude Satterthwaite #4

At the end of the rainbow, a man lies dead.

The apparently motiveless murder of a man outside the home of controversial equalities activist Claud Blackwell and his neurotic wife, Natalie, is shocking enough for a peaceful local community. When it's followed by another apparently random killing immediately outside Claud's office, DCI Jude Satterthwaite has his work cut out. Is Claud the killer, or the intended victim?

To add to Jude's problems, the arrival of a hostile new boss causes complications at work, and when a threatening note arrives at the police headquarters, he has real cause to fear for the safety of his friends and colleagues…

A traditional British detective novel set in Cumbria.

ACKNOWLEDGMENTS

There are too many people who have helped me with this book for me to name them individually: I hope those I don't mention will forgive me.

I have to thank my lovely beta readers – Amanda, Frances, Julie, Kate, Katey, Liz, Lorraine, Pauline, Sally and Sara – who not only read and commented but also produced support and suggestions throughout the process. I'd also like to thank Graham Bartlett, who kindly advised me on aspects of police procedure.

Finally, as before, I owe a huge debt of gratitude to the eagle-eyed Keith Sutherland, for proofreading.

Printed in Great Britain
by Amazon